THE OPPOSITE OF LONELY

ABOUT THE AUTHOR

Doug Johnstone is the author of sixteen novels, many of which have been bestsellers. *The Space Between Us* was chosen for BBC Two's *Between the Covers*, while *Black Hearts* was shortlisted for the Theakston Crime Novel of the Year and *The Big Chill* was longlisted for the same award. Three of his books – *A Dark Matter*, *Breakers* and *The Jump* – have been shortlisted for the McIlvanney Prize for Scottish Crime Novel of the Year. Doug has taught creative writing or been writer in residence at universities, schools, writing retreats, festivals, prisons and a funeral directors. He's also been an arts journalist for twenty-five years. He is a songwriter and musician with six albums and three EPs released, and he plays drums for the Fun Lovin' Crime Writers, a band of crime writers. He's also co-founder of the Scotland Writers Football Club. Follow Doug on Twitter @doug_johnstone and visit his website: dougjohnstone.com.

Other titles by Doug Johnstone, available from Orenda Books

THE SKELFS SERIES
A Dark Matter
The Big Chill
The Great Silence
Black Hearts

Fault Lines
Breakers
The Space Between Us

THE OPPOSITE OF LONELY

DOUG JOHNSTONE

**ORENDA
BOOKS**

Orenda Books
16 Carson Road
West Dulwich
London SE21 8HU
www.orendabooks.co.uk

First published in the United Kingdom by Orenda Books, 2023
Copyright © Doug Johnstone, 2023

A catalogue record for this book is available from the British Library.

ISBN 978-1-914585-80-7
eISBN 978-1-914585-81-4

Typeset in Garamond by typesetter.org.uk

Printed and bound by CPI Group (UK) Ltd, Croydon CR0 4YY

MIX
Paper | Supporting responsible forestry
FSC® C171272

For sales and distribution, please contact info@orendabooks.co.uk or visit www.orendabooks.co.uk.

This one is for Andrew and Eleanor,
who set me on this path.

1

DOROTHY

The tide made Dorothy nervous. She watched the waves splashing at the rocky shore and tried to judge how much they'd advanced in the last few minutes. Checked her watch. The thumping bass of an old Orbital tune made it hard to concentrate, and they were near the end of the window for getting off the island.

She tried to calm herself, listened for the lapping waves through the music. She looked across the Forth at Inchmickery, its crumbling concrete wartime defence buildings. It looked like a ghost ship. In the other direction were the three bridges, like architect's models from this distance. Closer was a flotilla of tankers, clustered around the Hound Point oil terminal.

'This is quite something.'

Indy's voice made her turn. Her granddaughter-in-law was in her funeral suit, turquoise hair in a bun, same colour of brooch on her jacket. Big brown eyes, smile on her face. Her luminous running shoes were a concession to the Cramond terrain.

'It is,' Dorothy said.

Beyond Indy was the funeral party for Arlo Wright, one of the older members of the travelling community who'd pitched up at Cramond a few months ago and never left. Here on the north side of the tidal island they were far away from prying eyes, couldn't see the causeway or the village to the south. Another reason Dorothy was nervous, she had no idea how much the water had come in over the causeway. Tourists were always getting stuck on the island and rescued by the coastguard.

Arlo was wrapped in a winding sheet and lying on the remains of a Second World War gun emplacement, an elevated concrete horseshoe with amazing views down the firth. On either side were ruined buildings – gun turrets, searchlights, stores, engine rooms and barracks, all covered in graffiti, colourful shapes and tags. Between the buildings were broken tarmac, overgrown bushes, rocks, scrub grass and rusted metal girders. In amongst it all were twenty people of all ages dancing and drinking, passing round joints and bottles, waving their hands in the air like they just didn't care.

Dorothy cared. She cared that they might not get Arlo back to the mainland.

The Orbital song was replaced by The KLF. Arlo had been big into the rave scene of the early nineties, fought against the Criminal Justice Bill. There was a healthy anti-establishment, counter-cultural vibe to that scene, it made sense that Arlo would end up in a travelling community. Life is about finding a way through, Dorothy knew that well enough. Although it always ended the same way, as Arlo had found out. His death was sudden, an aneurysm in his sleep. Dorothy also wanted a quick exit, nothing drawn out or painful, not to be a burden to Jenny and Hannah.

She checked her watch again. 'We need to go.'

They walked over to the mourners, Indy's hips shimmying with the beat as she bounced like a mountain goat over the rocks. Dorothy picked her way carefully. She was in trainers too, but being in her seventies meant she was less agile, less confident. And a busted ankle here would not be good.

She passed a tumbledown building, windows long gone, sagging roof. In amongst the random graffiti – a woman with a third eye, a black cartoon dog, the *Ghostbusters* symbol – she saw the phrase 'Fuck Tha Police' in thick letters.

She spotted Fara McNish by Arlo's body, nodding her head to the beat as she accepted a spliff. She was mid-twenties, tall and rangy, round glasses, wavy blonde hair with a red-and-white polka-dot headscarf like Rosie the Riveter. Bracelets and necklaces, dungarees and vegan Docs, scarlet tattoo of a handprint on her shoulder. Fara had come to the Skelfs to arrange Arlo's funeral a few days ago, knowing exactly what she wanted. This was it, and Dorothy was regretting it. She was all for a party but would've preferred if they weren't about to get stranded.

'Fara.'

'Dorothy.' Fara hugged her and Dorothy felt the genuine warmth of her affection. 'Have a toke.'

'Not while I'm working.' Dorothy pulled at her shirt cuffs. 'Fara, the tide has turned, we need to go.'

Fara looked around. 'Maybe we should stay until the next one.'

'We went over this. You wanted the funeral as green as possible, so Arlo isn't embalmed. If you keep him here for another eight hours, it won't be pretty.'

Fara passed the joint to an older woman then stuck two fingers in her mouth and gave a sharp whistle. 'Move out.'

The party started to shift, a young woman pulling the orange PA speaker on wheels, two men lifting the ropes attached to the ends of Arlo's body. One was round his ankles, the other looped under his armpits. They slung the ropes over their shoulders and walked, Arlo hanging between them like a deer from a successful hunt.

Indy joined Dorothy at the front as they led the funeral party across the island. They trekked through the trees, past the remains of teenage piss-ups – ashes, blankets, beer cans and vodka bottles. They walked up the hill and Dorothy saw the Dragon's Teeth, the extended row of large sawtooth concrete structures that marked the causeway. Originally submarine defences, now rotting along with the rest of the wartime detritus.

'Come on,' Dorothy called over her shoulder. Indy shared a look with her. The party was strung out behind them, swaying to Leftfield on the PA, the beats coming and going in the wind.

Indy picked the route to the beach, Dorothy and Fara behind. Dorothy saw a low wash sliding across the causeway. The tide came in quickly.

Indy waited for Dorothy and Fara, then they turned to look back. The two tall lads carrying Arlo were kicking up sand, some stragglers behind them.

'I don't know,' Dorothy said, looking at the water. 'It's already coming in.'

'It's fine.' Fara stuck her chin out and whistled like a builder again. 'Let's go!'

The crowd picked up speed as Fara ushered Dorothy and Indy forward. Dorothy splashed onto the causeway, soaking her trainers, low ripples runnelling across the concrete and seaweed. She started to jog – she was fit for her age but not fast. Indy was at her side, slowing her pace to stay near. Dorothy didn't want to look back, the path underfoot was uneven and slippy, she could easily trip. The concrete teeth loomed over her as she ran. She heard the thud of techno still coming from the speaker behind her, the splash of twenty pairs of feet through the rising tide. It was past her ankles now, quickly at her shins, soaking her trousers, the cold creeping up her legs, then she was wading through water over her knees.

Indy pulled her elbow. Dorothy risked a glance behind, saw a thrash of water around everyone's legs as if they were being attacked by piranha, then the music cut out as water got into the PA. The woman pulling it struggled then left it as water reached her thighs. Alongside her, a young couple had toddlers in their arms. Near the back were the two men with Arlo's body low in the water, the soaked winding sheet clinging to him.

'Hurry up,' Indy said, pulling Dorothy's arm.

She turned and waded as fast as she could, strong currents tugging at her waist, almost knocking her off balance. The raised walkway was up ahead. Indy dragged her along now, the two of them panting, Dorothy swearing under her breath. The steps to the walkway were a few yards away when her foot skidded from under her and she splashed face first into the wash. The icy snap of the water was shocking, pushed the air from her lungs. She scrambled and flailed. Indy yanked her upright, then she staggered a few more yards and felt the first step, pulled at the supporting rope and hauled herself out of the water to the safety of the walkway.

She fell to her knees, struggling to breathe.

'Are you OK?' Indy was next to her, panting and spitting out seawater.

She heard footsteps, swearing and grunting as others made it to dry land. They lay around like landed fish, sunshine on their faces, wet stone under their bodies, relief in the air.

Fara stared wide-eyed towards the causeway. Dorothy followed her gaze.

The two men were up to their chests in water, struggling to pull Arlo's body, waves thrashing through the Dragon's Teeth and rushing across the firth. A strong wave tore the ropes from their hands. They grasped to get them back but failed. Arlo floated away on the tide, bobbing in the wash like an inquisitive seal, as he made his way out to sea.

2
JENNY

She took a mouthful of coffee and looked out of the kitchen window at Bruntsfield Links. It was busy at lunchtime, pupils from Gillespie's spilling over the grass, students on their way to classes, workers sprawled out and eating sandwiches. The undulations made it look like a calm, green sea, blue skies above studded with little fluffy clouds. Jenny thought about the bodies buried way below in the old plague pit from five hundred years ago. Her dad's ashes were scattered there more recently, his atoms now spread out into the universe. Hannah always talked like that, she must be rubbing off on Jenny.

She looked down to see Schrödinger scrape his claws along the back of the armchair, pulling at loose threads. Stupid cat had shredded his favourite place to sleep. He yawned and settled, and Jenny walked to the opposite wall, two huge whiteboards and a giant map of Edinburgh.

The map was dotted with red pins marking places they visited for work – cemeteries, crematoriums, care homes, hospices, hospitals. The hidden spider's web of the funeral business. One whiteboard was for funerals, names of the deceased, next of kin, notes for the service, cremation or burial, if a viewing was needed. The other whiteboard was for cases. As private investigators, they picked up jobs through the funeral work, plus walk-ins sometimes. Always people in need, worried about partners, kids, parents, money, status, whatever. People didn't come to a PI if they were happy.

Jenny sipped more coffee. It had been almost four years since she got sucked into the family businesses, but it felt like longer. When Jim died, Dorothy needed her daughter around, so Jenny moved back in and never left. Now, she struggled to remember what life was like before. Simpler, probably, but less meaningful too.

She put her mug in the sink and walked downstairs, closed her eyes and breathed, imagined the smell of smoke. She opened her eyes.

The reception area looked brand new, considering the place had almost burned to the ground a year ago. The case of her ex-husband had gone badly wrong, and her former sister-in-law tried to torch the place. It took six months to get the house into shape again. New wallpaper, floorboards and carpets, furniture and fittings. Tasteful, Scandi-clean lines, more modern than the heavy old oak stuff from before. The inside of the house finally reflected the fact they weren't conventional funeral directors.

Jenny was supposed to be covering reception, but things were quiet. There was probably paperwork to do, but fuck that. Dorothy and Indy were out at some hippie funeral in Cramond, Hannah was at uni, Archie through the back, at the business end of the building.

Jenny walked that way and got a small carved fox out of her pocket, felt the smooth wood as she rubbed it. It was the *netsuke* Archie made for her a year ago. She'd kept it close ever since, a small token of friendship that she clung to amidst therapy and drinking, self-destruction and hatred. Weirdly, it had helped. A simple object to focus on while she trawled through PTSD and self-sabotage, pushing away loved ones. She smiled at the fox now and rubbed it for luck. She felt much better than she had any right to, couldn't have imagined it a year ago.

She stood in the embalming-room doorway and watched Archie. He was taking care of an elderly woman on the metal table, the embalming machine pushing pink milkshake into her carotid artery. Her blood was forced out by the pressure and drained through the jugular vein, running down the gutter at the side of the table and collecting underneath. He held her hand as if reassuring her, but Jenny knew it was to make sure the fluid got to the ends of her fingers so they didn't rot.

She stepped closer and saw that he'd done her face – mouth and eyes sewn shut, cotton wool up the nose in case of purging. Same down the bottom end, she presumed. Archie kept an eye on the woman's arms in case of embalming-fluid leaks – old, thin skin or IV holes could do it. Jenny knew all this stuff from hanging out with him, a world of expertise at his fingertips.

'Hey.'

Archie turned. 'Hey.' He nodded at the woman on the table. 'Wendy Watson, old age, died in her sleep.'

She took him in – late forties, shaved head, neat beard, kind eyes. Sturdy, a little taller than her but not much, solid, reliable. He'd certainly been that over the last year, a shoulder to cry on when things got too much, a release valve from her darkness. They'd taken to going out walking through the streets together, getting to know the nooks and crannies of the city they were both raised in. There was always an undiscovered corner, an unknown vennel or pathway. Edinburgh had centuries of secrets piled on top of each other, and she enjoyed uncovering them with him.

'Was there something?' Archie said, checking the pump.

'Just wanted to say hi.'

'Hi.'

'Hi.' She laughed and sounded younger than forty-eight. Almost happy.

She touched his shoulder then left, back to reception and out the front door, up the path to the wind phone in the corner of the garden. It was a phone box gifted to them by an elderly Japanese client. He had his own in the garden of his Leith flat, and thought the Skelfs could use one. It had an old rotary handset in it, uncon- nected, the cable hanging down. He'd got the idea from another Japanese man who built one to speak to dead relatives. Then when the tsunami hit he was inundated with people wanting to use it to contact the dead. Most people talk to the dead all the time, of course, but there was something about the specific space of the white phone box that gave permission.

It had certainly been used plenty in the last year. The bereaved much preferred chatting to their deceased relatives or friends in the box than sobbing in a quiet room inside the house. It was wonderfully healthy. So much of traditional western funerals seemed to alienate those left behind from the grieving process. This gave it back to them.

She turned to the house, three floors of Victorian townhouse with Gothic trim, like the Addams family set in posh Edinburgh. She remembered that night a year ago when Stella tried to burn it down. Flames dancing in the doors and windows of the ground floor, smoke billowing into the darkness, their giant pine tree ablaze. Its huge trunk and branches were destroyed in the fire, but an expensive arborist examined samples from the roots, and now suckers were growing from the stump. The tree was reinventing itself, starting again after a hundred years. Jenny thought about that a lot.

She heard a vehicle go past in the street, had a flash of Stella driving away that night with the body of Jenny's ex-husband Craig in the back of the van. She still hadn't been found by police, who gave up after a few weeks. Jenny hadn't bothered looking, she'd gone down that rabbit hole before and more than once it had ended in her nearly dying. She concentrated on therapy, the here and now. Dorothy always talked about living in the moment, that Buddhist shit she was into, and Jenny tried to channel it in her own way.

She opened the door of the wind phone, thought she might have a few words with Dad, check how he was doing. She heard a phone ring. Stared at the handset, the cable dangling loose. Eventually she realised it was her mobile and smiled. She took it out and looked at the screen: Violet.

Her former mother-in-law, Stella and Craig's mum. She hadn't spoken to her in a year, since Stella went missing with Craig's remains.

Jenny stared at the name on the screen for a long time, thinking about messages from beyond.

3
HANNAH

The auditorium buzzed with anticipation. They were at the back of the National Museum of Scotland, the event part of the Edinburgh Science Festival, and Kirsty Ferrier had star power. Scotland's first female astronaut, six months spent on the International Space Station, retired now but in demand for public speaking and generally inspiring young women like Hannah. She looked around. The audience reflected that, mostly young and female.

'So how are results and analysis going?' Rose said to her.

Hannah rolled her eyes. She should probably hide the mundane truth from her supervisor, but Rose wasn't that kind of boss.

'You know the movie *The Road*, where they trudge endlessly down an apocalyptic highway with no end in sight?'

Rose laughed. 'Sounds familiar.'

Rose McAllister was late thirties, red hair, sparky energy and very cool. She'd done some consulting for NASA on a sabbatical, that's how cool.

'I'm sure you sailed through your PhD effortlessly,' Hannah said.

'I almost gave up at your stage. Considered becoming an actuary.'

'Not really.'

Rose leaned in. 'Two years in is hard. Nothing has gone as planned, and now you have to create some narrative about it for your thesis. Think of it as a creative-writing exercise.'

'I'm not sure my supervisor should give me that advice.'

Rose touched her arm. In truth, Rose's guidance was one of the reasons Hannah was still at the astrophysics department. Rose was also the reason they were here, she'd scored free tickets because she used to work with Kirsty Ferrier before she became a national treasure.

The lights dimmed and Kirsty walked on stage to excited applause, even a few gasps. Hannah understood, girls of a certain age latching on to a public figure who could show them how to be. She liked to think she was too old for that shit now, but she felt a trill in her belly all the same.

Behind Kirsty, the title of today's talk glowed on screen: *How To Be an Astronaut*. She smiled and took the applause. She looked younger than forty-three, lean and fit, black hair in a pixie cut, large-framed glasses. She started talking in her familiar Orcadian accent. On the screen, the title was replaced by a video of her on the International Space Station, the Earth visible out the window, Kirsty bobbing in zero G, a pencil floating past her shoulder. She talked about what it was like in that moment, four hundred and eight kilometres above Earth, one of only a handful of people to have left the planet in the history of humanity.

She talked about her past, Kirkwall Grammar then Edinburgh University to study astrophysics, like Hannah. Postgrad then postdocs at various international institutions, then a sideways swerve into the European Space Agency programme, first as technical advisor, then trainee astronaut, finally a goddamn spacewoman.

'Fancy it?' Rose said, nudging Hannah.

Growing up, Hannah had been obsessed with space and the astronauts who explored it. She pored over every detail of the moon landings, the workings of the ISS, the unmanned expeditions to Mars and further into the solar system, probes and satellites out there to glean knowledge of the universe.

These days, she still felt a thrill thinking about that stuff, and seeing Kirsty in the flesh was riveting. But something else gnawed at her. She remembered the first time she talked to Indy about the need for space exploration, not long after they started seeing each other. Indy didn't understand, pointed out the incredible cost, billions of dollars that could be spent on housing, sanitation or food on Earth. That argument was hard to counter, and Hannah found herself unmoored. But it wasn't either/or, she finally decided. Space travel for knowledge wasn't the enemy, rather it was the insane system of capitalism and commercialism at the expense of everyday people. That needed to change. Countless dollars on weaponry and armies, a corporate system that kills Earth's climate when there was sufficient technology to save it. The current trend for rich, white billionaires playing in space didn't help. The way Bezos, Branson and Musk treated space exploration as a personal pissing contest made her sick. And the idea that we would colonise the moon or Mars was ridiculous. Indy was right, we had to fix the planet we have.

But for all that, she was still in awe of the woman talking on stage.

Kirsty had moved on to the personal downside of space travel, the physical and mental-health impacts. Loss of bone mass, muscle wastage, fluid movement within the body that could lead to all sorts of problems, including potential blindness. Increased exposure to radiation, reduced red blood cell count, altered biome, the toll of isolation. Hannah hadn't really appreciated the stress of it all.

'So it's not all Bowie singalongs,' Kirsty said.

She paused to let the laughter subside, narrowed her eyes. 'But there was something very moving about being on the ISS, when we had a moment to reflect. I definitely experienced what some call the overview effect.'

An image of earthrise faded in behind her.

'The overview effect is a cognitive shift that some astronauts experience during spaceflight when viewing Earth. Looking at the planet where eight billion people are living and breathing, going about their days, and being separate from that, well...' She paused to gather herself. 'Let's just say, it makes you think differently about who we are and what we're doing to the planet.'

Another photograph appeared behind her, blackness above and below a blue curve, a speck of sunset in the middle. Hannah realised it was the surface of Earth from an acute angle, showing the thinness of the atmosphere.

'This is the thin blue line picture, taken from the ISS. It clearly shows how fragile we are, how little we're protected from the vast coldness of the cosmos.'

Hannah swallowed. She thought about the gravity holding her in her seat, the thousands of miles an hour she was travelling as the world spun on its axis. She was also hurtling around the sun, racing through the galaxy, always dancing, always moving.

'Bullshit.' The voice came from the front of the auditorium.

Kirsty placed a hand at her throat and peered into the gloom. 'What?'

'What did you see?'

Hannah saw the man, hoodie and baseball cap, sitting in the third row.

'I'm sorry,' Kirsty said. 'Do you have a question?'

'What did they do to you?' He was irate.

Two security guards strode down the aisle towards him. He spotted them and pointed at the stage.

'You're a fucking fraud, tell the truth. What happened up there?'

Kirsty was flustered, looked to the side of the stage, then back at the man as the security guards hauled him out of his seat. He kept shouting as they dragged him out of the fire exit.

'I'm so sorry,' Kirsty said under her breath. It was weirdly intimate, picked up by her mic, broadcast over the PA. 'So sorry.'

She looked at the fire-exit door, then around the dark room. She closed her eyes. Hannah wanted her to start talking again, find her rhythm and get the energy back. But she just stood there, saying she was sorry over and over.

4

DOROTHY

Dorothy looked around the chapel, renovated after the fire. They'd made a few improvements with the insurance money, including the extension into the garden to house the S900 resomator they bought from a death-research institute in Liverpool. Arlo was lying in front of it now on a gurney, still in his wet winding sheet. Fara stood alongside with half a dozen mourners from earlier in the day. The irony of water cremation for a body just recovered from the sea wasn't lost on Dorothy. She was mortified that they'd had to get the coastguard out to retrieve Arlo from the wash of the Forth.

Indy was explaining the process of water cremation to the gathering.

'Arlo goes in here,' she said, opening the large circular door. The resomator was a large stainless-steel tube, something between an industrial washing machine and a room in one of those Japanese pod hotels. The front door was thick glass, so they could monitor proceedings inside.

Indy pulled the body tray out of the machine. 'He slides in here, then these jets inside spray hot water at ninety-five degrees and a small amount of sodium hydroxide into the chamber, and Arlo dissolves. The sheet too, it's biodegradable.'

'Sodium hydroxide sounds like chemicals?' Fara said, ducking her head into the resomator.

Indy shook her head. 'It's the same process as natural decomposition, just speeded up. Sodium hydroxide is caustic soda, it breaks down body fat and tissue. Water cremation is legally called alkaline hydrolysis, it's the most eco-friendly funeral possible. It has a tenth of the carbon footprint of normal cremation, plus any heavy metals or plastics in Arlo's body don't get burned into toxins, they can be removed from his remains and disposed of properly.'

Fara nodded. 'What happens to his juice?'

'It goes down the drain to the water-treatment plant. It's actually a lot less polluting than the blood we remove from the deceased in embalming.'

'And what do we get back?'

'Only his bones are left. We usually grind them up in a cremulator, which gives you white ashes, not the grey stuff from a regular cremation. Pure calcium phosphate.'

'I think we'll just take the bones as they are.'

Dorothy tugged at her jacket and breathed, still trying to smooth out the adrenaline from earlier. She and Indy had changed their wet clothes for dry ones when they got back here, and the mourners had done the same before coming up the road. But there was a small pool of seawater under Arlo's gurney and a briny tang to the air. Dorothy recalled the coastguard boat thrusting into view from Port Edgar. They were used to fishing dead bodies out of the water near the Forth Road Bridge, a famous suicide hotspot. But Dorothy bet they'd never recovered a body from a funeral service before. They were nice about it, respectful when hauling Arlo into the boat, the same when they brought him to the concrete ramp.

Dorothy looked round the chapel now. She couldn't quite get a handle on these people. They weren't all dressed like Fara, one guy in jeans and a T-shirt, one with a side parting and button-down shirt, a young woman in yoga pants and strappy top. There was no clear demographic, no tribe she could pin down. Maybe they were just people who'd found each other and made a family. She got that.

'Any last words?' Indy said, hands clasped in front of her.

Fara shook her head and glanced at the others. No one spoke.

'We said it all on the island. That was his celebration.'

Fara came forward and touched her forehead against Arlo's through the sheet. The others came up and did the same, remaining around the body. Fara gave them a nod and they lifted Arlo from the gurney to the resomator tray then stepped back.

Indy slid the tray into the machine and closed the door. She pointed at the large green button to the side, looked at Fara.

'Do you want to?'

Fara stepped forward and put her hand on the glass door. She pressed the button and Dorothy heard the water jets flooding the chamber. It looked like a washing machine through the door and Dorothy remembered the water flowing over her shoes on the causeway earlier.

She looked at Indy. Water cremation was her idea and there were others too. Human composting, burial in a mushroom suit. They were trying to move away from embalming, had made it opt-in rather than opt-out. And Dorothy was talking to the council about buying land to create a natural-burial woodland. Indy and Hannah wanted to carve out a niche as the greenest funeral business in the country, and Dorothy couldn't be happier. She wouldn't be around to see what happened to the planet in fifty years, but she owed it to Hannah's generation to stop pumping chemicals into the ground and CO_2 into the air.

Fara moved away from the resomator window, signalling to the others to take a look. They took turns gazing at the chamber filling with water and caustic soda. When they were done, Indy held an arm out to usher them out of the chapel. The process took three hours.

Dorothy stepped to the machine and looked inside. She wanted to see something dramatic, like the Nazi face-melt from *Indiana Jones*, but all she saw was Arlo lying there, the water level rising, showerheads blasting, steam swirling. They'd saved Arlo from the water once today already but in three hours he would be returned to the water forever.

5

JENNY

Jenny wondered how many times she'd walked through the Meadows in her life. From their house in Greenhill Gardens, it was the main route to the centre of Edinburgh. As a kid she'd scuffed her way through the fallen cherry blossom, as a stoned teenager she lay down on the grass and gazed at the stars. As a journalist she traipsed through after hundreds of anodyne stories. As a young mum, she'd lingered with the buggy while Hannah picked up every stick she found. Stood watching her daughter captivated by squirrels darting up trees or magpies flitting between branches.

Now Hannah was married and lived down the road in Argyle Place with Indy, and Jenny was alone. Not completely, she had her mum, a friend in Archie. But she felt lonely. She'd had romances in recent years, and some unhealthy sex. And then there was Craig. His re-emergence in her life, his exposure as a murderer, their obsession with each other, his body washing up in Wardie Bay last year, only for it to be stolen by his sister.

Which was why she was here. She walked up Middle Meadow Walk, past a busker on the clarinet. Two girls with braided hair scooted past on roller skates, cyclists on racing bikes with padded shorts, an old couple wearing too many layers, arm in arm. Jenny felt a twinge at their devotion to each other.

She reached Söderberg and looked around. She didn't spot Violet at first, was looking for the trim, contained woman from a year ago. Then she scanned again, stopped at the woman in the fancy wheelchair with the young, muscular man by her side. He held a glass of iced tea while Violet tried to suck on the straw. She seemed so much smaller, had lost a lot of weight. Her hair had gone from neat white bob to straggly and yellowing. She had a blanket on her lap despite the warm sun dappling the trees, and her feet were turned inward on her wheelchair footrests. Jenny took her in. A year ago she had to identify Craig's bloated and burnt body in the mortuary, had to deal with her daughter stealing that body.

Jenny thought about the phone call earlier. She hadn't answered it, just stared at her mobile until it went to voicemail. When she listened back it was a man's voice, thick Highland accent explaining that Violet wanted to meet her, giving the time and place. Jenny assumed it was a solicitor or other representative. But this guy seemed more like her carer.

She walked to the table. 'Violet.'

The man put down the iced tea and stood. Violet's head was twisted to the side, a tremor running from her hands to her face.

The man put out a hand. 'I'm Norrie, I look after Violet.'

He had thick arms and Pictish tattoos, brown hair flecked with ginger, kind eyes and heavy stubble. Jenny shook his hand. Norrie pointed at a chair, and Jenny sat.

'Can I get you something?' Norrie said, looking for a waitress.

'No, thanks.'

Violet stared at Jenny, her head jerking like she was receiving signals from somewhere.

'Motor neurone disease,' Norrie said. 'Violet has been fighting it for about a year now.'

He reached over with a napkin and wiped some spit from the corner of her mouth. Violet's eyes followed him, then after a few seconds she spoke.

'Thanks.'

It seemed a huge effort of will to control her mouth. She trembled, and Norrie moved the iced tea to a safe distance.

'I've changed,' Violet said slowly.

The last time they saw each other, Jenny had harangued her on the Royal Mile, trying to find out where Stella had taken Craig's body. Turned out she didn't know any more than Jenny.

'Wondering...' Violet's shoulders jerked and she waited for it to pass. 'Why you're here?'

Jenny heard crows in the trees above their table, call and response between branches. 'Have you heard from Stella, is that it? She's still wanted for arson and attempted murder, so if you know anything, you should tell the police.'

Violet coughed and struggled to swallow. Norrie leaned in, held the straw to her lips. She sucked a small amount, coughed again. She breathed a few times, shallow ripples through her chest.

'The police gave up,' she said eventually.

This was true. Stella was a missing person, after a short window people forget and move on. Unless some glaring evidence dropped in the police's lap, they would do fuck all.

'Then what?'

Violet looked at Norrie, leaned on her headrest and closed her eyes. 'Dorothy?'

Jenny frowned. 'Mum's fine.'

'Retired?'

'I don't think she'll ever retire. She loves the funerals and everything else.'

Violet's head wobbled. 'Lucky. You and Hannah.' She coughed roughly, head banging on the wheelchair.

Norrie placed a hand on the back of her head to cushion it, then squeezed her hand. It looked like a crumpled piece of paper in his big paw. 'You're doing fine, Mrs M.'

Violet blinked. 'Mothers and daughters.'

Jenny tried to think what to say. She'd run the spectrum of emotions with Dorothy and Hannah over the years, but they'd always been there for each other when it mattered. 'I suppose so.'

Violet closed her eyes for a long time, then opened them.

'I'm dying,' she said with colossal effort. 'I need to see Stella. Will you find her?'

6

HANNAH

The roofs of the nearest buildings looked close enough to jump to. Edinburgh's Old Town was an insane jumble of structures, grown like mould over the last five hundred years. The rooftop clutter on the slope from the castle to Holyrood Palace looked like a crowd jostling to get a glimpse of the sea beyond.

Hannah walked around the rooftop terrace of the museum, ogling the view. South of the castle was Edinburgh College of Art, Heriot's private school, then the dome of McEwan Hall, where she'd graduated two years ago. Further south she saw another dome, the observatory on Blackford Hill, where she studied. Then east to the colossal knuckle of Arthur's Seat, glowing in low twilight. She imagined being a giant, striding through the streets, tourists diving for cover as she lumbered around the city's hills, lifting roofs, finding secrets underneath.

'Hannah.'

Rose held two champagne glasses and offered her one. She took it and looked around. Maybe a hundred people, and she wondered how many had been at Kirsty's talk, or if they just wanted to be in the proximity of celebrity. Maybe that was unfair. In amongst the invited guests were lots of museum staff, and Hannah wondered if there was any security here. She thought about the event derailed by the heckler, how Kirsty eventually got things back on track, answering questions, then finishing a few minutes early.

'The uni are paying for all this,' Rose said, waving a hand. 'And yet they just cut my pension by thirty percent.'

Edinburgh Uni had a shit ton of money – you didn't own large swathes of property in a medieval city without making a few quid. And they were constantly throwing up new student flats to coin in more money. A lot of pomp and circumstance at official functions, yet students and staff got shafted. Before she started her PhD, Hannah had a notion of a future in academia, gentle research, corner office, funded conferences. But now, at the business end of her studies, she didn't see it at all. But what else could she do with an astrophysics doctorate?

'Kirsty.' This was Rose speaking over Hannah's shoulder.

Hannah turned and saw Kirsty with another woman she knew to be her wife, Mina. Both of them were tall up close, striking. Kirsty had a youthful glow, while Mina had a model's cheekbones and air of confidence. They were a power couple for sure, Mina big in biotech.

Kirsty and Rose hugged, then Kirsty introduced Mina.

'And this is Hannah Skelf, who I told you about,' Rose said.

'You did?' Hannah said.

'All good stuff, I promise.' Kirsty's accent made everything seem friendly.

'I'm a huge fan.' Hannah's cheeks flushed. She felt like a wee girl with a pop star. 'You're an inspiration.'

Kirsty grinned and Hannah felt the full force of that smile, just for her.

'Thinking of following in my footsteps?'

Hannah had imagined being an astronaut when she was younger, but that was silly, unrealistic. But Kirsty was standing here, another Scottish woman from an ordinary background. Why the hell not?

'She could,' Rose said. 'She's certainly smart enough.'

Hannah sipped her drink to hide her embarrassment and shook her head. 'I don't have the right stuff.'

Kirsty laughed, but not unkindly. '"The right stuff" is such alpha-male bullshit. It's a twentieth-century mindset, men puffing their chests out to be the most heroic. I know you didn't mean it like that, but the idea that only extraordinary people do this sort of thing is something I've struggled against my whole career.'

Mina leaned in with raised eyebrows. 'You've touched a nerve.'

Kirsty nudged her wife and Mina spilled a little from her glass. They both smiled.

'It's about collaboration and community,' Kirsty said. 'Helping others. But you know that already, right? You're kind of famous yourself, the Skelfs, private investigations and funerals.'

Hannah felt blood rise to her face again. She would never get used to the fact her family were famous in this town. Infamous, more like. Over the last few years, all the bullshit with her dad had been big news. How he murdered Hannah's friend, Melanie. Escaped on the way to court, kidnapped Hannah's half-sister Sophia, then been found and killed by Jenny. It was like a cheesy soap opera, except it was her life, trauma she had to come to terms with. It had taken time and understanding from Indy and others, but she finally felt on an even keel.

'Sorry,' Kirsty said, seeing her reaction. 'I didn't mean to be flippant about what you've gone through.'

Hannah shook her head and took another drink. The noise of the crowd swamped over her. Somewhere down in the street, a police siren wailed.

'Not at all, it's fine.'

Mina touched Kirsty's arm, reminding her of something.

Kirsty cleared her throat. 'But you're an investigator, right? You find things out for people.'

'I help when I can.'

Kirsty side-eyed Mina and clinked her wedding ring on her champagne flute. 'I might need your help.'

Hannah thought back to earlier in the auditorium. 'Is this to do with the heckler?'

'Not exactly.'

She shared another look with Mina, then glanced around the room. Hannah followed her gaze, half expecting the same mouthy idiot to appear, pointing and shouting. People were looking at Kirsty while pretending not to, that famous-person-in-the-room vibe. One woman wearing a museum name badge stared. It must be weird to be so well known.

'Maybe this isn't the best place to discuss it.' Kirsty handed Hannah a card with her address on it. 'Why don't you come to ours for dinner tomorrow?'

Hannah looked from Kirsty to Mina, who nodded.

'I'd love to.'

7

JENNY

Jenny watched her mum take the veggie lasagne out the oven. Dorothy touched the small of her back once she'd put the hot dish on the table and straightened up. Just a twinge from age. Jenny thought of Violet, unable to take a drink without help. She was only three years older than Dorothy, fit as a fiddle a year ago.

Jenny lifted bowls of salad and garlic bread to the table as Hannah and Indy arranged cutlery, glasses, a jug of water and a bottle of Rioja. Her daughter was happy, healthy, hopelessly in love, lucky to find a soulmate so early in life. Jenny wondered if Dorothy considered Jim her soulmate. They'd been married for fifty years, so what else? Dorothy had Thomas now, a second chance at love, they obviously cared deeply for each other. Jenny wondered if she would ever have that again in her life. The one time she'd felt it, it was destroyed so brutally.

Dorothy dished up lasagne as Indy poured wine. Dorothy always tried to get them together for an evening meal. It started when Jim died, company to banish the grief, but had turned into something more, the glue between them. When Jenny was a young mum with Hannah, there was a lot of bullshit parenting advice about 'quality time'. But there was no such thing as quality time, just time. Just be there, that's your fucking job.

Jenny wondered if Hannah needed her anymore. She had Indy, and a close connection to Dorothy, two spiritual souls with a wider vision of the universe. Jenny felt like a Neanderthal next to them, but maybe she was being hard on herself. She was here, wasn't she?

Dorothy and Indy recounted the craziness of this morning's funeral ceremony on Cramond Island. Thank God neither of them had been washed away. Jenny thought again about Violet in her wheelchair. Dorothy had slowed down over the last year, more considered in her movements. Jenny didn't want to picture her running to escape a rushing tide. She realised she'd been watching her mum as she served food, looking for hand tremors, momentary slips, early signs.

'What about the ashes?' Hannah said.

Dorothy shook her head. 'They want bones, not ashes. I'm taking them to Fara later.'

Hannah talked about her day meeting a famous astronaut. Jenny recognised the name but didn't know much about her. Maybe there *was* such a thing as quality time, she should've got involved in Hannah's science interests when she was younger. Maybe Jenny was a terrible mother after all.

Hannah waved a card in the air. 'So we're going to theirs for dinner tomorrow.'

Indy raised her eyebrows. 'We?'

'She said I should bring you.'

Hannah pushed back her chair and walked to the PI white-board, wrote *Kirsty Ferrier*.

'She has a case?' Dorothy said.

'She mentioned something at the reception, that's what tomorrow's about.'

Jenny marvelled at her daughter, studying for her PhD, married, solving mysteries, meeting famous astronauts. She remembered the little girl, so confident and bold, with an inner strength that astounded Jenny. Hannah had always known who she was and Jenny envied that.

'I saw Violet today,' she said as Hannah sat down.

Dorothy turned. 'What?'

'She called, I went to meet her.'

Hannah frowned. 'Has she heard from Stella?'

This was the hard bit. Violet was Hannah's other gran, after all. Craig was her dad. They were all so intertwined.

'No.' Jenny went to the whiteboard and wrote *Violet McNamara*. Dorothy bent down and picked up Schrödinger, who'd sauntered over to the table looking for scraps. She stroked his back. 'What did she want?'

Jenny glanced around the room then out of the window. Dark already, autumn closing in. Streetlights fizzing amongst the trees, the city going about its business, oblivious to their little dramas.

'She wants us to find Stella.'

Dorothy narrowed her eyes. 'What about the police?'

'She has no faith in the police, says they've given up. She has a point.'

'I'll talk to Thomas about it.'

Jenny shrugged. 'I think we should do it anyway.'

Dorothy shook her head. 'That's not a good idea, Jen, you're too close. Remember what happened last time?'

Jenny hadn't stopped thinking about it since she met Violet. The look on Stella's face as she set fire to the house, as she beat Jenny.

She stared at her mum. 'Like you've never taken on a personal case.'

'This is different.'

'Because I'm not as strong as you?'

'That's not what I meant.'

'What then?'

The question hung in the room like mist.

'Why now?' Hannah said, flicking Kirsty's card in her fingers.

'What?'

'Why does Nana want to find Stella now? It's been a year. What changed?'

Jenny swallowed and kept her eyes on Hannah. 'She's dying.'

8

DOROTHY

The Cramond Arms was ragged around the edges, an old pub that hadn't jumped on the 'traditional' bandwagon. Smattering of shoogly tables, the smell of the drip trays, lights too bright, TV showing Formula One, a spread of regulars nursing lagers. Dorothy stood at the bar, no sign of any staff. Eventually a middle-aged woman rolled her hips into view and scowled at Dorothy, who ordered an IPA.

The door behind her opened and Fara came in, looking nervous. The old guys at the bar shifted their weight when they saw her, stared at their pints. Dorothy sensed the atmosphere change. The barmaid returned with the cloudy pint, head too large, and stared at Fara.

Fara stuck her chin out. 'Another of those, please.'

The barmaid hesitated then poured it.

'Can we grab a table outside?' Fara said. 'We're not too popular in here.'

Dorothy clocked the barmaid's frown at Fara as she paid.

Fara picked up the pints. 'Come on.'

Dorothy shook her head and followed to a table outside. The bar was on the waterfront, view over the River Almond to the trees beyond, a flock of seagulls bobbing on the water amongst anchored sailing boats, rigging clanking in the breeze. Twenty-five years ago in the silt of the river mouth, a ferryman found a Roman sandstone sculpture of a lioness eating a man. There were more Roman ruins up the hill behind them. Dorothy pictured centurions marching into the village and declaring it Roman, what the locals must've thought.

The briny smell reminded Dorothy of earlier, water rising up her legs, Arlo escaping into the firth. She had his remains in her small backpack, took it off and put it at her feet.

Fara glanced at the pub door. 'They hate us in that place.'

'Why?'

Fara shrugged and glugged her pint. 'They hate us everywhere. It's just part of the life. Small-minded locals think we're hippie freeloaders. Plenty of us have jobs and pay tax, we always clean up our mess, never harm anyone. But check out any local Facebook page when a community like ours turns up. Moral outrage. It's deep-rooted insecurity and jealousy. They see us enjoying life and they hate it.'

Dorothy was well aware of that narrow mindset. It maybe wasn't as bad as it used to be, but it was still prevalent. And social media had made it fester and grow in some people's hearts. She couldn't understand the negativity, had spent a lifetime trying to see the positive in people. But she knew some were super-resistant to change, preferring to wallow in misery and anger.

'Can I ask you something?' she said.

Fara smiled and leaned in.

'How did you come to this life?'

Fara's smile flickered. 'I would love to say idealism. I mean, I do believe in it, deeply. Humans have been nomadic for thousands of years longer than they've been settled. And we try to leave as small a footprint as we can. But the truth is, I was chucked out of my home. The usual – strict parents, rebellious teenage daughter, drugs and an unwanted pregnancy. It got to the point where I wasn't welcome, and I couldn't live like that. I knew Arlo and a couple of others, hitched a ride, never looked back.'

Dorothy thought about not putting down roots. She'd had her feet embedded in number zero Greenhill Gardens for half a century, but it was almost taken from her in last year's fire. Could she have walked away and started again?

'That was amazing earlier,' Fara said.

Dorothy took a moment to think what she meant. 'Losing Arlo?'

Fara laughed. 'No, but that was memorable, right? Life is about experiences, and I won't forget it in a hurry.'

'It's one for the memoirs.'

Fara touched Dorothy's hand. 'You should write a memoir, it would be amazing. You have a great energy, and the stories you could tell.'

Dorothy wasn't convinced she had stories to tell, or that anyone would be interested. She never understood the compulsion to revisit the past. It influenced us, of course, made us who we are. But she'd never been one to dwell on it, life was like water in the river, moments slipping away.

'I meant the resomation at your house,' Fara said. 'I'd never heard of water cremation until I read your website.'

'We're trying to move into the twenty-first century.' Dorothy sipped her drink. 'It's insane how damaging traditional funerals are to the environment.'

'Well, you got Arlo's funeral because of it.'

'Speaking of which.'

Dorothy unzipped the backpack and took out the box of Arlo's remains. They had fancier boxes and urns, but Fara wanted the recycled cardboard. Dorothy put it on the table between their pints.

Fara opened the flaps. A scatter of bones, thin and brittle from drying out, sat amongst the dust of disintegrated fragments. It was all dazzling white. Nicer to think of our essence that way, rather than the dull grey they usually handed over.

Fara lifted out a femur, rubbed her hand over the bulbous end. She waved it like a lightsaber then held it by the ends like a scroll. She placed it back in the box and picked out the skull. The jawbone had crumpled and there was a hole on the left side of the parietal bone. Fara turned it in her hands like Hamlet.

Two women Dorothy's age walked past with their terriers, stared at Fara and gave each other a look. They didn't like what was happening here, or they didn't like Fara.

'What are you going to do with him?' Dorothy said.

Fara placed the skull in the box and traced a finger through the white powder lining the bottom.

'Not sure yet. Arlo wasn't bothered. We'll take a vote, that's how we settle things.'

'Does that work?'

'Better than you think,' Fara said. 'As long as there's empathy, we get along fine. I'm not kidding myself, this isn't a model you can expand indefinitely. It works because we know and support each other. It's when people can be anonymous that they behave with no respect.'

Fara was talking about her caravanners, but it was the same everywhere. A lack of responsibility for your actions meant you could hurt others with impunity. Dorothy thought the world had got better in her lifetime – look how far we'd come with racism, homophobia, all the rest. But seeing aggressive online tribalism, or the reactions of the Cramond locals to a different way of life, made her wonder.

She heard slapping footsteps and saw a young woman running towards them. Dorothy recognised her from the ceremony earlier, remembered her dancing with Fara on the island.

Fara spoke as the woman reached them. 'Billie, what's wrong?'

Billie was panting, placed a hand on her chest, the other pointing behind her.

'There's a fire. Me and Ruby's camper. Quick.'

Dorothy looked behind her. Streetlights along the riverside, smoke in the sky above the headland.

Fara launched out of her seat and ran, Billie behind.

Dorothy grabbed Arlo's box and shoved it in the backpack, then followed. As she turned the corner she saw caravans and campers sprawled across the sandy grass. One on the right was blazing with fire. She heard a crackle as the frame buckled, the roar of the flames. Thought about her own house a year ago, the damage it caused, the misery.

People were standing close to the inferno, helpless, some holding each other.

Fara and Billie raced to the flames but were pushed back by the heat.

Dorothy took out her phone and called 999.

9

HANNAH

Mortonhall Crem would've been a disconcerting building even if it wasn't a place to burn your dead. Hannah glanced up as she waited to go inside with Indy and the body of Elsie Schumann. The façade was made of tall, thin concrete slabs leaning against each other like ancient standing stones. Hannah wondered if the entrance lined up with the solstice sunrise. The whole effect was austere brutalism, something from a 1960s sci-fi movie.

The last mourners were filing into the chapel, Hannah giving out orders of service. She'd been roped into this morning's funeral last minute because something had come up with Dorothy, to do with yesterday's thing at Cramond. So here she was in her grey trouser suit, white blouse and black hair tied up as neat as she could, which wasn't very.

She looked at an order of service: 'In Loving Memory of Elsie Schumann, April 1944 – September 2023'. What it didn't say was that Elsie suffered the bizarre death of being struck by lightning. While out walking her dog, an elderly schnauzer called Mr Pickles, in Saughton Park. On came the rain, umbrella up, and zap, over she went. She was found later with burn marks on her arms and neck, like she'd been possessed by a demon. Archie tried his best to cover those marks for the viewing.

The picture her children had used for the front of the order of service was from a few years ago, a smiling woman with white hair and thick glasses. Hannah wondered what she was like as a girl or a young woman. Did she live life to the full or filled with regret? We always say nice things at funerals, but some lives are sad. Hannah hoped Elsie had a great one.

As the final mourners entered the chapel, Indy came over and raised her eyebrows.

'See that guy?' She nodded towards a young man, off-the-peg suit, wavy dark hair. He had a restless energy, gangly arms and legs, black trainers. He was good-looking in a gormless, vacant way.

'What about him?'

'Funeral crasher. He's been at half a dozen in the last two weeks.'

'Is that really a thing? I know that's how Gran met Archie, but that was because of his Cotard's syndrome.'

Indy shrugged. 'All I know is he's regular as clockwork, looking sad and shaking hands with the bereaved.'

'Maybe he's just unlucky.' Hannah lifted an order of service and waved it. 'Elsie Schumann was.'

'There's no harm in it,' Indy said. 'If you want to grieve for strangers, that's up to you.'

Indy went to organise the pallbearers at the hearse, showed them how to pull Elsie from the back of the vehicle, share the weight. They were Elsie's grandchildren, three men and one woman.

Hannah thought about the funeral crasher. Indy was right, there was no harm in it, not to the mourners, unless they felt it cheapened their own grief. But what about the crasher, was he in a good place?

The grandkids carried Elsie into the chapel, Indy at the front, Hannah behind. They walked down the nave to the altar and laid the coffin on the plinth in front of a powder-blue curtain. The business end of proceedings was behind it. Hannah thought of the Wizard of Oz: pay no attention to the man behind the curtain. In this case it was a body furnace that would roast Elsie to a thousand degrees Celsius, belching her smoke into the air via the industrial chimneys, reducing the rest of her to dust.

Hannah cringed at the thought of all that CO_2 billowing into the atmosphere. But Dorothy was right, not everyone was ready to change, and older clients wanted familiar rituals. Of course, the worst excuse in history for not changing things was 'we've always done it that way'. Tradition was ninety-nine percent bullshit.

She sat in the front row of hard pine benches cemented to the floor and thought about Kirsty Ferrier. The overview effect, how she'd come back from space a different person, with a newfound respect for the earth, and disgust at the way we hurt each other and the planet. Everything needed overhauling for a new millennium. It was so obvious to Hannah's generation that industrial capitalist bullshit hadn't worked, yet the old dinosaurs were holding on to power, in politics, industry, everywhere.

'You're in a dream,' Indy whispered in her ear, as the crem filled with organ music.

'Just thinking about the overview effect.'

'What?'

'Kirsty talked about it yesterday. A new perspective you get when you've been in space.'

'On first-name terms already?'

Hannah's cheeks reddened, though she knew it was a tease. 'You'll like her.'

A short, stocky minister gave an account of Elsie's life, skirting over the lightning strike, then led the congregation in song and prayer. Finally the blue curtains opened and the coffin slid into the back area, ready for cremation. Curtains down, show's over.

Hannah and Indy escorted the family out, where they did the line-up. Hannah never really understood that – at the worst time in your darkest grief, you glad-handed a bunch of people you barely knew? But each to their own, and the Schumann clan were up for it.

Hannah blinked in the sunshine as she left the building. She examined the crowd until she spotted the funeral crasher, nodding in sadness, shaking hands with Elsie's children in turn. He shook the final hand and left, squinting at the sun streaming through the trees. He breathed deep and shook his head, as if trying to clear a bad dream. He rolled his shoulders and walked along the path to the car park. Hannah was only a few yards away on the grass. As he passed her, he glanced up then lowered his head.

'Excuse me,' Hannah said.

He kept walking.

She followed. He increased his pace, looked to the side.

'Excuse me.'

He kept at the same pace, shoulders tense under his jacket.

Hannah reached him and touched his arm. 'Excuse me.'

He stopped and turned, tears running down his cheeks, lip quivering, face crumpled.

'Are you OK?' Hannah said.

He took a stuttering breath and shook his head, then fell into her with a hug she was surprised by.

'No,' he said into her shoulder. 'Not at all.'

10

DOROTHY

The stench of burnt wood, scorched metal and molten plastic in the morning air was triggering. Dorothy remembered the first sight of her home, after the fire a year ago. They were so lucky the fire fighters suppressed the blaze quickly, limited the worst damage to a few ground-floor rooms. She swallowed thinking of what could've happened, the house destroyed, Hannah, Indy or Jenny dead.

She looked around Cramond Beach, counted nine campers and caravans parked in a rough circle. She remembered the old Westerns where they would circle the wagons against indigenous attacks. Shocking, looking back, how racist the culture was, centred on the white experience. There was one gap in the circle here, the charred remains of Billie and Ruby's campervan. All that was left was the lower part of the chassis, black and dirty, melted tyres on the buckled wheels.

This part of the beach consisted of compacted sand and scrawny grass, sitting above the tide line, between sea and promenade. Dorothy looked at the island, glowing in sunshine. The tide was in and the tips of the dragon's teeth looked like a column of infantrymen marching to land. She turned to the prom, busy with joggers, dog-walkers, two mums pushing babies in buggies. They looked at the burnt remains of the camper then turned into the village.

'Hi, Dorothy.' Fara wore a biker's jacket and tweed trousers that somehow worked together. Her blonde hair was loose, sombre look on her face.

Dorothy nodded at the burnt-out remains. 'I wanted to see how you were doing.'

'Not great.'

'How are Billie and Ruby?'

Fara considered the question. 'They'll be OK. They're young and elastic, they'll bounce back.'

The girls were late teens, and Fara couldn't have been older than twenty-seven. At that age, ten years felt like half your life. From Dorothy's end of the telescope, it was a blink of the eye.

'They seem very young to be living like this,' Dorothy said. 'How did they end up here?'

Fara shrugged. 'You'd be surprised what people have lived through, even at their age.'

She walked to the remains and Dorothy followed. The ash was still damp from the fire-engine water jets, puddles and mud underfoot.

'Were they able to salvage anything?'

'They didn't have much. You learn to travel as light as possible in this way of life. Leave no trace and all that.'

Dorothy thought about that. What if her house *had* burnt down? She wasn't one for reminders or keepsakes, organised photo albums. Her leaning towards Buddhism meant she wasn't inclined to hold on to material possessions. But the house had been her home for five decades, the idea of it gone made her heart flutter. Maybe this life of Fara's was easier, not putting down roots.

'Any idea how it started?'

Dorothy saw the charred and soggy pages of a book. A melted cushion in a puddle, the blackened neck of a guitar, strings broken. Jesus.

'The girls weren't in when it happened, they were at Parker's place.' Fara nodded at a rusted old caravan across the circle.

'Parker?'

'Billie's boyfriend.'

In the space in the middle of the camp were a handful of foldout chairs and two wooden pallets. Sitting on the furthest pallet were Billie, Ruby and a guy Fara's age, presumably Parker.

Billie was small and thin, strawberry-blonde hair piled on top of her head, gold hoop earrings, wearing a white crop top and leggings, oversized denim jacket like someone from an eighties pop band. Her leggings were covered in ashen smears from the fire. Ruby was a similar build, brunette, nose stud and a snake tattoo on her arm. Parker was very tall, wiry, curly black hair tangled over his face, skinny black jeans and a gold chain over a Misfits T-shirt. He was decades too young for Misfits, but whatever.

Fara led Dorothy over.

'How's it going?' she said to Billie, who was smoking a large joint. Dorothy saw it was a hollowed-out cigar, full of skunk by the smell of it.

Billie held her toke, blew it out, passed the joint to Ruby. She stared with narrow eyes at Fara and Dorothy, then shrugged.

'Fuck, you know?' She waved a hand at her campervan.

Her left leg twitched and Dorothy saw her trainers were caked in mud.

Fara nodded at the girls. 'Dorothy was just asking how it happened.'

'Fuck,' Billie said again, drawling it out.

'What did the police say?'

Billie spat out a laugh. 'Fucking whatever.'

Ruby passed the joint to Parker, who inhaled deep.

'Useless,' Ruby said, touching Billie's arm.

Both she and Billie had strong Doric accents. What were two Aberdeenshire girls doing here?

'An accident?' Dorothy said.

'Fuck accident,' Ruby said.

Fara walked over and lifted something from behind a pallet. It was a blackened metal jerry can, the kind you fill at the petrol station.

'The fire fighters found this.'

'Someone torched our home,' Ruby said.

'And the police confirmed that?' Dorothy said.

'Did they fuck,' Ruby said. 'Cunts didn't listen.'

Fara was back at Dorothy's side. 'The police don't treat us with much respect.'

'But this is obviously arson.'

Billie widened her eyes. 'The cops don't give a fuck about likes of us.'

'Who would've done this?' Dorothy said, pointing at the jerry can.

Billie sat up, took the blunt off Parker and inhaled. She blinked several times, exhaled, pushed her shoulders back.

'Why do you care?' She scoped Dorothy up and down. 'You some kind of detective?'

'That's exactly what I am,' she said. 'And I want to help you guys.'

Billie flashed a smile then sighed. 'Honestly, don't bother.'

Dorothy caught Ruby frowning at Parker. They were concerned about Billie's flat answer, and so was Dorothy. Something about this didn't add up and Dorothy knew she would have to find out what.

11

JENNY

Jenny would never feel comfortable around cops. She hadn't trusted the police since she was a student, on marches and protests, faced down with heavy-handed tactics by arsehole officers, men who enjoyed the power their uniform gave them over young women. Not all cops, blah, blah, blah, of course, but enough were attracted to the service for the wrong reasons. The dickhead lads at her school all joined the army or police, which spoke volumes. Things were probably a little better know, but the uproar around Black Lives Matter in the States, and the subsequent spotlight on Scotland's force suggested otherwise.

She tried to tally these feelings with Mum's boyfriend. It was ridiculous to call a police officer in his late fifties the boyfriend of a woman in her seventies. But what else – lovers, fuckbuddies? Get it where you can, Mum. Jenny was envious, she hadn't fucked anyone in a year and missed it. Though the sex she was having before she stopped wasn't exactly healthy, so maybe she was better off temporarily celibate.

She watched two very young officers walk through reception. Police stations didn't feel like police stations anymore, St Leonard's was more like an anonymous office space, apart from the uniforms and security.

Thomas appeared through the door and hugged her. He smelled of sandalwood and calm. She wondered what the young female officer behind reception thought of him. He was an oddity, for sure, a black Swedish guy who'd kept his head down and worked his way through the Scottish ranks after moving here for love three decades ago. She couldn't imagine the shit he must've got, not fitting in as one of the lads. But he was still here, that's all any of us can do.

She looked at him as they separated. He was a silver fox, white flecks through his short hair and beard, trim body in a sharp suit. Dorothy had done well, but she was a catch for her age too. Years of yoga, meditation, drumming and hydration made her look at least a decade younger than she was. Jenny felt like a lump of lard in comparison, becoming more shapeless with every passing year, the weight of those years on her face, in her heart.

Thomas ushered her upstairs to his office. Not huge, but tasteful furniture and an amazing view of Salisbury Crags and Arthur's Seat out of the window.

'How are you?' he said.

Jenny sat. 'Good. Haven't seen you in a few days, everything OK with Mum?'

He waved at his messy desk. 'So much more paperwork than we used to have. That's all I do now.'

Better than going out and cracking skulls, Jenny thought.

'So.' Thomas raised his hands.

Jenny glanced out of the window. Parts of Salisbury Crags had been closed to the public recently because of falling rocks. Last weekend, someone had to be helicoptered off a scree slope. It was weird having something so wild and dangerous squatting in the middle of your city. Today she saw the tiny outlines of tourists on the cliff, specks of dust with lives, hopes, dreams, grief she would never know.

'Violet McNamara came to see me.'

He nodded but didn't speak. He employed the same silent technique as Dorothy to get people to open up.

'She wants me to find Stella.'

'That's an open missing-persons case.'

Jenny leaned forward and touched the desk. 'How many man-hours were costed to it last month?'

'Our resources are stretched. We have to prioritise.'

'Exactly.' Jenny smiled. 'I'm here to help you by taking the case off your hands.'

'You think that's a good idea?'

His measured manner was starting to irritate her. She didn't do measured.

'I'm a new woman compared to last year.' Jenny's voice was too eager, like someone had injected her with positivity serum. 'Therapy has me on an even keel.'

'Nevertheless.'

He didn't say anything else and Jenny decided to wait him out. Two could play at that game.

'You're too close,' he said eventually, smiling. He knew what she was doing.

Jenny tapped the side of her head, then realised it was a sign for being crazy. 'That's why I'm the right person for it, I know the family.'

'You knew Craig, you don't know Stella.'

Jenny splayed her hands out on the desk. 'I might have some insight.'

'You think that's why Violet came to you?'

Jenny saw two figures on the edge of the cliff outside. Imagined one of them tumbling to the rocks below, the other distraught at the top.

'No, she asked me because she's dying and the police aren't doing anything.'

Thomas cleared his throat. 'I'm sorry about Violet, but I did say our resources—'

'I'm not blaming anyone,' Jenny said. 'I just hoped you could let me see the file.'

Thomas pressed his lips together. 'That's technically illegal.'

'You've done other technically illegal things for us.'

He tilted his head. Jenny glanced behind him, the figures were gone from the cliff. Maybe they jumped off together, holding hands on the way down. Or maybe they just walked to a café for cake.

'What does Dorothy think of this?'

'She *loves* the idea.' Jenny couldn't keep the sarcasm from her voice.

'I bet.'

She held his gaze, fronting him out.

'I've taken the case already, Thomas, I just hoped you might help.'

He stuck his lip out then started typing on his laptop. She watched him for a moment then looked out of the window again, hoping for some drama.

'There's not much,' Thomas said.

He turned the laptop screen to her and she leaned in. A brief summary of the original investigation a year ago. The registration and hire company for the van, which was never recovered. A list of people they interviewed. No phone usage since that night at the house. A few thousand pounds withdrawn earlier that day, no other transactions since.

'Pretty cold trail,' she said.

'I told you.'

'Can you email this to me?'

'I already have.'

'The money means she was planning to stay low for a long time, right?'

'It seems so.'

'So how does someone disappear like that? Even with cash. She has to be living somewhere, paying rent. Earning money for food.'

Thomas turned the laptop back and closed it down.

'It's easier to disappear than people think. You know that.'

She did. Much of her recent life had been spent chasing shadows, hunting ghosts, finding people who didn't want to be found. She looked out of the window and imagined being on the edge of Salisbury Crags, looking down over the city, searching for a sign that would reveal the truth. Something to help her find Stella and Craig.

12

DOROTHY

She loved playing with The Multiverse. That was the tongue-in-cheek name Hannah had given the band Dorothy was in, and they decided to keep it. Fifteen of them were crammed into the second-floor attic studio of Dorothy's place, the heat from their exertions giving the air a sweaty glow.

By the open window were the ten members of the choir, organised by a local community group based in one of the churches on Holy Corner at the top of Morningside. Dorothy wasn't religious, but a lot of good people used their beliefs to help people. Katy was one of life's organisers – she met isolated refugee families through her work at a foodbank, and had corralled a gang of mostly young women from Syria, Afghanistan, Somalia, and latterly Ukraine, into singing together. And they were good, confident and strong when belting out in their second, third or fourth languages. The grins on their faces made Dorothy's heart swell.

The rest of the band had coalesced around Katy's husband Will, a skilful guitarist across half a dozen genres. Young Zack was on bass, floppy fringe and teenage acne, his girlfriend Maria on piano and keyboard. Then there was Gillian, a lanky German multi-instrumentalist, who found the right flourishes of violin, trumpet or percussion, whatever was needed. And Dorothy on drums, of course.

Dorothy checked the setlist at her feet. It was hard to define this band. Hannah described them to Indy as a gospel, blues, country-rock sideshow community revival, and Dorothy couldn't think of anything better. The setlist had songs by Wilco, Low and Lambchop, but also the likes of Brittany Howard, Mavis Staples and Aretha Franklin. They'd worked out gospel-tinged versions of pop bangers by Katy Perry and Lorde, and would sometimes delve into the country-rock archive, like the next song.

Dorothy counted them into 'The Weight' by The Band, a song that made her body ache for the California of her youth. She pictured walking along the shore of Pismo Beach with a pale-skinned Scottish boy on her arm who would become her life for five decades, the pair of them impossibly young, full of energy and promise. When you got to her age, it was easy to forget what it was like to be young and bursting with life. A lifetime ahead of you to create yourself.

This song was perfect for The Multiverse with its message of sharing the load – especially if you're half-past dead, travelling the world like some of this choir had done, looking for sanctuary and the kindness of strangers. It was simple drumming in the verses, straight fours on the snare, kick and hi-hat, small flourishes leading into the chorus where she could open up a little. But this wasn't showy drumming, just about sitting in the pocket, riding the groove. The song was about camaraderie, playing a small part in a bigger whole. All music was like that to an extent, but drumming in particular. Doing just enough to lift things overall. Dorothy was here to support the choir as they sang about the load they carried. Christ, these people knew about carrying a load. She couldn't begin to imagine what their lives were like before winding up in this sweaty loft making a racket.

The overlapping vocals of the last chorus faded. They rattled through the riff four times and ended with a flourish, toms rolls and cymbals for Dorothy, ad-lib scales for the musicians, a single note from the choir, then silence.

Dorothy shared a wide grin with everyone in the room.

The door opened and Hannah spotted Dorothy. 'The guy we spoke about is downstairs.'

It was the end of rehearsal, so Dorothy made excuses and followed Hannah downstairs. It always took ages to wrap up band practice, packing gear away, the choir hanging out rather than go back to their refuges, hostels or high-rise flats in housing schemes. Normally Dorothy liked to hang out too, share coffee and cake, listen to the hubbub of different languages, the hand gestures, body language. But she'd heard from Hannah and Indy earlier about someone crashing funerals, and she had an idea.

'Brodie Willis,' Hannah said over her shoulder at the bottom of the stairs. She crossed to an unused viewing room.

Dorothy touched Hannah's arm. 'And you don't think it's like Archie? He's not ill?'

Hannah pressed her lips together. 'I think he's just grieving.'

They went in. Brodie had kind grey eyes, a lopsided smile. He wore a green hoodie and black joggers and was rubbing at the material. He had a flash of panic in his eyes and Dorothy imagined him bolting for the door.

'Please sit,' she said, then took the chair opposite. Soothing light in the room, ambient seascapes on the wall, a low coffee table with a box of tissues, a bouquet of carnations and roses adding colour.

'I'm Dorothy.' She held out her hand.

His grip was firm and dry. 'Brodie.' He looked at his lap.

Dorothy liked him. Instinct went a long way. She wasn't always right, but had a good batting average. She leaned forward. 'Hannah told me about this morning.'

Brodie glanced at her, then Hannah, then back at his lap.

Dorothy held out her hands. 'You've been to a few of our funerals recently, I hear.'

'I didn't mean any disrespect, I just...'

'It's OK.'

The silence was loaded, like silence always is. Brodie pulled at his earlobe. Dorothy watched him, razor rash on his neck, brightly striped socks between joggers and trainers. He smelled of blossoms and nerves.

'Do you want to talk about it?'

He started rocking in his seat.

'You're not in any trouble.' Dorothy wanted to give him a hug. 'And you don't have to be here. But I have a feeling you want to talk.'

Brodie looked at Hannah, who smiled at him.

'You're really her granddaughter?' he said.

Hannah nodded.

Brodie rubbed his chin and looked around the room. 'You don't want to hear what I have to say.'

Dorothy angled her head to the side a little. 'Of course we do.'

Brodie sighed and looked round the room again. Pulled his earlobe some more.

'I had a son,' he said eventually. 'He was stillborn.'

'I'm sorry,' Dorothy said.

'This was months ago, it was...' His eyes welled up and he swallowed hard. 'The thing is, everyone was great with Phoebe, that's my girlfriend.'

He closed his eyes for a long time and breathed deeply.

'Ex-girlfriend.' He nodded to himself. 'Her family were all there for her, shoulders to cry on. I felt lost but I wanted to help her too, make her feel better.' Tears fell onto his knees. 'But I couldn't grieve, I had to be a man about it, keep it all together. Nobody ever asked how I felt. No one.'

Dorothy shifted her weight but didn't speak.

'We called him Jack. Had all these toys, a fucking cot and a buggy. As far as I know, that's all still at her place.'

He wiped at his nose with the back of his hand, voice a tremor.

'Phoebe and I stopped talking, like, completely. I couldn't stand to look at her, and she was the same with me. I moved out. I'm living in my fucking car. I lost my job, just stopped going in. I couldn't sit at the desk and pretend everything was OK. I set up an email address for Jack, and I email him all the time.'

Dorothy thought of the wind phone outside, how she used it to speak to Jim, how their clients used it to speak to those they'd lost.

Brodie sniffed and wiped his eyes, then turned to Hannah. 'When you asked me if I was OK this morning...' He took a shaky breath, seemed like he might fall apart any second. 'It's just too much.'

He stuck his chin out, blinked, breathed out heavily. Straightened his shoulders and looked at Hannah then Dorothy.

'Sorry, I've never told anyone all this. It just came out.'

'Don't apologise.' Dorothy smiled. 'Everyone needs someone to talk to.'

She recognised the despair, the loneliness of grief. She'd seen it a million times, but she'd also lived it now, felt it in her bones.

'I have an idea.'

She looked at Hannah and thought about how Indy had come into her life. How Archie had come to work for them. Even Schrödinger. Her family of strays.

'How would you like to work for us?'

⁂

Webster and Low sounded like a neighbourhood bakery rather than two detective sergeants. Dorothy took them in as they all settled in the interview room. Don Webster was the bigger of the two, slicked-back hair, blue eyes, gym-bunny pecs. Ben Low was taller and thinner, an overbite giving him a goofy demeanour. He slouched to hide his height, or in deference to Webster.

The interview room was like an office, thin brown carpet, metal table and blue plastic chairs, posters on the wall for crime prevention and community outreach. A row of police cars sat outside the window, razor wire along the wall. Imagine having the balls to steal a police vehicle.

This was a different environment to Thomas's office upstairs, but she didn't want to exploit her privilege of knowing the boss, that would just get these guys' backs up. Webster and Low were investigating Billie and Ruby's camper fire, and Dorothy wanted to keep them onside.

'So,' Webster said, leaning back and spreading his hands out. 'To what do we owe the honour?'

She was a well-known face at St Leonard's. Being a private investigator in your seventies made you stand out. And they all knew about her relationship with Thomas, break-room scuttlebutt for sure.

'The suspected arson at Cramond Beach.'

Webster raised his eyebrows. 'Are you investigating it?'

'I am.'

'On behalf of the girls?'

They were young women, but Dorothy let it slide. 'On behalf of the whole community. They deserve to have this investigated with as much rigour as anyone else.'

Webster held his hands out in acquiescence. 'Hey, I agree. But we're not exactly swimming in budget for this one. Low and I have interviewed the people there, asked some locals. It's a dead end.'

'What about forensics?'

Webster smiled. 'You know it's not *CSI*, they're only a small department with a ton of work on.'

'But?'

Webster tapped on a cardboard folder on the desk. 'But they did confirm signs of an accelerant.'

'Yes, I saw the jerry can.'

'It contained turpentine.' Webster glanced at the folder. 'You can buy it anywhere, unfortunately.'

Dorothy nodded at the desk. 'Can I see the report?'

Webster looked at Low then slid it over to Dorothy. She'd read forensic reports before, didn't care for the convoluted language. She scanned the introduction and conclusion, which confirmed what Webster said.

'Can I get a copy of this?'

Webster raised his eyebrows. 'I don't think so. But I guess you could always go over our heads.'

She didn't resent the tone, they were just trying to do their jobs without some old busybody sticking her beak in. Nevertheless, that's exactly what she intended to do.

13

JENNY

She sat in the traffic jam outside Perth and sighed. The A9 was the shittiest road in Scotland. She'd spent a frustrating morning in Pitlochry sniffing around Stella's past and come away with nothing except a resentment for the rarefied air of the Perthshire town. There was something about the place that made her feel inferior, tearooms and woodland walks and turreted baronial castles, straight out of fucking *Trumpton*. It was a gentrified version of the Highlands for American tour buses, no real energy.

The traffic hadn't moved, an accident at the roundabout ahead. She smelled petrol and fertiliser. She lifted her phone from the passenger seat and flicked through Stella's file on her email. Craig and Stella grew up in Pitlochry, and the well-to-do atmosphere went some way to explaining Craig's sense of entitlement. He'd always had his privilege to boost him, give him the confidence and charisma that had fooled Jenny.

Stella had left the town for twenty years but found her way back, like a lot of folk do with small-town Scotland. You grow up desperate to escape your parents, then you become them. Jenny was the same – had hated the death industry as a teenager, tried to make her own way in the world. Now she was back sharing a roof with Mum, working on cases and deaths. She pictured Dorothy in a coffin and shuddered, then jumped as the car behind honked his horn. She realised the traffic had moved forward and waved an apology.

Stella had wound up working in a café kitchen on Atholl Road. None of her former colleagues knew her well, either that or they were good liars. The head chef put Jenny on to two of Stella's school friends, but they hadn't been in touch with her much before she went missing, and certainly not in the last year. Maybe Jenny couldn't tell when someone was lying. Craig had lied to her over and over and she'd hoovered it up.

She was past Perth now, on the motorway south. Raindrops thudded on the windscreen. It always rained in this part of Fife, some horrible micro-climate. It was mostly farms along the road-side, and she spotted two detectorists in a field. She imagined them turning up Roman gold or a Viking hoard. She glanced at her phone on the passenger seat, imagined it was easy for treasure to reveal itself. She drove on, chewing over her next move. Stella could be anywhere. It would've been hard to leave Britain with a stolen van and a decomposed corpse, an arrest warrant for arson out on her. But there was a lot of country to hide in.

She thought about the caravanners in Cramond, making a new home in a different place when they got sick of the old one. But even they left a trace, no matter what they said. Dorothy said they had jobs, paid tax, claimed benefits.

As she got closer to the Queensferry Crossing, she felt something in her stomach, a muscle memory of driving the other way to find Craig two years ago. She turned off the M90 and headed towards Elie, past Lochgelly and Kirkcaldy, anxiety rising as she covered the miles. There was no reason to this, but why not see it through.

She breathed deeply as she came into Elie, the rain stopping, and turned along the main road. She parked and got out, found the same path between houses down to the beach, windblown sand filling every corner.

She walked along the backs of the houses, over the grassy sand dunes, looking in the windows. A young family eating at a table, an older couple pottering about, two kids playing with a puppy. She reached the house where Craig had been living, where he'd beaten her, pointed his gun, told her the truth about them, they would always be connected. The house looked solid, but one day the sand would wear it away, the sea would rise and drown it, all this would be gone from the planet, along with all of humanity, and no one would remember.

'Can I help you?' A man in his forties stepped into the garden from the back door, steaming coffee mug in hand. He was a few years younger than Jenny, than Craig. A small girl, maybe seven, clung to his plaid shirt, shy around this strange woman.

Jenny thought how to answer, but couldn't come up with anything.

'Sorry,' she said, pointing vaguely. 'Wrong house.'

She turned and kicked up sand as she hurried down the dune to the beach. Remembered coming this way at gunpoint with Craig, the beating, petrol, flames, violence, death.

She reached the shore, calm sea glistening in the afternoon sun. She took off her trainers and socks and stepped into the waves, felt the cold on her skin, tremors through her body. Thought about how all the lands of the world were connected by seas, every living thing in an inconceivable network, a web of intertwined meaning and possibility. She looked at the water and felt connected to Stella and Craig. She knew she would find them, just knew it.

14

HANNAH

Hannah was fuzzy from the red wine. She wasn't used to drinking, felt the blood flush her face as she looked around. She imagined this was the future of the planet – four cute lesbians around a dinner table, an astronaut, a biotech businesswoman, a private investigator and a funeral director. It sounded like the start of a crap joke. Kirsty and Mina were quizzing Indy about the death business, and she replied with authority. Hannah glowed as she watched her wife, full of enthusiasm, brimming with compassion and sexy as hell. Shit, she'd definitely had too much wine.

The room was all clean lines and pale wood, like something from a Danish cop drama. In the bay window was an expensive telescope which Hannah had already looked through. The house was a pristine Victorian semi on Cluny Drive, not as ostentatious as some of the Morningside places up the road, but still worth a shitload. She wondered if that money came from Kirsty or Mina. How do you make money as a retired astronaut, apart from writing books, giving talks, sponsorship? Mina was probably the money, she had the air of rich business about her.

The table was covered in the detritus of a good meal, smeared plates, demolished cheeseboard, wine and port and coffee. A lithe tortoiseshell cat slunk into the room and Kirsty fed it a few crumbs of Lanark Blue.

'This is Yuri,' she said. 'After Gagarin.'

Yuri raised his tail then settled under the table.

The flickering candles highlighted Mina's cheekbones and gave Kirsty an angelic aura. Mina produced a joint from a carved wooden box and lit it. Hannah blinked heavily. She'd self-medicated with weed and other stuff in her teenage years, trying to deal with depression and anxiety, and was reasonably straight-laced now as a result. She was a little nervous about getting high in this company, but she also had a Pavlovian reaction to the smell, felt herself getting drawn towards it.

'And what about you?' Kirsty said. It felt like a spotlight had been beamed into Hannah's eyes, and she straightened in her seat.

'What about me?'

'The famous private investigator.'

Hannah blushed. 'I'm really just a student. I do that other stuff in my spare time.'

'As well as helping me out,' Indy said, touching her hand.

Hannah stared at Indy's wedding and engagement rings, a trill in her stomach when she remembered for the millionth time she was married to this beautiful woman.

'You wanted to speak to me about a case,' she said.

Kirsty took the joint from Mina and inhaled. 'I really don't think it's anything.'

'It's something,' Mina said, leaning forward. 'Kirsty can be annoyingly understated about this shit.'

Kirsty passed the joint to Hannah. 'It feels weird talking about it.'

'It's not weakness to ask for help,' Mina said. 'And the police have been fuck-all use.'

Hannah hesitated then took a hit on the joint, felt herself dissolve a little. 'You've gone to the police already?'

Mina sighed. 'Waste of time. You'd think someone with Kirsty's profile would get respect. But being a lesbian still matters to those knuckle-dragging fucks.'

'It wasn't anything like that,' Kirsty said.

'Sure it was, you're just too nice to see it.'

Hannah tried to focus on the power dynamic here. She and Indy were almost half the age of the other two, so it felt odd for the older women to come to the young ones for help. She took another hit of grass that she didn't need, then passed it to Indy.

Kirsty drank some port and swallowed in exaggerated fashion. 'I've been getting some low-level harassment since I got back from the ISS.'

'That guy in the auditorium?'

'I don't think that's connected.'

Mina snorted. 'Of course it is.' She turned to Hannah. 'She gets that at every public appearance now.'

'From the same guy?'

Kirsty frowned. 'No, that's just it.'

'It's orchestrated,' Hannah said, nodding.

Mina pointed at her and smiled. 'You get it. There's some fucking alt-right, white-bros sub-Reddit, and they're piling on her. It's making her life a misery.'

'It's not that bad.'

'It's getting worse.'

Kirsty had the joint again. 'It started online, hundreds of bull-shit comments every time I posted. But we got media training at the European Space Agency, it's nothing I can't handle.'

'What sort of stuff?'

'Standard misogyny, you can imagine. And a wee bit of anti-Scottish shit from dickheads.'

'But it gets weirder,' Mina said.

Kirsty sighed, like she had no time for this. But she'd asked Hannah here for a reason. 'There's a conspiracy theory about me.'

Indy leaned in.

Kirsty gave the joint to Hannah and laid her hands on the table. 'It's not exactly clear. All sorts of shit doing the rounds, you know what these sites are like. Some think I saw things on board the ISS. That I had some kind of first contact with aliens.'

She laughed nervously at the word 'aliens'.

'They really believe that?' Hannah remembered a previous case in which a disturbed young man thought he was being sent messages via astronomical data from deep space. What we project around us, what we glean from the cosmos.

She took a toke, felt the burn in her lungs. Handed it to Indy.

Kirsty shrugged. 'You name it, there's a conspiracy theory for it. I don't know if they mean alien probes up the butt or what. Or maybe that I *came back wrong*.'

'What?'

Mina shifted her weight.

Kirsty smiled. 'It's a trope with these guys. Someone goes into space, or down in a submarine, or visits a haunted house, and they come back different.'

'Anything more specific?'

'Some of them think I've been replaced. Like *Invasion of the Body Snatchers*.'

Hannah looked at Kirsty for a long time, then at Mina.

'Needless to say,' Kirsty said slowly, 'it's all nonsense.'

'Of course,' Hannah said.

Mina waved her hand and almost burned it on a candle. 'But it's not just online anymore, that's the worry. You saw the guy yesterday.'

'Who was he?'

Kirsty shrugged. 'No idea.'

'Have you seen him before?'

'I don't think so.'

Mina sat back, more agitated. 'And we've been doxxed, our address is on all these sites. I swear there's been folk going through our rubbish, walking past the house taking pictures. The doorbell goes and there's no one there.'

'And the police did nothing?' Hannah said.

Mina rolled her eyes. 'We had to explain to them what doxxing was. They're not exactly up to speed.'

'They should still take harassment seriously,' Indy said, passing the remains of the joint to Mina.

Mina rubbed her forehead. 'You know how women get murdered, then it all comes out about the stalking, harassment and abuse that went beforehand? I don't want Kirsty to become one of those stories.'

'That's ridiculous,' Kirsty said.

'Is it?'

Silence around the table as Kirsty placed a hand on Mina's. She looked at Hannah.

'We talked about it, and it would be great if you could find info on these guys, the ones who come here. Then maybe the police will take it more seriously.'

Hannah thought of Thomas in his office, always moaning about lack of funds. Maybe her job now was doing the police's work for them. She looked at Indy, who smiled in a way that suggested she had complete confidence in her.

'I'm happy to do it,' she said.

Kirsty took the stubby roach of the joint from Mina.

'We can give you what we know so far,' she said. 'I have a file, I'll email it.'

Mina pushed back from the table and picked up a couple of plates. 'Hannah, could you help me clear up?'

Hannah followed Mina to the kitchen carrying plates. Yuri emerged from under the table and followed them looking for scraps. Mina placed her plates on the worktop next to the dishwasher and fed Yuri some more cheese.

Hannah was about to walk away when Mina touched her arm.

'There's one more thing,' she said, looking around the room as if ashamed.

Hannah glanced at the open doorway. 'What?'

'Can you keep an eye on Kirsty for me? I'm worried about her.'

'You think she's in danger?'

Mina leaned in. 'Yes, but also...'

Hannah felt her heartbeat in her ears, a faint ringing. The air in the kitchen seemed clammy and thick. 'What?'

'She seems different somehow,' Mina said.

Hannah stared at her, then at Mina's hand on her arm. 'You think she came back wrong?' She had a nervous laugh in her voice.

Mina looked shocked at the words, the first time she'd confronted them.

'Maybe, I just...' She looked at the door as if Kirsty would magically appear. 'Keep an eye on her, let me know what you think.'

15

JENNY

Their sushi arrived. If she was an Insta daftie, she would've taken a picture. Brightly coloured creations – snow crab hand rolls, eel nigiri, yellowtail maki and a bunch of other stuff Jenny couldn't remember. She was drinking some cocktail of prosecco and chilli plum sake in a flute, Archie's yuzu margarita in a coupe glass half drunk already.

This was part of Jenny's unofficial therapy. She and Archie went on long walks every couple of weeks, exploring different parts of the city, always ending up eating at some place they'd never been before. This time it was Kanpai on Grindlay Street, across from the Lyceum. Sometimes they went far afield – Corstorphine one week, fish and chips in Newhaven the next – other times they stuck close to home. They headed out after hours and just wandered wherever, not talking much for long stretches, comfortable in each other's company. Archie lived alone in an Abbeyhill colony flat, though she'd never been there. He missed his mum, like she missed her dad. They didn't talk about their grief or troubles, just lived in each other's space for a moment, enjoying the proximity.

And the incredible food and drink. Jenny had done her fair share of Edinburgh socialising, but not in the last few years. The restaurants that had recently emerged astounded her. Case in point, this amazing snow crab she was trying to negotiate into her mouth with chopsticks. Archie was much more nimble, deftly flicking bluefin tuna into the soy sauce then his mouth.

'This is amazing,' Jenny said.

She raised her glass and they clinked and smiled.

Their walk earlier took them through Grassmarket, up Victoria Street onto the Royal Mile, down Johnstone Terrace. Familiar for tourists, but Jenny hadn't spent any time in the city centre for years, locals never did. They cut into St Cuthbert's Kirkyard from King Stables Road, looked at the ancient, worn gravestones. There were plaques up for the occasional famous corpse but Jenny never read them. Probably a bunch of old slave traders or something – only the rich could afford headstones in the castle's shadow.

A compact and serene waitress brought more food – seaweed salad, shrimp fishcakes, feathery and light tofu tempura. Holy crap, this was good.

'So,' Archie said.

Jenny knew what was coming. They never usually mentioned Craig but he was back in her life, and Archie was the only one she could talk to.

'So,' she said.

He raised his eyebrows.

She wiped her mouth with a napkin and took a hit of spicy cocktail. Bubbles up her nose. She took the *netsuke* fox from her pocket and rubbed it with her thumb, placed it on the table.

Archie looked at it. 'It's getting a little worn.'

'I like that.'

'It makes my carving look slapdash, like I didn't know what I was doing.'

Jenny ran her tongue around her mouth. 'I like to touch it. The worn part reminds me of your kindness.'

She'd never seen him blush, and wasn't sure she'd be able to through his beard. She wondered what that beard would be like against her cheek, then shook the image away. They were friends, and that had been good for them.

'You avoided the question,' Archie said, sipping his drink.

'There wasn't a question, you just said "so".'

Archie put his glass down, popped a salmon sashimi in his mouth, chewed and swallowed. 'Craig.'

Jenny clutched her chest like she was being stabbed in the heart, made a strangled noise.

Archie smiled. 'At least you can joke about it.'

'Gotta laugh, et cetera.'

He waved his chopsticks. 'Come on. This thing with Violet dropped out of the blue, it must've had some impact.'

His tone was serious and she decided to stop joking. He deserved that. 'I honestly don't know. I just think, why not try to find Stella for her dying mum?'

'And all the business with Stella a year ago?'

'I mean, I'm not happy about that, but...'

'How do you think you'll feel if you find her?'

'I guess we'll see.'

'And Craig's body?'

Jenny thought about their wedding day, young and naïve, full of hope, bursting with love. It seemed like that happened to a different woman. She felt no connection with her younger self and she wondered about that.

The waitress appeared with more food – grilled scallop, yam noodles, crispy lotus slices.

'We ordered too much,' Jenny said.

She ignored Archie's frown and got stuck in, thinking about her younger self, if she even knew that woman anymore.

16

DOROTHY

Dorothy watched Thomas plate up tagine and couscous, yoghurt and coriander leaves on top, then bring the plates to the table. It smelled spicy and sweet, apricots, chickpeas and lamb in the stew.

'This looks amazing.'

They clinked wine glasses, a Malbec they'd already half finished. 'I hope it's OK.'

She liked that he cooked, something sexy about that. Cooking was self-expression, even if it was only Moroccan stew. The fact he was willing to knock this together for them in her kitchen said something too. He was comfortable here.

Early in their relationship, they'd established that they preferred to hang out at her place. She'd been to his flat in Marchmont, of course. He said that he and Morag loved the location, the student vibrancy with a bohemian edge. Better than the New Town, sterile and soulless, half empty at weekends.

The same went for her place. Old John Skelf couldn't have known a hundred years ago, but their location was a perfect site amongst the lively animation of Tollcross, the Links and the Meadows out the window.

She tasted the tagine and it was amazing. 'Wow.'

He smiled.

She thought about the meals she'd eaten here with Jim over the years. Before Thomas. She had to keep reminding herself not to compare them, they were different men for different times in her life. Jim could cook too, but didn't very often, usually wiped out by the funeral work he took on. But maybe that was just an excuse from a different century. She worked like hell too, raised Jenny, helped out with the business, kept the house running. And she still had time for friends, yoga, drumming. Expectations were different back then, of course. Jim was a good man, caring husband, attentive father. He was open-minded and generous, which went with the job, of course, but he was like that outside work too. Just because he didn't vacuum or do the school run, didn't make him bad. But now she had this other man, who'd made this amazing tagine.

'Jenny came to see me today,' Thomas said, sipping Malbec.

'She said she would.'

'I can't imagine you approve of her taking the Stella case.'

'She's a grown woman, she makes her own decisions. Who cares what I think?'

'I do.' Thomas touched her hand. 'I'm sure she does too.'

'Jenny hasn't cared what I think since she was thirteen. But that's fine.'

'You're underestimating yourself. You must know how big a part of Jenny and Hannah's lives you are.'

He was right but it was hard to admit it. Mothers and daughters always had fraught relationships, that was perceived wisdom, right? She felt a distance from Jenny for a long time, especially when she was first with Craig. When Hannah was born, Dorothy welcomed the opportunity to be the doting grandmother and free babysitter. That contact had waned as Hannah grew older and more independent. But Dorothy was grateful she still had her daughter and granddaughter in her life, and she was determined to let them live their own way.

'Jenny's in a good place,' Dorothy said. 'I think this might even be helpful.'

Thomas nodded, but clearly didn't agree.

'What about the Cramond thing,' she said. 'Where's the investigation?'

Thomas gave her a look. Dorothy had stepped on the toes of police business a few times now. She knew it put him in a difficult position, but she had to follow her gut. She had some faith in the police, but more faith in Thomas doing the right thing. She remembered her mother telling her, if you wanted something done right, do it yourself. She'd found that out since Jim's death, all the cases she'd solved.

'We're doing as much as we can,' Thomas said.

'Like?'

Schrödinger wandered into the room and rubbed against her leg. She picked him up, imagined herself a Bond villain as she stroked him. She breathed in, tried to smell the fire damage, but couldn't. She'd always assumed this house would outlive them all. Jenny taking over from Dorothy, then Hannah and Indy from Jenny, then their kids if they had any, into the future. Discovering better ways to care for the dead without killing the planet.

'A couple of officers spoke to the people at the camp,' Thomas said.

'Webster and Low. They weren't very impressive.'

Thomas gave her a stare. 'When did you meet them?'

'Earlier, I went to have a look at the forensic report.'

Thomas sighed. 'Dorothy.'

She held out her hands. 'What else have they done?'

He waited a few moments before speaking. 'They've talked to locals in the pub and on the prom.'

'Stopping people on the street, really?'

'You know I have to leave officers to conduct their own investigations.'

'What's the point of having a cop boyfriend if he can't interfere?'

She was winding him up, but they both knew there was a grain of truth. She liked the access Thomas gave her, but the way the police worked was frustrating. That's why PIs existed, they did the shit that the police didn't.

'They're doing just fine without interference,' Thomas said.

'You know how it'll go, they'll ask a few more questions, find out nothing, it goes away.'

Thomas looked at her for a long time.

'I'm sorry,' Dorothy said.

'Don't be.'

She had to remind herself of his point of view. He'd lost his wife and was in a relationship with an annoying older woman who wouldn't let things lie.

'I'm thinking of retiring,' Thomas said, matter of fact.

Dorothy stared at him and he shrugged.

'I'm fifty-seven, I can cut a deal.'

'Why?'

Thomas breathed out. 'I used to think I made a difference, made the world a better place. I'm not sure anymore.'

'What changed?'

'I did. I thought you could change the culture from the inside, that was the mantra. There are occasional bad apples but if you stick at it, make the right choices, employ good people, the police get better.' He looked around the kitchen for answers. 'But the culture hasn't changed, the focus is all wrong. Community groups and charities do a better job of helping people than we do most of the time.'

Dorothy reached for his hand and squeezed.

'But you're one of the good ones, Thomas. If you go...'

He shook his head. 'I'm so tired. Don't you get tired of fighting all the time?'

'It's not a matter of fighting, it's about finding a way through.'

There was more she wanted to say, a deep-felt belief in something she couldn't express. Maybe there weren't words for it. She held his hand for a long time.

'That's just it,' Thomas said. 'I can't see a way through.'

17

HANNAH

The stars glowed overhead, embers in a black sky. They walked home from Cluny Drive through rich neighbourhoods, Indy on her arm, her head resting on Hannah's shoulder. Hannah could smell her perfume. She kissed Indy's hair, then on the lips, and they stumbled a little.

'So now we're pals with an astronaut,' Indy laughed.

Hannah shrugged as they turned up Canaan Lane. 'I've taken a case for her, that's all.'

'Come on, we just got stoned with them over dinner.'

Hannah couldn't deny the thrill of being at close quarters to a heroine. She looked at the sky, imagined being on the International Space Station, whizzing around the planet at unimaginable speeds. You could sometimes see the ISS scudding across the darkness, she had an app on her phone which told her when it was overhead. She imagined seeing it now, a sign. Because of the satellite's speed, astronauts on board saw sixteen sunrises a day. Would you ever get tired of that? Another sunrise over everyone who's ever lived – human, animal, plant, dinosaur, microbe.

She thought about the overview effect. She craved that kind of transcendent experience, wanted to feel like she was a part of something more. She had a feeling Gran glimpsed that through meditation. Hannah sometimes caught it out of the corner of her eye with astrophysics, the interconnectedness, the immense scale.

They walked along Hope Terrace into Marchmont Road, almost home. Hannah wondered about this conspiracy-theory stuff, angry white men sitting at home, keyboard warriors who thought they knew some hidden truth that idiotic sheeple had missed. She'd read a book once about conspiracy theories, how they stem from the mind's need for order. We want to think someone's in charge, someone bigger than us. That used to be religion – when apes form bigger social groups, they demonstrate awe of things like volcanic eruptions and lightning, as if they're caused by some being they can't perceive. But as religion has declined, we've found that sense of control from elsewhere. If the governments of the world don't know what they're doing, if random bad things can happen to anyone, maybe there's a secret order, a cabal behind the scenes causing this bad shit. From there it's a short leap to the New World Order. Then aliens, viruses, 5G, mind control, all bets are off. And right-wing governments fuel these conspiracies, the rich exploiting the chaos for money and power.

She saw a light in the sky moving west and wondered if it was the ISS, off to catch another sunrise. But the light got bigger, resolved into an aeroplane, turning over the Forth and approaching the airport. She wondered who was on it, where they'd been, what they wanted from life.

Indy squeezed her shoulder as they reached their flat at the bottom of Argyle Place. Hannah felt her phone buzz in her pocket, took it out:

I need to see you, now. Radisson Blu. Violet x

Hannah checked the time, almost 2am. She showed the screen to Indy, who took a moment to focus.

'Shit.' Indy looked up.

Hannah stared at the screen. 'You think Mum got this message too?' She dialled Jenny's number, voicemail. She hung up and looked at Indy. 'I should go.'

'So go.'

Hannah nodded to herself. 'OK, I'll see you in a bit.'

Indy angled her head. 'What are you talking about, I'm coming too.'

'You don't have to.'

'Yes, I do.'

They headed through the Meadows. Hannah felt suddenly sober, as if the message had cleared her brain. Violet wasn't exactly an estranged grandmother, but she hadn't been very present either. Things became more complicated after Craig's bullshit three years ago, but when she'd turned up last year to identify his body, there was some reconciliation. Acceptance that they'd all suffered at the hands of the same man.

They turned down Chambers Street, the road empty except for taxis, two drunk students. A night bus on South Bridge, folk spilled from the shawarma shop, homeless people in sleeping bags on Hunter Square.

The hotel receptionist was younger than Hannah, heavy brows, big glasses, name badge said Claudette.

'I need to see Violet McNamara.'

Claudette looked over her glasses. 'We wouldn't normally ring a room this time of night.'

'She just messaged me.' Hannah held out her phone.

Claudette pushed her glasses up the bridge of her nose, lifted the phone. She introduced herself, explained, nodded a few times, then hung up.

'Room 427.' She looked at the lift.

'Thanks.'

They went up, Hannah feeling a weight in her gut.

They came out and walked down a long corridor, got to the end. Hannah glanced at Indy, who rubbed her back. She knocked and waited. About to knock again when it was opened by a large man with tattoos.

'Hannah, I'm Norrie, your gran's carer. I messaged you for her.' He glanced at Indy, but didn't say anything. 'Come in.'

She was shocked at the sight of Nana. She was in a motorised wheelchair with a head support, back reclined. She was so thin, grey skin, eyes closed, fingers curled in her lap. She had an oxygen mask over her mouth. Her eyes opened as Hannah approached.

Norrie lifted the mask from her face. Violet blinked heavily. Her eyes were red and dry, sunken cheeks, lips cracked. Norrie put a straw from a glass of water in her mouth, but she struggled to sip.

'She gets very dry.'

Violet's lips moved. Norrie put his ear to her mouth.

'She's asking about Jenny.'

Hannah glanced at Indy then shook her head. 'I called her. I don't know where she is.'

Violet seemed to understand. She looked at Norrie, who leaned in again then straightened up.

'She says she missed you, and she loves you.'

'I love you, too.' Hannah wondered if she was saying it automatically. She didn't have the same bond with Violet as she did with Dorothy. Was that all love was? It had to be more. She knew from the funeral business that being near the end made people think about the stuff they'd fucked up or missed out on, the regrets.

'She's dying,' Norrie said.

Indy frowned. 'Should we do something, call an ambulance?'

Norrie shook his head. 'She has a DNR, she knew this was coming.'

Hannah took Violet's hand. 'I'm so sorry.'

She *was* sorry. That she hadn't tried harder to stay in touch, that she'd ghosted Nana after Mum and Dad's divorce. That was cruel and she hated herself for it. She wanted to feel Violet's hand squeeze hers.

Violet's eyes went to Norrie again, and he leaned in. When he straightened up, Violet was staring at Hannah.

'She wants you and Jenny to make sure Stella's OK. Lay your dad to rest.'

Violet closed her eyes. Hannah squeezed her fingers, looked at her chest for signs of breathing. Wanted to climb onto the wheelchair, push life back into her body. Norrie touched Violet's neck, two fingers where a pulse should be. He stood there for a long time in silence. Hannah imagined a death rattle, a final resignation. But there was nothing. Eventually Norrie turned and shook his head.

Hannah kept hold of Violet's hand for a long time.

18

JENNY

Morning sunlight striped the far wall of her room. Jenny lay in bed trying to hold on to the dream. Craig was in it, but it wasn't a nightmare. It was long ago, the two of them drinking in a dive bar in Hamburg on their first trip together, schnapps sticky on her fingers, his tongue in her mouth. She didn't know if good dreams of Craig were better than nightmares.

She checked her phone and saw a message from Violet, shook sleep from her mind and got up. Threw on an old Napier Uni sweatshirt and walked to the kitchen, stopped in the doorway when she saw Dorothy and Hannah with drams in front of them.

Dorothy looked up and ran her tongue around her teeth. 'Violet died last night. Hannah was there.'

Jenny sat. 'Holy shit.'

Hannah took a sip of whisky and shivered. Jenny smelled the antiseptic burn and liked it.

'Just like that,' Hannah said, clicking her fingers.

'But I saw her two days ago.'

'Her carer said it can happen like that with MND. Like only willpower is keeping you alive.'

Dorothy placed her hand on Hannah's. 'A lot of deaths are like that, people just decide it's time.'

Hannah shook her head.

Jenny watched Schrödinger stretch in the sunlight at the window, oblivious to them. Outside, the world was the same. To Jenny, this was her ex-mother-in-law, but for Hannah it meant more.

'I should've known her better,' Hannah said, as if reading Jenny's thoughts. 'I should have made more effort to stay in touch.'

Jenny scratched at the wood grain of the table, decades of wear and tear. 'You did nothing wrong. When Craig and I split, I didn't want his family to have anything to do with you. It's my fault you never spent much time with her.'

Hannah stared at her. 'I'm a grown-assed woman, I make my own decisions.'

Dorothy stood and put the kettle on. 'It's the easiest thing in the world to blame yourself. Sometimes you need to forgive yourself, that's much harder.'

Hannah drank her whisky. 'That's such an easy thing to say.'

Silence stretched out for a long time. Jenny heard traffic noise from Bruntsfield, the beep of a truck reversing. She felt a rock in her stomach as she looked at Hannah. Her daughter had spiralled as a teenager through depression and anxiety, self-medication, a phase of cutting her arms, medications which eventually righted the ship. She gradually weaned herself off pills, but it was always there in the background, the possibility of falling again.

Hannah cleared her throat and slid her whisky away. She got up and walked to the PI whiteboard.

'Mum, where are you with finding Stella?'

'Violet just died, honey.'

'Her dying words were that she wanted us to find Stella and lay Dad to rest.'

'Christ.' What a weight to put on your granddaughter.

Hannah tapped the board with a marker pen. 'Well?'

Dorothy put a pot of coffee on the table, poured out three ceramic tumblers. 'Are we sure about this?'

The look in Hannah's eyes told Jenny they didn't have a choice.

'We have to,' she said.

Hannah looked relieved.

Jenny joined Hannah at the board. 'I didn't get anywhere in Pitlochry. Spoke to a few folk she worked with, school friends. She hasn't been in touch with anyone back there.'

'What about the police file?'

'The trail's cold.'

Hannah went to the window. 'There has to be something. It's easy to disappear if no one is looking for you. But now we're looking.' She tapped on the glass with the marker. 'Where are you?'

Dorothy sat down and sipped her coffee. 'Haven't you got your hands full with the astronaut?'

'Kirsty's thing isn't too bad. Indy will help.'

Dorothy rubbed at the palm of her hand. 'Just be careful, harassment tends to escalate.'

'I can handle myself.'

'I don't doubt it.'

'I wonder about Mina, though.'

Jenny perked up. 'How come?'

Hannah touched her earlobe. 'She seems to have some sympathy for the conspiracy nuts.'

'Why?'

Hannah shrugged. 'I don't know. She thinks Kirsty has changed since she was on the ISS.'

Dorothy nodded. 'That experience would change anyone.'

There was a low purr from Schrödinger on the armchair.

'What about your thing, Mum?' Jenny said. 'The campervan fire.'

'I'm heading to Cramond to ask around. You know what it's like with locals, wary of incomers.'

Jenny walked to the table and drank her coffee. 'Not everyone is as full of love as you, Mum.'

Dorothy stood and rolled her shoulders. 'You want to come?'

Jenny pictured Stella out there with Craig's body, Violet dead in her hotel bed, Kirsty zooming around the world above it all in her space station. But no one was above it all, and Jenny liked being down here in the thick of it. Bring it on.

19

DOROTHY

Dorothy looked at the pub's dirty pebbledash and weather-beaten sign. The sun shimmered in a muggy haze. She was surprised, usually there was a fresh breeze off the firth. She looked at Jenny then pushed the door of the Cramond Arms. It was busy for the morning, air freshener and bleach hanging in the air. A dozen old punters, mostly men. There was a sign behind the bar for an OAP offer, nip and a pint for a fiver before noon.

She'd already had a dram this morning, didn't need a pint on top. The same woman from before came from out back, eyeing up her and Jenny. This was a drinking place, not for twee old ladies. This was useful for investigations – people always underestimated an older woman, assumed Dorothy was useless.

She ordered two coffees, a look of disdain from the barmaid. She was short and wide in the hips, curly chestnut hair, gold-link chain round her neck, patterned blouse. Old school.

She made the coffees and Dorothy paid.

'Place is busier than last time I was in.'

The woman narrowed her eyes as the gears churned in her mind. 'You were in with that gypsy.'

'She's not a gypsy.'

The woman sucked her teeth. 'Doesn't matter, it's a disgrace what they're doing out there.'

'What are they doing?' This was Jenny, sitting on a bar stool.

Dorothy smiled. Jenny was playing the idiot to get her to talk. The woman scoped Jenny up and down. Maybe she realised she was being played. People often did, but they went along anyway, happy for an excuse to air their grievances.

'Make the place look like a midden.' The woman folded her arms. 'I've heard there's been human excrement found on the beach and floating in the sea. They dump their chemical toilets in there. They should be arrested.'

Dorothy couldn't help herself. 'Have you seen any evidence?'

'Dogs running around bothering folk on the prom.' The woman was on a roll now. 'Kids in just their nappies, playing in dirt. Those young girls dressed up, showing everything. Jailbait.'

How much bigotry could you fit into one rant?

Jenny nodded noncommittally, sipped her coffee.

The woman didn't care Dorothy was here with Fara two nights ago. Another bigot emboldened to speak her mind, air her toxic shit.

The woman ran her tongue around her mouth, as if clearing it out. 'The quicker they move on the better.'

'To where?' Jenny said, innocent voice.

'Anywhere.'

Not in my back yard. Dorothy looked at her coffee. A greasy film on the top, a smudge of dirt on the rim of the cup. She wasn't putting that to her lips.

Two old guys with yellowing beards sat along the bar listening in. The whole pub was probably listening, it felt like a Wild West saloon.

The nearest guy wore a stained fisherman's jumper, worn at the elbows, homemade tattoos on his fingers. He sipped a whisky and wiped his mouth.

'Cunts don't pay taxes, can't expect to use the council's amenities. Yet the police do fuck all, too scared they'll get it in the ear from the woke brigade.'

Dorothy sighed. 'Most of them work and pay taxes, maybe they just prefer that lifestyle.'

'Fucking layabouts.'

'What if they can't get on the housing ladder, Edinburgh is crazy.'

The barmaid leaned forward. 'Stop drinking Starbucks, then. Save a few quid, that's what I did.'

Dorothy turned to the guy at the bar. 'Are you on a pension?'

'What if I am?'

'That's benefits.'

'Benefits I paid for in tax when I worked.'

'Benefits are to help people who need it.'

'Fucking scroungers.'

Dorothy breathed deeply, blinked twice. It was so easy to get entrenched in your views, believe what the *Daily Mail* told you about refugees, Travellers, homeless, anyone who doesn't fit into your conventional ideas of society. She was always wary of falling into that trap. Keep an open mind, see the other side, think about what it's like to be someone else. It seemed simple, but maybe it wasn't.

'What do you think happened the other night?' Jenny said, cutting in with that innocent voice again. Dorothy was amazed, given how jaded she usually sounded.

The barmaid raised her chin. 'The fire? Probably stoned and fell asleep. Lots of drugs over there.'

Dorothy wanted to point out she was standing behind a bar with thousands of pounds' worth of legal drugs.

The old guy wrinkled his nose. 'They're always wasted, don't know how they afford it.'

Dorothy straightened her shoulders. 'Maybe someone set fire to the caravan. Wanted them gone.'

The barmaid stared at her. 'I don't like what you're insinuating.'

'I'm just saying it's possible.'

The old guy prodded the Tennent's towel on the bar. 'We want them gone, but we wouldn't do that.'

Dorothy looked around the bar. The others avoided her eye. 'You speak for everyone, do you?'

'I think you should leave,' the barmaid said.

'Like Fara and the rest of them.'

The old man shook his head. 'We're law-abiding citizens minding our own business. If you want to find out who set fire to their caravan, ask them. I've seen the Ferguson lads over there a few times, the police breaking things up.'

Jenny finished her coffee. 'Fergusons?' She sounded like butter wouldn't melt.

The barmaid threw a thumb over her shoulder. 'Biggest gang in Muirhouse. We've had trouble with them in the past. They run that estate and bring half their shite down here. Drugs, booze, all-nighters on the island. Scramblers and quad bikes up and down the prom, over the causeway, terrorising the locals.'

'And you've seen them with the caravan community?' Dorothy said.

'Like flies round shite,' the old guy said. 'Drug dealing and sniffing around the lassies. Surprised none of them are up the duff.'

Dorothy thought about Billie and Ruby, how vulnerable they seemed in the ashes of their home. Was that it, jealous boys?

'And the police know about it?' Jenny said, glancing at Dorothy. The meaning was obvious – had Thomas mentioned this?

The barmaid nodded. 'Aye, there's been cop cars along the prom loads recently. What with these lot, the Muirhouse crew, and the Travellers up at Gypsy Brae, they've had their work cut out. Still not doing enough, likes.'

Dorothy wondered if the barmaid wanted a purge, a Dredd-style clean-up campaign. She thought about Thomas and what he'd said about quitting. And she thought about those girls, lucky not to be dead in a fire. All the hatred circling their little community, how the hell to untangle it all.

20
HANNAH

Archie pulled the van over on a double yellow line and switched the hazards on. Van guys could park anywhere if they were working.

Hannah looked up at the tenement. They were at the bottom of Easter Road blocking a left-hand turn into Duke Street, Leith Links spread beyond the junction. Lots of traffic, just what they wanted when they were removing a body. Also, the deceased was on the top floor.

'Flat 3F2?'

Archie sighed as he undid his seatbelt. 'Yeah.'

Mostly they collected bodies from care homes, hospices, hospitals and the mortuary, but sometimes they got them from private homes. If there were no suspicious circumstances and the deceased wasn't whisked off in an ambulance, it was down to whoever was left behind to sort it. Calling a funeral director was such a hard thing to do if you've just found somehow dead. These days, more people were choosing to die at home if possible, rather than spend their final hours surrounded by beeping machines and strangers. Hannah understood that.

They got out, and Hannah buzzed the intercom while Archie pulled the gurney from the back of the van.

'Mr Coulson? It's the Skelfs Funeral Directors.'

'Oh, right.' He sounded surprised. Not his first surprise today.

The door buzzed and Archie pushed the gurney in, then collapsed the wheels and they lifted it upstairs. Three flights was easy with an empty gurney, though Hannah noted the tight corners in the stairwell, tried not to scrape the paintwork.

Mr Coulson stood at his door as they reached him, out of breath, Archie punching the gurney wheels back out and locking them.

'Hi, Mr Coulson,' Hannah said, putting her hand out. Her palms were red from lifting the gurney.

Mr Coulson looked at her hand like he'd never seen one before.

'Call me Eric.' He led them through the flat, it was dark, smelled of cigarettes and mould. He shuffled down the hall and Hannah wondered about him up and down all those stairs. He wore brown slacks and a thick jumper, unshaven, sallow face, a curve to his shoulders. He stopped at the living room.

Anita Coulson was on the floor, arms by her side, skin grey.

The paramedics had left her in a decent state. Hannah wondered how she looked when they arrived.

'She was cold when I woke up this morning.'

Hannah swallowed and glanced at Archie, who touched Eric on the shoulder.

'Maybe you could pop the kettle on?' he said.

This was a common tactic, it gave the bereaved something to do. Otherwise they tended to hang around and watch their loved one wrangled onto the gurney. Anita didn't look too bad, her legs were straight, so if rigor mortis had started they wouldn't have to massage it away to get her on the stretcher.

Eric nodded, keeping his eyes on his wife of forty-five years. Indy took the call earlier, passed on the information. Dorothy and Jenny were out investigating the arson, Indy had to manage the office, so here she was with Archie doing the donkey work. Hannah wondered about Brodie, the funeral crasher Dorothy had asked about a job. She hadn't officially employed him yet, otherwise he could've been doing this. And Dorothy had something up her sleeve anyway, Hannah could tell from the way she talked to him.

Hannah wasn't in the right frame of mind for this. She remembered Violet last night, her frail body giving up. And now, twelve hours later, Hannah was about to manhandle another poor sod onto a gurney, into the van, off to the afterlife.

Eric was still in the doorway, blocking Archie and the gurney.

'That cup of tea?' Archie said softly.

Eric nodded and patted his pockets, as if he might find the meaning of life amongst his tissues and lip balm, then wandered to the kitchen. Archie brought the gurney alongside Anita and folded the legs till it was on the floor. He took the body bag from underneath, unrolled it alongside her, then unzipped.

'You OK?' he said to Hannah, who hadn't moved.

Hannah nodded, swallowed, went to Anita's feet. She preferred the bottom end, didn't have to look in their eyes. Anita's were open, a reflex from lack of moisture for a lot of deceased. If needed Archie would sew them shut for a viewing. If he closed them now, chances were they'd pop open again and give everyone a fright.

Archie had his hands under Anita's armpits. 'Ready?'

Hannah gripped her calves and nodded.

They lifted her onto the body bag and Archie zipped her in. Hannah saw a wet patch on the carpet where Anita had been. She leaned over and sniffed, only urine, could've been worse. She wondered if she should tell Eric. The last communication from his wife's body, a piece of her left behind in the worn fabric, a drop of her humanity forever soaked in, there with him. Or just a piss stain, depending how you looked at it.

They strapped Anita in then raised the legs of the gurney.

Eric arrived with a tray of cups, teapot in a knitted cosy, small sugar bowl.

They sat and drank tea, occasional small talk, an unbearable weight pressing on Eric, hunching his body. Hannah thought about Violet, Stella, her dad. About Kirsty in space, coming back different. But we're always different, right? Everything we do changes us, we leave a little something behind, like Anita's piss in the carpet, we pick something up from our surroundings. We're always part of something bigger, changing as we move through the universe.

'We'd better get on,' Archie said, placing a hand on Eric's wrist.

Eric nodded but didn't look up. Didn't want to see Anita leaving him for the last time.

Hannah stood. 'We'll be in touch about arrangements.'

Eric nodded again, looked at the teacup in his hand.

They left him there and Hannah was grateful he didn't come to see them out. Having him at the front door while they negotiated Anita downstairs wouldn't be great.

Archie collapsed the gurney again and went first, taking the majority of the weight and handling the corners skilfully. Hannah felt the strain in her arms from lifting her end above the stone steps. They were round two corners when they met a woman and her young daughter coming up.

They paused, Hannah's muscles burning, Archie smiling. The woman realised and her eyes went wide.

'Oh. Mrs Coulson?'

Hannah nodded.

'What's that, Mummy?' the girl said, reaching out to touch the gurney. Just natural inquisitiveness. Her mum grabbed her hand and pulled her upstairs into their flat, thumping the door closed. People don't like to be confronted by death. Hannah frowned. We need to be more open, have more of a connection with the process, see it as an essential part of life.

They got Anita downstairs, into the van, then drove off, Hannah wondering about Eric. Whether his neighbours would visit, make him feel less alone. Not easy in an anonymous city, so many of us felt alone.

'You OK?' Archie said.

He seemed to take everything in his stride, but then he was around death eight hours a day, five days a week. She didn't really know him. He was a still pond on the surface, but everyone has an inner life, everyone is going through stuff you have no idea about. She wondered about Violet, dying without knowing where her children were.

'I'm fine,' she said, not feeling it. 'You?'

Archie seemed surprised that she'd asked, but considered the question. 'I'm OK.'

He'd got closer to Jenny in the last year, and Hannah wondered about that. It seemed like they were just friends, but maybe it was more. Whatever, it'd had a great effect on Jenny, pulled her together in a way she hadn't been for years, since Dad. Maybe all you need is a friendly face once in a while, someone to listen to your bullshit and not judge. Hannah had read once about a man who succumbed to suicide on the Golden Gate Bridge. He left a note at home before walking there, which said that if one person smiled at him on the journey, he wouldn't jump. Maybe all we need is a smile to stop us jumping.

21

JENNY

Cramond Vale was only a short walk up the hill from the beach, but it had a very different vibe. Sixties, brown-brick semis, neat wee gardens and short driveways out front. Jenny smelled cut grass. Behind the hedges at the bottom of the road was the River Almond, then fields and woods, but this felt like a contained slice of suburbia.

She rang the bell at number twenty-three. The door opened and there was Fiona, the woman who used to be her nemesis. She grinned, grabbed Jenny in a hug and ushered her inside. Jenny followed her to the kitchen. She was the same age as Jenny but looked younger, a pint-sized bundle of energy, blonde hair in an expensive cut, smart blouse and skirt despite working from home, big blue eyes.

She'd stolen Craig from Jenny twelve years ago, an affair which turned into divorce for Jenny and a second marriage for him. And a second daughter, Sophia. But then the shit hit the fan three years ago when they found out he'd had another affair with Hannah's uni friend Mel, then murdered her, setting off a chain reaction of pain and violence. Jenny and Fiona became unlikely allies when he escaped on the way to court, then more so when he abducted Sophia. The fact that Jenny tracked Craig down and returned Sophia meant they were bonded forever. Fiona said repeatedly she would do anything for Jenny. They were sisters-in-trauma, understood what that bastard had put them both through.

'Sit.' Fiona pointed at a chair by the kitchen table.

The table was covered in paperwork and an open MacBook, a large pot of coffee. Fiona got a mug from a cupboard and poured

Jenny some. This kitchen was a seventies throwback, wooden décor, chunky old appliances, flocked orange wallpaper. Totally at odds with Fiona's style, but this was her mum's place. Fiona and Sophia moved in when she had to sell her place. The similarities with Jenny went on and on – both middle-aged women back living with their mums after their shitstorm lives. Jenny had resented it originally, but now she couldn't think of anywhere she'd rather be than at the Skelf place. That realisation scared her.

She sipped her coffee. 'How's Sophia?'

Fiona beamed. 'Going great guns at school, into volleyball, cheerleading, skateboarding, a good bunch of pals. She's a resilient wee thing.'

'Just like us.'

'Maybe it takes us a little longer to recover from things.'

'Just a wee bit.'

They'd already chatted on the phone about Stella. Jenny called the other day, after Pitlochry, asking if Fiona could think of any other leads. It was a long shot, but Fiona had known Stella more recently than Jenny had.

Fiona sighed, she knew what it meant to be raking all this up. 'Are you sure this Stella thing is a good idea?'

Jenny looked out of the window, beech trees waving in the breeze. 'Sometimes I feel like you're the only one who understands.'

Fiona squeezed Jenny's hand.

Jenny drank more coffee. 'I'm honestly OK about it. I obviously had PTSD last year and tried to drink and fuck it away. I see that now. But I think looking for Stella is good for me.'

'How's Violet coping?'

Fuck. Jenny realised she'd called Fiona yesterday evening, before she found out about Violet.

'Sorry, Fiona, shit, I forgot I hadn't told you. She died last night.'

'But you met her two days ago.'

'She wasn't well, but I didn't think she was that close. Hannah was there.'

'What?'

'At her bedside. Her carer messaged both of us late last night. I didn't see the message, Hannah did.'

'Christ. How is she?'

Jenny thought about it. How was Hannah? 'Violet's dying wish was for us to find Stella and put Craig to rest.'

Fiona laughed nervously. 'Fuck, she was always one for the dramatic. Sorry, I just ... Violet is dead, holy shit, and she didn't know where her kids were. I mean, I never got on with the old bird, but that's a shit deal.'

Jenny knew what she meant. 'It hits differently when you're a mum.'

Fiona finished her coffee and cleared her throat. 'So, I did have one idea about Stella.' She tapped the laptop screen. 'I ran through all the old clients, the same rogues gallery we tried when Craig disappeared. But none of them knew Stella, as far as I know, so I don't think any would've helped her. Especially given she was wanted for arson and driving around with a dead body. But there was a guy.'

'Like a boyfriend?'

'I was never quite sure. She lived with him for a while, me and Craig met him. Older than her by quite a bit, and rich. Old money, Barbour jacket and red cords, a hat with earflaps.'

'Sounds like a weird fit for Stella.' She didn't know Stella well, but she always seemed down to earth, no nonsense. Not the sort to get mixed up with landed gentry.

'She introduced him as Bill, he had one of those posh surnames. I wracked my brains and eventually remembered. Porterhouse, like the steak. He made that joke at dinner.' Fiona turned the laptop to face Jenny, tapped the screen. 'Sir William Porterhouse, the fifteenth Marquess of Longniddry.'

'Wow.' Jenny scanned the wiki page, minimal details, but it did mention an estate in East Lothian near Aberlady. Lots of room for a van, lots of space to live off-grid. Maybe.

'Feels like I should speak to him,' Jenny said. 'Want to join me?'

'I mean, I'm tempted.' Fiona waved around the kitchen. 'But I'm kind of OK here, you know? I don't need this like you and Hannah need it. I have to think about Sophia.' She raised her eyebrows at the paperwork on over the table. 'Plus, I have a shit-ton of work.'

Jenny understood. She'd warmed to PI work but it wasn't for everyone. She didn't feel obsessed about Stella the way she had about Craig, and that felt better, like she might actually do the job properly. And it had been Violet's dying wish, after all. If nothing else, this would get that weight off her and Hannah's backs.

'I understand.'

They sat in comfortable silence for a moment, before Jenny nodded out of the window. 'What do you know about the caravan fire the other night?'

'At the beach?'

Jenny nodded.

Fiona smiled. 'Don't tell me you're investigating that too?'

'Mum is.'

'Of course, I heard you guys did the funeral and lost the body.'

'We got it back.'

'I heard the coastguard got it back.'

'What else did you hear? Cramond is a wee place.'

Fiona waved her finger in the air. 'It's all second hand from Mum.'

'What has Betty heard?'

Fiona shifted in her seat. 'Mostly a lot of unkind bullshit from people who should know better.'

'Yeah, I experienced some of that in the pub earlier.'

'That place is a shithole.'

'Weird, for such a genteel village.'

Fiona laughed. 'On the surface, maybe, but it's like *Hot Fuzz*, all sorts of nasty shit underneath.'

'Like what?'

Fiona shook her head. 'It's the usual misogynistic bullshit. But I heard there was stuff going on in Silverknowes woods.'

'What sort of stuff?'

Fiona shrugged as if trying to shake the dirty feeling from her shoulders. 'Group-sex stuff. The camper girls involved. It's just rumours – you know what dickheads guys can be.'

'With local guys? You think one of them set the fire?'

Fiona picked up her coffee cup and realised it was empty, poured some more and nestled the cup in her hands. 'I wouldn't trust a fucking word any of them said, put it that way.'

Jenny nodded.

'I feel sorry for the caravan folk,' Fiona said. 'They're just trying to live their lives, right? Like any of us.'

Everyone just trying to get to the end of the day and hoping tomorrow would be a little brighter. We didn't need our homes torched, our dead ex-husbands disappearing, all the hate and bullshit in the world coming to kick us in the arse.

❧

Jenny was about to walk over to the caravans when she saw Billie coming along the prom. She recognised her from the picture Dorothy had pinned to the whiteboard back at the house. She was coming from Silverknowes. Jenny thought about what Fiona said and felt disgusted with herself. That's the way bullshit works, it infects anyone who hears it, colours their opinions, consciously or not.

Billie wore black leggings and a pink crop top, chunky white high-tops. She frowned as Jenny approached with her arms out.

'Billie, right?'

She stopped and looked around. 'Who the shit are you?'

'I'm Jenny, Dorothy's daughter.'

It took her a moment to twig, then she sighed. 'What do you want?'

Who wouldn't be defensive if their home was burned down and there were rumours of gangbangs? The shit these girls put up with.

'I was in the neighbourhood, thought I'd drop by. Are you OK?'

Billie swallowed. 'Has *your* home ever been torched?'

Jenny laughed. 'Actually, yes, this time last year. The fire fighters managed to restrict damage to the ground floor.'

Billie stuck her bottom lip out. 'Must be nice having more than one floor.'

'It's a beautiful place, I'm not going to apologise for that.'

Billie raised her eyebrows. 'So who did your place?'

'My ex-husband's sister. My ex is dead. She stole his body and disappeared.'

'Wow.'

'My daughter and her wife were inside the building when it went up. They're not much older than you. They just got out.'

Jenny felt her throat tighten. She could smell the smoke in her nostrils, felt dizzy. She closed her eyes and when she opened them, Billie was staring at her. She could smell the salt of the sea, the tang making her eyes water.

'So who torched your place?' Jenny said.

Billie shrugged, looked down. 'No idea.'

'Really?'

Billie pushed her shoulders back. 'Of course. I would say if I knew anything, wouldn't I?'

'Would you?'

Jenny checked herself. It was easy to combat defensiveness with aggression, so natural to Jenny. She wanted to tell Billie this pain would pass, she'd find a way through. But she didn't believe that enough to say it, it would've sounded hollow.

She pulled a business card from her pocket and held it out. Maybe with a bit of time, Billie might be more forthcoming. 'Take it.'

Billie stared at it like it was an ancient artefact, who has business cards these days? But she took it, twirled it in her fingers.

'Please,' Jenny said. 'If you want to talk, just call me. OK?'

Billie chewed her lip and nodded, but Jenny knew she wouldn't call.

22

DOROTHY

'Empathy is the most important thing in this business.'

Dorothy sipped her tea, then put her mug down on the kitchen table. Across from her, Brodie nodded and looked at the funeral and PI whiteboards on the wall, the giant map covered in pins.

'I guess I never thought about the funeral business,' Brodie said.

He wore the same hoodie and joggers as yesterday. She'd told him there was no need to dress up, he was just going to be shown the ropes today. He seemed a little more together, less on the edge.

'The work is actually pretty easy,' Dorothy said. Schrödinger sauntered over to the table and wrapped himself round her legs. 'Indy and Archie will show you that stuff in a bit. Answering the phones will be one of your duties. Indy has been doing that for years, but she's graduated to funeral director and taking on more responsibility. Archie is the engine room, deals with the deceased. Picks them up, prepares them for the funeral. How do you feel about dead bodies?'

Brodie shrugged. 'I don't know.'

Dorothy thought about what he said last time he was here – about his stillborn son. Maybe seeing dead bodies all day wasn't the best therapy, or maybe it was exactly what he needed. Time would tell.

'Archie also constructs the coffins and does some hearse driving. We need you to do some of that too. I have plans to expand and I need Archie for that.'

'What kind of expansion?'

'We're trying to be as green as possible. You'll see the resomator downstairs, Indy will explain how it works. But I'm also looking at buying a site for a natural burial woodland. The plan is that Archie would look after that.'

'Sounds like a lot of work.'

'And I'm working on something else with the council. Did you know dozens of people die in Edinburgh every year with no friends or family to take care of the funeral?'

Dorothy remembered the funeral she took on last year, for a middle-aged woman in exactly that position. She had a distant cousin in New Zealand who paid for the ceremony, but no one came to her cremation except the Skelfs, Archie and Indy. That was the seed of this idea, which she'd been nurturing ever since.

'In the Netherlands and Belgium, there's a project called The Lonely Funeral. A network of poets in different cities find out what they can about the deceased, write a poem for them and read it at their funerals.'

'I'm telling you now, I'm not a poet,' Brodie said.

Dorothy smiled. 'We don't need to do that. But I've made an arrangement with the council, they'll donate their small budget for those anonymous funerals to us, and we'll carry out the ceremonies.'

'Won't you make a loss?'

'It's not about money, it's about empathy.'

'The Lonely Funeral sounds a bit sad. It reminds me of the loneliest whale, ever heard of that?'

Dorothy tilted her head. 'No.'

'For decades, oceanographers detected the call of a single whale singing at fifty-two Hertz. Its call is different from all other whales, the pitch is higher. The other whales can't hear it, so it's spent decades calling out to no one.'

'Wow.' Dorothy walked over to the map on the wall. The Firth of Forth was a blue expanse to the north of the city, peppered with islands. She placed a finger on the mouth of the firth, imagined a whale weaving its way through the depths, calling out year after year.

She turned back to Brodie, whose leg was twitching.

'I think you'll fit in fine around here,' she said, waving at the door. 'Let's go and see the rest.'

At reception Indy said hello, and Dorothy stood aside while she showed him the phone and computing systems, all the rest. She watched how he interacted with Indy, attentive, respectful.

They went through to the back and met Archie, Dorothy watching as Brodie was shown Archie's job. Archie checked with Brodie first, then opened one of the fridges. Brodie didn't baulk at the body, just nodded as Archie explained the various processes.

Then they went to the coffin workshop, sawdust caught in sunbeams through the window, that wonderful smell in here, the sense of real work being done. She caught a glance from Archie over Brodie's shoulder, thought she knew what it meant. She got the same from Indy, they had a good feeling about him. Gut instinct was underrated. She'd made mistakes, who hadn't? But her gut brought Archie and Indy into her life, Schrödinger too. Where would she, Jenny and Hannah be without them?

When Archie finished showing Brodie the guts of the operation, Dorothy took him to the front garden. His Hyundai was parked in the driveway, and she remembered he was living in it. She saw the sleeping bag inside, thought of another man in another car, one who crashed into her life a few years ago, died in the process.

'And this is our wind phone,' she said, pointing at the white telephone box in a secluded corner.

She explained its purpose as he examined it. It was such a simple idea. We always tell the bereaved they can talk to their loved ones anytime, but physically setting up a space to do it made a huge difference. She used it often to talk to Jim, and she knew Indy used it to speak with her parents. Jenny and Hannah both used it too, maybe to talk to Craig, although that wasn't something they'd discussed.

'Can I?' Brodie said, touching the door handle.

'Of course.'

He slid inside and touched the cord dangling from the old handset on the shelf. He nodded, arranged himself in the small space. Then he picked up the handset and listened. Dorothy remembered what he'd said about never being allowed to grieve for his son.

After a while he spoke into the phone and she turned away to look around the garden, at their pine tree sprouting from the stump left behind. At Schrödinger, walking along a high wall between here and the park, whiskers in the air. The sound of kids playing in Bruntsfield Links beyond. The sharpness of autumn in the air.

She turned when she heard the wind-phone door open. Brodie stood in the doorway breathing deeply, blinking.

'You OK?'

'I think so.' He closed the door. 'Are you sure you're OK with me working here?'

'I have a good feeling about you. You can start straight away if you like.'

He raised his eyebrows. 'I'd like that.'

Dorothy turned and looked at his car.

'One more thing,' she said. 'Do you need a place to stay?'

23

HANNAH

A knot of sparrows fluttered between branches in the oak tree above her. They moved in synchronicity, as if guided by telepathy. Hannah had read in *New Scientist* that there still wasn't a proper theory to describe how flocks of birds or schools of fish moved with a single intention. It was impossible to mathematically simulate a murmuration of starlings, the rhythms and fluxes. And what was it all *for*? So much of the world remained inexplicable. She loved science, believed in observation to support theory, but our understanding of so much fell pitifully short.

'Hey.'

Hannah snapped out of it and saw Mina standing at her table outside Söderberg. She lifted her aviators to reveal her sharp green eyes. Her cheekbones and cropped red hair gave her a vintage Bowie look, and Hannah imagined her with a lightning flash down her face. She wore a boxy peach blouse that only someone skinny could pull off, and baggy three-quarter-length trousers. Hannah thought of *The Man Who Fell to Earth*, and the reason she was here. Speaking of which.

'Where's Kirsty?'

Mina pulled up a seat. 'Last-minute television interview. The BBC wanted a talking head to discuss the new NASA ten-year plan.'

'But Kirsty has nothing to do with NASA.'

'BBC don't know the difference. A telegenic woman astronaut with opinions is all they want.'

She waved a finger in the air and a graceful waitress came over, took her order for a berry hibiscus tea.

She placed her glasses on the table and ran a hand through her hair. 'I thought I'd just catch up with you myself, if that's OK?'

Hannah was distracted by the helicopter-whirr of sparrows' wings above her, chirping in the air. Two magpies had landed higher in the tree, making the sparrows anxious. How easily their world was unbalanced.

She smelled Mina's tea as it arrived, more sophisticated than her black coffee. She tried not to be in awe of Mina and Kirsty, knew that wouldn't help with the investigation. Role models were a lame idea, but what else would you call a successful and beautiful middle-aged lesbian couple living in an expensive house down the road? One of whom was a goddamn astronaut.

'So,' Mina said, cricking her neck unself-consciously. 'Did you take a look at the stuff I sent?'

Hannah had read the material that morning between everything else, but didn't have time to go deep. With online abuse, it was easy to go down a rabbit hole and never emerge. The abuse Kirsty got on socials was familiar, anonymous keyboard warriors, always men, middle-aged or older, being offensive to anything she posted. It was the same playbook as any right-wing campaign – throw so much shit out there that it drowns the voices of ordinary people. But Hannah couldn't work out the end game. Like a snowball down a hill, it gathered momentum until it was self-fulfilling. But who started this shit and why?

'I had a quick look,' Hannah said. 'But I haven't had time for a deep dive yet.'

Mina sipped her tea. Hannah caught the sharp tang of berries. 'It's escalation I'm worried about. Pencil-dicks shouting homophobic and misogynist abuse is our bread and butter as *high-profile lesbians*.' She made a goofy face at that last phrase, and sounded like a television announcer. 'But now they know where we live, it's different. Are you fitting the cameras tonight?'

Hannah nodded. It was something they could do for themselves, of course, plenty of folk had doorbell cams for burglars and deliveries. But there was something reassuring about an independent person taking charge that appealed to clients. Also, it didn't hurt if things got to the courtroom, having an independent witness to corroborate harassment. God knows, the scales weren't balanced when it came to burden of evidence in such cases.

Hannah went to drink her coffee but realised it was finished. The magpies clacked in the tree and she saw branches rustling.

'I was interested in something you said last night.'

'Oh?'

'In the kitchen, you asked me to watch Kirsty.'

Mina looked at her nails, played with the arms of her sunglasses. Hannah watched her. 'And you didn't want Kirsty to know.'

'I'm just worried about her.'

'You said she changed in the ISS.'

Mina's shoulders began to hunch into a cringe, but she fought it off. 'It's nothing.'

'It didn't sound like nothing.'

Mina shrugged. 'Of course that experience changed her. You went to her talk, the overview effect, all that. She's bound to be different.'

Hannah examined Mina's face. 'But that's not what you're talking about, is it?'

'Of course it is. What else?'

Hannah swallowed. This had been bothering her since last night. 'You think she came back wrong, don't you?'

Mina snorted with laughter. 'You had too much wine last night, that's not what I said.'

'It's not what you *said*, but it's what you think.'

'Not at all.'

Hannah shook her head. 'It's just, if you really think something happened up there...'

'I don't.'

Hannah stuck her lip out. 'Then it sounds like you have some sympathy with the guys harassing her.'

Mina stared at her long and hard. 'How dare you. I love my wife.'

'But?'

'There's no "but", I'm just worried about her. That's more than can be said for these wankers hassling her.'

'It sounds like you know them.'

Mina pushed away from the table, scraping her chair legs on the concrete.

'Look, you've got the wrong idea. I don't know what you think you heard last night. That weed was pretty strong. All I want is for Kirsty to be safe, and for this hassle to stop. Are you going to help or not?'

She stood up and grabbed her bag from the table.

Hannah narrowed her eyes against the sunshine behind Mina. She looked like a visiting alien, Bowie fallen to earth.

'Of course, I'll be round tonight at eight.'

❧

She stood on the mezzanine and watched the millennium clock tower burst into life, clangs and bells, cranks and groans. It was a colossal wooden spire on the ground floor of the Museum of Scotland on Chambers Street, surrounded by little kids. Hannah remembered sitting in front of it at that age, mesmerised by the weird carvings and moving parts, a grotesque medieval puppet show. From where she was now she could see the belfry carvings clearer – naked figures depicting war, famine, slavery and more. She loved that this was a tourist attraction for wee kids.

'Hannah Skelf?'

She turned and saw a woman in her late twenties, tall and lithe, straight black hair in a fringe, wearing the museum uniform of purple blouse and navy suit, which somehow fit her really well. Her nametag read Nadia North.

Hannah recognised her. 'You were at Kirsty Ferrier's reception.'

Nadia smiled. 'So glad to have someone like her appear here.'

Hannah had called ahead to the museum, asking to speak to someone about security at the event. After being passed around the system for a while, she landed on Nadia. The museum was only five minutes away from Söderberg, so she'd popped in.

Hannah looked around. An exhibition on the history of anatomy to the left, a swanky gift shop to the right. 'What exactly do you do here, Nadia?'

'Public Liaison Officer is my official title. Anything outward facing, really.'

'So you organised Kirsty's talk and reception?'

Nadia straightened her blouse collar. 'One of the team.'

Hannah wasn't sure where she was going with this, sometimes just talking threw up something weird.

'Did Kirsty's team mention anything about security beforehand?'

'For sure. There have been other incidents, abuse from randoms. That's why we had those security guys there.'

'Are they museum employees?'

'Agency, I can get you their details if you like.'

'Do you know anything about the guy harassing Kirsty?'

'Sorry, the security guards just threw him out. I don't suppose they thought they needed to contact the police.' Nadia touched her earlobe. 'I don't feel I'm being much help. What's this about, exactly, are you working for Ms Ferrier?'

Good question, what was this about, exactly?

Nadia straightened her skirt. 'I know that she's been getting online abuse too.'

'Did Kirsty mention that?'

Nadia shook her head. 'Seen it on socials.'

'Did you speak to Kirsty before the event?'

'Only briefly,' Nadia said.

'Did she seem OK?'

Nadia shrugged. 'I guess so. I don't know her, so it's hard to say.'

'Was she quiet or nervous?'

'Nervous, I suppose. She was about to give a public talk, I'd be nervous. But then I'm not an astronaut.'

Hannah smiled, recognised a fellow fan. Kirsty had that effect on young women, showed them the way. At least that's what Hannah used to think. It all seemed more complicated since last night's dinner, and she couldn't explain why.

'One thing,' Nadia said, frowning. 'Her partner.'

'Mina, what about her?'

'She did seem weird, really edgy or something. I mean, she wasn't the one giving the talk, what did she have to be nervous about?'

24

DOROTHY

'Are you sure about this?' Archie said.

He drove the van up the hill of Crew Road South, past the Western General Hospital to the large roundabout, then headed left. They turned down Pennywell Road into Muirhouse, the street lined with scruffy older tenements and blocky new flats. Like a lot of the poorest parts of Edinburgh, Muirhouse received a lot of recent funding for improvements, but it only went so far.

'We're investigating, right?' Dorothy said.

'Confronting the Muirhouse Young Team doesn't seem the safest idea. Wouldn't you rather have Thomas and some back-up?'

'Police cars will make them run a mile.' Dorothy smiled at Archie. 'You're forgetting how disarming a little old lady can be.'

Archie frowned.

The light was fading in the west as they drove past Craigroyston High onto Marine Drive, the high-rise blocks on Muirhouse Parkway casting long shadows.

Marine Drive was typical of the weird juxtapositions in Edinburgh. Brand-new professional flats alongside waste ground, a stately home hidden behind high hedges across the road from a caravan park. A halfway house for released prisoners and a temporary home for refugees in amongst a golf course. No city would plan this shit, but that's how real cities grew, old bumping hips with new, derelict next to developed. What always seemed the same was that the poorest people got the shitty end of the stick, and that was certainly the case in Muirhouse.

They reached the end of Marine Drive and parked. Dorothy saw Fara down the grassy slope on the promenade. Silverknowes

Beach was underused – a beautiful stretch of seafront with only a single ice-cream shop for miles. She remembered visits to Venice Beach in her youth, hundreds of tiny shop fronts along the shore for miles, a ramshackle sense of community, before bylaws made it more for tourists, less for locals. That was the mantra the world over, and it definitely applied to Edinburgh. The city was known globally as a picture-postcard dream of ye olde Scotchland, castle and mountains, cobbled streets and history. But the northwest edge of the city was definitely just for locals.

She and Archie walked to Fara, who nodded east. Dorothy had already spotted them, heard the quadbike engines along the prom. She'd asked Fara to call her when the Fergusons next turned up.

'Did you speak to them?' Dorothy said.

'Not yet.'

Dorothy peered in the twilight. There was a bonfire two hundred yards away, most likely a bunch of wooden pallets thrown together and sprayed with lighter fuel. Dorothy saw an armchair on top, lopsided and melting, black smoke pluming into the sky. There was a makeshift ramp alongside, concrete blocks underneath plyboard sheets to raise one end. A quadbike approached then launched off the ramp, fat tyres bouncing as it landed.

Fara started walking towards them, Dorothy and Archie following.

'For what it's worth, I don't think they had anything to do with Billie and Ruby's camper.'

Dorothy had to raise her voice to be heard over the engine revs. 'Why not?'

'We've never had any trouble. The locals hate them, but the locals hate us too, so maybe we're natural allies. My enemy's enemy and all that.'

There were eight of them, the boys in hoodies and joggers, puffy jackets making them seem bigger, the girls in tight leggings, crop tops, shivering in the chill. There were bottles going round, two lads throwing junk on the fire, two others examining the quadbike. In the lull, Dorothy heard the lap of water on the shore. Blackness above the Forth, peace and quiet trying to spread over the land.

'Hi there,' she said as she reached the bonfire.

This surprised them. Little old ladies didn't usually approach them.

One of the quadbike lads sauntered over, used to controlling situations. He was about seventeen, short and wiry, buzzcut blond hair, scar on his chin.

'Aye?'

'I'm Dorothy.' She heard tittering from the group at the bonfire. 'This is Archie and Fara.'

The kid glanced at Fara, spent longer taking in Archie, a middle-aged man of decent size. He nodded at Fara. 'One of the fucking hippies.'

Dorothy marvelled that the concept of hippies still existed for a Muirhouse teenager in 2023. She wondered what the counter-culture dropouts from the sixties would make of that.

'Are you one of the Ferguson brothers?'

He stiffened. 'The fuck is it to you?'

'Some Cramond locals said I should speak to you.'

He snorted with laughter, the gang behind joining in. 'Those stuck-up cunts can get tae fuck.'

He was hoping to shock her, maybe.

'Those "stuck-up cunts" suggested you might know something about the campervan fire the other night.'

Ferguson stared at her, then at Fara, then Archie. 'Who the fuck are you?'

'I'm a private investigator.'

Ferguson made a show of laughing too loud, turning to his posse for effect. 'Auld cunt like you?'

'Yes, an old cunt like me. Is that a problem?'

He clearly didn't know what to make of her. Dorothy had banked on that.

He shook his head. 'That shit had fuck all to do with us.'

'But you've been down there bothering them.'

He took a step towards Fara. 'Is that what you telt her? That we've been fucking with you?'

Fara straightened her shoulders. 'I said you'd been down to our camp, that's all.'

Dorothy stepped forward to distract him from Fara. 'Are you dealing?'

Ferguson turned again to his gang for show. The girls were high, passing a vape around, and Dorothy wondered about their safety here. Some of the boys were staggering too, slow movements. Only Ferguson and one other lad seemed with it.

'Do we look like dealers?' Ferguson grinned, arms wide. He waved at the bonfire, the quadbike, out to sea. 'Innocent laddies like us? Just cos we're fae Muirhouse.'

Dorothy shook her head. 'I'm just trying to find out what happened.'

'You've got us all wrong,' Ferguson said. 'It's drugs all right, but we're no the ones dealing. That cunt Parker has some of the best brown and blues I've ever had, cheap as fuck. Maybe ask him who torched the caravan. The amount he's dealing, he must know some heavy cunts.'

25

JENNY

Jenny drove the hearse between the huge sandstone gateposts of Longcraig House. Something was written in Latin on the archway over the road, but she couldn't make it out in the gloom. A small gatehouse was connected to the stone structure, lights off inside. She drove up the huge, winding drive to the big house in the distance.

This amount of opulence always made Jenny queasy. She'd checked online maps of this part of East Lothian, and was shocked at how many stately homes and castles were peppered along the coast. Gosford House, Luffness Castle, Fenton Tower, Seton Palace. Some were now tourist attractions, others converted into executive self-catering or wedding venues, always money to be made. She thought about the aristocracy who used to live in these places, what they would think.

This was one of the few that seemed to still be in private ownership, and she wondered how the Marquess of Longniddry made his money. She'd done as much online research as possible, but this place was suspiciously secluded. There were high brick walls on all surrounding roads, thick trees forming a further barrier. The grounds were several square miles, a lot of space for privacy. According to Google Maps the estate also contained a lake and woodlands, livery and stables, and a mausoleum that looked like a scaled-down version of the Great Pyramid of Giza.

The house was intimidating up close, reminded Jenny of Monty Burns' place in *The Simpsons*. She pictured him upstairs at a huge mahogany desk, stuffed polar bear beside him, pressing the button to release the hounds.

She parked on the gravel and walked to the house, then pulled the doorbell, an old-school brass knob that clanked and chimed inside. The building still breathing after centuries. A lot of these places stayed afloat with guided tours around the grandeur but not Longcraig. Jenny wondered at the irony, that the house name contained 'craig'. But half the placenames in Scotland had 'craig' in them, which meant a rocky hill. She couldn't start reading signs in things.

She was surprised when Sir William Porterhouse opened the front door himself, she'd expected a manservant. He was older and more dishevelled than his online pictures. His wispy white hair stood up in spikes, and he wore a linen shirt under dirty denim dungarees and work boots.

He smiled at her as if he was always getting knocks on the door from randoms, then glanced behind her.

'Am I dead?' he said, grinning. 'Have you come to take me away?'

She was confused for a moment then realised about the hearse. 'Sorry, no, that's just my car.'

'Right.' He stretched out the vowels. His voice had that incredibly posh Scottish accent that seemed fake, indistinguishable from posh English, the product of a boarding-school education.

'I should explain,' Jenny said, feeling flustered.

He had that natural authority thing she despised, and she felt inferior despite decades of trying to knock that shit out of herself.

'My name is Jenny Skelf, my family runs a funeral directors, hence the hearse. But I'm here about something else. Sir William Porterhouse, right?'

'Call me Bill.' He was amused, tilted his head to the side. His eyebrows were bushy and white, and she could see hair coming from his nose and ears. But he looked lean under the clothes, like he did plenty of manual work around the grounds.

'I'm trying to find Stella McNamara, and I was hoping you'd seen her?'

His eyes widened at Stella's name. 'Has something happened recently?'

'How do you mean?'

'I spoke to the police when she went missing a year ago. Told them I hadn't seen her in months and I still haven't. I just wondered why you're looking now.'

Jenny looked beyond his shoulder, saw pink marble banisters on two curving staircases. A colossal Asian vase on a table, huge-framed portrait above a fireplace to the side. She wondered what it cost to heat this place, then hated herself for having sympathy for him.

'Her mother just died.'

'I'm sorry to hear that. Stella will be distraught.'

'I'm trying to find her to let her know.' That wasn't strictly true, or was it?

'Can I ask how you found your way to me?' There didn't seem any malice in his question. He played with a shock of hair, tried to smooth it down, but it sprung up again.

'Craig's ex-wife Fiona remembered meeting you.'

'Ah yes, I hope she's well?'

All so civil and nice. It was easy to be civil in a place like this. 'She was fine once she got her daughter back from Craig.'

Bill frowned and nodded. 'Of course, you're Jenny. I'm sorry you had to go through all that.'

She hated that her personal shit made the news, but murder, prison escape and kidnapping tended to do that.

'I suppose you have a vested interest in finding her too.'

No point denying it. 'For sure. So anything you can tell me...'

Bill shook his head and pushed his fists into his dungaree pockets. 'I'm afraid I don't have anything. We dated for a while. But I hadn't seen her in months when all that happened last year.'

'How did you two meet?' Jenny waved a hand at the sculpted gardens and groomed driveway. 'If you don't mind me saying, you seem like an odd couple.'

He gave a hearty laugh. 'I suppose we were. I go shooting on my friend's estate in Perthshire, and we sometimes go out in Pitlochry in the evening. I met Stella working in a restaurant and we just got on.'

'"She was working as a waitress in a cocktail bar"', Jenny said under her breath.

'I'm sorry?'

'Nothing. And you got on?'

Bill nodded. 'It's not easy to meet genuine people when you live somewhere like this.'

Jenny wondered what Stella saw in this rich guy and his stately pile. Or maybe it was genuine, maybe Jenny was just cynical.

'But you stopped seeing her?'

Bill cleared his throat, glanced around as if spilling a secret. 'She didn't handle Craig's disappearance well. All that business with you, Fiona and the girl. And the other things he did before that, to that young woman. It really knocked her for six. I tried to look after her, she moved in here for a while. But she pushed me away, pushed everyone away. Went back to live with her mother for a while, then I suppose the next thing was taking Craig's body.'

Now she was supposed to feel sorry for Stella.

'I know it's not easy from your point of view, but she's very sensitive and she loved her brother very much. It was quite devastating.'

Jenny looked behind Bill again and he laughed. 'You think I have her hidden inside?'

Jenny didn't answer.

Bill stepped aside. 'Please, be my guest. It might take you a while, there are twenty-five bedrooms and as many public rooms. But I have no secrets.'

She considered taking him up on it, wavered on the doorstep. She took a step forward and he made way. She stopped. If Stella really was inside, he wouldn't be so welcoming. And something else bothered her. Would someone like him hide an arsonist?

Someone wanted for attempted murder? Someone with a decomposing corpse in their van? She looked around, acres of secluded woods and parkland, easy to bury a body, or cremate him, or chuck him in the mausoleum.

But it was Bill's reputation Jenny was thinking about. Rich people got away with plenty, but for someone like him, life was all about reputation. Prestigious hunting and shooting trips, invited to the right balls, the perfect gentlemen's club. She didn't think he'd risk all that for a waitress.

'Do you have any idea where she might've gone?' Jenny said, stepping back. 'How does someone just disappear?'

'You need money and empty space, and I have both. But I promise, she's not here. The police searched the house and grounds a year ago, and you're free to do the same. As for where she might be, I don't know. She always had a nomadic streak, liked the idea of life on the road, living off the land. That's easier said than done, of course, but it's possible.'

'That doesn't help.'

Bill smiled. 'Honestly, she could be anywhere.'

Jenny decided to believe him. She might have to come back, she might have to stake out the place, although was that even possible with such a big estate? But for now she believed Bill Porterhouse. Stella could be anywhere.

26

HANNAH

Hannah kissed Indy goodbye at reception and left the big house. Her backpack contained a handful of spy cameras, and she felt a trill in her stomach. She was heading to Kirsty's place to install them and was nervous about seeing her again, but wasn't sure why. She thought about Mina earlier, maybe Hannah *had* been too stoned last night, maybe she was imagining things.

She heard footsteps on gravel and saw a young woman at the end of the driveway. Black leggings, high-tops, outsized denim jacket. Hannah recognised Billie from her picture on the whiteboard upstairs. Billie took a few steps forward, then jumped as Schrödinger emerged from a hedge and sauntered across her path. She was flicking a card between her fingers.

'Billie, right?' Hannah said.

Billie frowned. 'Everyone seems to know who I am.'

'I'm Hannah Skelf.'

'Another Skelf?' Billie looked past her at the house. 'Any more in there?'

'Three's plenty.'

Billie nodded and looked at the card in her hand. 'Is Jenny about?'

Hannah shook her head. 'Sorry.'

'Dorothy, then?'

Hannah held her hands out. 'Just me, and my wife's inside.'

Billie smiled. 'Wife? Cool. Boys are fucking trouble.'

'Can I help?'

Billie shifted her feet and played with a big hoop earring. 'Dunno.'

'Want to come inside?'

Billie shook her head. 'Fine here.'

'OK.'

Billie was maybe four years younger than Hannah, but her face said she'd seen plenty. Living like she did was tough, it could harden you. Hannah had a flash of gratitude for all she had in her life, easy to fall between the cracks otherwise.

Billie looked at the card again. 'Is Jenny your mum?'

Hannah nodded.

'And Dorothy's your gran, then. Must be nice to have family.'

'We're lucky.'

Billie gave her a look she couldn't fathom. It wasn't aggressive but it wasn't friendly either. Maybe world-weary.

Hannah cleared her throat. 'If you came here to tell us something about the fire, I can pass it on. I'm kind of involved in investigating stuff too.'

'Yeah?'

Hannah patted her backpack. 'I'm off to install some spy cameras.'

Billie pouted. 'Nice. Could've done with some of them the other night.'

Her face fell and she shuffled her feet again.

'Please,' Hannah said. 'If there's anything you can tell me that might help us.'

Billie chewed that over for a long time. She looked around the garden, spotted the white phone box. 'What's that?'

'A wind phone. A present from an old Japanese client. It's for talking to the dead.'

'What?'

Hannah walked her over to it. 'There's an old, unconnected handset. We use it to talk to dead relatives or friends.'

Billie ran a hand over the door, her fingers resting on the handle. 'What about?'

'Anything you want.'

'Who do *you* talk to?'

Hannah swallowed. 'My grandpa. And my dad.'

Billie looked at the handset on the shelf then back at Hannah. 'Were they good guys?'

Hannah felt a flush in her cheeks. 'Grandpa was. Not Dad.'

Billie nodded. 'Fucking dads.' She opened the door. 'Can I?'

'Of course.'

Billie went inside and Hannah stepped away, turned to look at the house, the tree stump, Schrödinger now walking amongst the flowerbeds. She heard Billie's voice, quiet at first, then angry. She walked to the other end of the garden, turned and saw Billie waving a hand around, leaning into the mouthpiece and shouting, shaking. She took the handset away from her mouth and stared at it, eyes wide. It looked like she might smash it to pieces. But she just stared for a long time, then placed it back in its cradle and left the box, shaking her head.

'Fucking dads,' she said again.

Hannah had to agree.

❧

She rotated the camera until it was pointing at the front doorstep. Stepped back and checked the image on her phone app, waved at the camera and saw herself. She looked ghostly in black and white, needed some sun. She walked down the path then back up to see when the camera picked her up.

She headed back inside to the kitchen, where Kirsty was sitting with a glass of Shiraz and a half-smoked joint. Yuri was mooching his way around the edge of the room, then squeezed out the cat flap on the side door. Hannah's glass of red was sitting along from Kirsty, untouched. Not a good idea to set cameras under the influence.

Kirsty looked as tired and pale as Hannah's ghost on the camera footage. She seemed a long way from the radiant presence she was on stage. Maybe that was to be expected, we perform in public then hide our true selves until we're home. But now her home was being threatened, that's why they had five cameras around the perimeter.

She held the joint up to Hannah.

'I shouldn't.'

'Come on, we're friends.'

Hannah felt a fire in her belly at that word. They were *friends*.

She had a small toke and passed the joint back, then took a sip of wine.

'Show me,' Kirsty said, waving her phone.

Hannah took it. Kirsty had downloaded the app and Hannah set her up with a login and password.

'It's simple,' she said. 'You have access to all the footage. They're motion triggered, so there won't be anything unless someone's in your garden or at the door. You'll get false triggers from Yuri – does he do a lot of outdoor exploring?'

'Yeah.'

'And triggers from wildlife too – foxes, maybe badgers or hedgehogs. You'd be surprised how much shit is out there.'

Kirsty's throaty chuckle filled Hannah's heart. She still couldn't really believe she was drinking wine and sharing a joint with an astronaut.

'OK, I'll expect lots of rogue moles digging away.' Kirsty took another swig of wine.

Hannah held Kirsty's phone up. 'There are five cameras. Front and back doors, two at the side of the house, and one at the bottom of the garden, in the oak tree. That should give you a good spread of angles and sightlines.'

Kirsty put her glasses on to see the phone screen and touched Hannah's hand as she pulled the phone closer to her face. Hannah felt her smooth skin, smelled her perfume, dark and woody.

'Mina not around?' Hannah handed the phone over and took a sip of wine, cradling her glass in both hands.

'At a work thing.' Kirsty slid her phone across the worktop.

'What exactly does she do?'

'Cutting-edge biotech stuff to do with human interfaces.'

'Interfaces?'

'The senses.'

'Like wetware, connecting your brain to the internet?'

Kirsty laughed. 'I don't think we're quite at the singularity yet. And given my socials, I'm not sure we need to be that connected. No, they're working on tech for people who've lost one of their senses. A vibrating watch to help folk hear, or implants that can retrigger smell or taste.'

'Wow.'

Kirsty passed the joint and tapped her temple. 'The brain can be retrained in all sorts of ways. Folk think it's set in stone when you're an adult, but the old dog *can* learn new tricks. After all, our brains change with every experience.'

Hannah thought about the overview effect, tried to imagine the mindfuck of seeing Earth from space. She remembered the Total Perspective Vortex from *The Hitchhiker's Guide to the Galaxy*. It was a device designed to demonstrate the infinity of creation, which became a torture device because people couldn't handle that perspective on their insignificant lives. The joke was that egomaniac Zaphod Beeblebrox survived it because it told him he was the most important person in the universe. The overview effect was similar, it could either inspire awe and change in a person, or totally fuck them up. Maybe a bit of both.

'I met Mina today,' Hannah said.

'I know.'

'She's worried about you.'

'I know.' Kirsty touched her neck. 'But I don't want to talk about Mina.'

The wine and the grass and thinking about the overview effect had made Hannah dizzy. She only now realised that chilled beats were playing in the kitchen.

'You must get asked this all the time,' she said. 'But what was it *really* like in space?'

Kirsty smiled and looked into her eyes. Hannah felt herself disappearing in that gaze.

'I can never say what I really think, not in public.'

Hannah watched Kirsty's lips, waiting for the next word. They were dark red from the wine.

Kirsty leaned closer and spoke softly. 'It was fucking *insane*. Like, totally … mind-blowing doesn't cover it.'

She put her hand on Hannah's, warm and comforting.

'The trouble is,' she whispered. 'We just don't have the words. Humans can't describe shit like that. It changes you.'

Hannah felt the warmth from Kirsty's hand spread up her arm and through her body, making her shiver.

Kirsty leaned in and kissed her, and Hannah felt the tingle on her lips for a moment before she straightened her back and pulled away, sliding her hand from under Kirsty's. She lifted her wine and took a drink, looked around the room and wanted to scream.

'I'm sorry.' Kirsty slid her hands across the worktop. 'I thought I was getting a vibe.'

'No, I'm sorry. I just…'

Kirsty shook her head. 'Forget it.'

Hannah swallowed hard. 'What about Mina?'

Kirsty angled her head. 'We have an open relationship, I thought that was obvious.'

'I didn't realise.'

'She didn't mention it when you spoke to her earlier?'

'No.'

'I kind of thought that's *why* she met you.'

Hannah tried to think. 'She sounded like she wanted you to go back to who you were before you went to space.'

Kirsty sucked her teeth. 'We've had that conversation. She doesn't like that I care about stuff.'

'But she helps people with her work.'

'Maybe. But there's a lot of ego involved too.' She laughed. 'Like I can talk.'

Hannah couldn't believe she'd just been kissed. And she couldn't believe they were now chatting like nothing happened.

There were two pings from her and Kirsty's phones.

'Probably Yuri,' Kirsty said.

Hannah opened the app and saw someone in a hoodie and face mask running up the back garden towards the house.

She jumped as the kitchen window smashed, showering them with shards. She ducked too late, felt glass in her hair. She saw a brick on the floor.

Kirsty slid off her stool and picked it up like it was a wild beast.

Both their phones pinged again, and Hannah saw the same figure at the side of the house then on the front-door camera. She ran to the door and flung it open, saw the person go through the gate and turn towards Blackford Hill. She ran after, trainers slapping the pavement, adrenaline and grass and wine in her system, breath hammering in her chest. She was gaining on them. They disappeared around the corner and she followed, then rounded the hedge.

She felt it before she saw it, a wooden plank from some scaffolding swung at her head. She turned enough for it to miss her nose and crack against her temple, the wood splintering as she collapsed to her knees, head pounding, breath knocked out of her lungs, her palms on the rough paving stones. She closed her eyes and slid into the gutter.

27

JENNY

She felt warmth on her chest, tugging her out of sleep. She thought of Craig, how they would fuck early in the morning when they were first together, that half-sleep making it seem like a weird horny dream.

She opened her eyes and saw Schrödinger's arsehole, his tail flicking at her face. Sunlight slipped through the cracks in the curtains. She sighed and shoved the cat aside, his claws digging into her skin then releasing. She felt discomfort at the scar tissue on her stomach, ran a hand along it, thought about Craig slipping a knife inside her, just as easily as he used to slip inside her in bed.

'Stupid cat.'

She got out of bed, stretched her shoulders and neck. More and more these days she felt sore waking up. She was the target audience for all those memory-foam mattresses and knee pillows, but she couldn't face being that old. She stepped out of the bedroom in a ratty old Rage Against the Machine T-shirt and pants, then stopped at the kitchen doorway.

A man she'd never seen before sat at the kitchen table drinking coffee. He was half her age, cute in a babyish, dishevelled way, stubble and bed hair, plain white T-shirt and skinny jeans. He was looking out of the window at Bruntsfield Links and hadn't spotted her.

'Excuse me, who the fuck are you?'

He jumped at her voice and scraped his chair away from the table, splashing coffee into the bargain.

'Shit.' He put his mug down and got a cloth from the sink, swiped at the table then the base of his mug, nervous and clumsy.

Jenny thought about her bare legs on show. She should cover up, but this was her house.

'I'm Brodie,' the guy said, the cloth in his fist. 'Brodie Willis.'

'And what are you doing in my kitchen, Brodie Willis?'

He took a step towards her and offered a nervous hand, then dropped it when Jenny stared at it.

'You must be Jenny,' he said. 'Dorothy told me all about you.'

'I wish I could say the same.'

'I started work here yesterday.'

Jenny raised her eyebrows. 'What?'

'I thought you knew.'

He looked beyond Jenny into the hall, maybe wishing someone would come through the door and save him. Jenny was enjoying his embarrassment and she was glad she hadn't covered her legs, it gave her a sense of power.

She saw a half-full cafetiere, grabbed a mug and poured herself a good dose, took a swig and turned. His gaze switched from her legs to her face and she wondered about that. Sexist bullshit, of course, but it was nice to know your forty-eight-year-old legs were worth looking at.

She pointed at the table.

'Why don't you sit down and tell me about it.'

She pulled up a seat. He moved like a wary fox and sat, picked up his coffee.

'It was actually Hannah who first spoke to me.'

Jenny raised her eyebrows. Dorothy and Hannah were always in cahoots. Part of her resented that, but part of her liked the two women she most loved getting along so well. If she had to stay out of it, fair enough.

'Wait, are you the funeral crasher?'

He cringed.

'Indy mentioned some guy had been coming to funerals.'

He looked at his hands, scratched at the table. 'I guess that's me.'

'Why?'

'You're quite up front, eh?'

Jenny sipped her coffee. 'I don't see any point in beating around the bush.'

The word 'bush' made him blush and look away.

'My son died. In childbirth.'

Jenny put her mug down and touched the table. 'Fuck, I'm sorry.'

He waved that away.

Jenny cleared her throat. 'I was being a dick. I'm sorry.'

'It's OK.'

Jenny heard kids screaming outside in the park, as if on cue. The nursery along the road often took them out to play games, four-year-olds in tiny hi-vis vests, trying to catch a spongy ball.

Schrödinger sauntered in, tail high, and made straight for Brodie, rubbed against him. Dorothy always said the cat was a good judge of character, but he'd always been standoffish with Jenny. That spoke volumes.

'So Mum just gave you a job?'

Brodie raised his head. 'I lost mine. Split with my girlfriend. I'm a bit all over the place.'

Jenny thought about that. Dorothy brought Archie and Indy into the family that way. Pretty obvious pattern – find a lost soul, welcome them with open arms.

'I told her I only need to stay here until I find somewhere else.'

'You're living here?'

His face reddened. 'Sorry, I thought you knew. I'm crashing on the futon in the studio upstairs.'

'Wow.'

He stood up and stared at the floor. 'You're right, I shouldn't be here. This was stupid.'

Jenny looked at him, panicking like a kid on a first date.

'Wait,' she said. 'I overreacted. It's just a surprise.'

He pressed his lips together like he was about to say something, but didn't.

So this young guy was now sharing their house. He could be a fucking axe murderer. Dorothy liked to talk about gut instincts, but Jenny didn't believe that bullshit. Her own gut had got her into all sorts of trouble over the years, murderous, violent trouble. Brodie looked harmless enough, but who knew?

'I don't want to cause any trouble between you and Dorothy,' he said.

Jenny chewed her lip. 'I just wish she'd spoken to me first.'

He rubbed his palms together and glanced at the doorway. 'Anyway, I'd better get downstairs. Archie and Indy have stuff for me to do.'

Jenny nodded as he took his coffee mug to the sink, rinsed it out and placed it upside down on the draining board.

On his way out the door he nodded at her chest. 'Nice T-shirt, by the way.'

'Christ, I thought for a second you were going to say, "nice tits".'

She meant it as a joke, but he looked mortified that she'd mentioned her tits. Good, she still had some power to offend.

28
DOROTHY

St Leonard's canteen was scruffy and gloomy, small windows out to the car park at the back of the building. The smell of bacon fat hung in the air as Dorothy looked around. It was busy with uniformed officers, detectives in suits, office staff and IT guys with lanyards. She spotted Webster and Low in the corner with Lorne sausage rolls and milky tea, went over and sat alongside.

Webster frowned at her. 'What the hell are you doing here?'

'Just wanted a quick catch-up on the arson case.'

He waved his roll, a blob of brown sauce dripping onto the table. 'We're on our break, you shouldn't even be in here. I suppose your boyfriend swiped you in.'

'Thomas doesn't know I'm here. It's easy to get into a police station, you should tighten your security.'

Low slurped his tea. 'It's getting out of the station most folk worry about.'

Webster straightened his shoulders and stared at Dorothy. 'Look, we met you last time as a courtesy to Olsson, but this is ridiculous. You're not entitled to regular updates.'

'Did you speak to the Muirhouse gang?' Dorothy said.

Low scoffed. 'I don't think those bampots would have a useful contribution.'

Webster glowered at his partner.

'Not even to eliminate them?' Dorothy said.

Low went quiet and Webster took a bite of his roll, wiped sauce from his fingers, then had a sip of tea. 'Fuck it, I'll play along. Why would the Fergusons give a shit about the crusties on the beach?'

Dorothy narrowed her eyes. Webster didn't look old enough

for 'crusties', that was an early-nineties phrase for rave-scene drop-outs. She would've put him at late thirties, not late forties, maybe he'd just aged well.

'I spoke to Niall Ferguson last night.'

Low perked up. '*You* spoke to the Fergusons?'

'Yes.'

'Alone?'

'With a friend.'

Webster looked annoyed at Low. 'What did he say?'

'I asked if they were selling drugs to the caravaners.'

Webster took the final bite of his roll, smudging sauce on his chin. 'And?'

Dorothy ran a finger across the table. 'I thought they would've been on your list of people of interest.'

'Out with it.'

'Niall could've been lying, of course, but he said it was the other way round. They buy drugs from someone at the site.'

'The girls?'

What Dorothy had done was basic police work that Webster and Low should've already covered. 'No, Billie's boyfriend, Parker. They got uppers and downers from him. Niall reckoned it was quality stuff, so Parker might have a connection up the food chain.'

She was reluctant to give this away without speaking to Parker first, but she'd already been down there early this morning, and he, Billie and Ruby weren't about. She wondered about that – if they hadn't stayed the night at the camp, then where? But Dorothy also wanted to keep the police sweet, she might need their help.

'Interesting.' Webster turned to Low. 'Did we see Parker at the site?'

Low stuck the tip of his tongue out between his teeth. 'He wasn't around.'

'That's convenient.'

'Sounds like you've really got stuck into it.' Dorothy regretted the words as they slipped out, but she couldn't help it. Fara and her friends weren't a priority for the police. Webster and Low thought Billie and Ruby were second-class citizens, not worth the effort. So Dorothy had her answer. The police would turn up nothing, even if she gave them leads. It was down to her to help the Cramond community, because no one else would.

She pushed her chair back and stood, pointed at the brown sauce on Webster's chin. 'You missed a bit.'

29

HANNAH

Her fingertips hovered above her temple as she looked at herself in the bathroom mirror. An obvious lump surrounded by a crescent of lilac bruising, the skin grazed and raw in the middle. She rubbed arnica on the injury and sighed. She'd pretended to be asleep earlier when Indy went to work, keeping the injured side of her head against the pillow. It was stupid, she wouldn't be able to hide this, but she needed more time to figure it out. And in the back of her mind she was more worried about kissing Kirsty than the plank of wood across her head.

She splashed water on her face and patted it dry, then walked to the kitchen. She made a cup of herbal tea and stared at the tenement windows across the communal gardens. Far enough away that it didn't feel as if they were staring at her, but close enough that she could catch glimpses of her neighbours' lives – students waking up, young parents exhausted after a sleepless night, the old widower who sat with his crossword every day, pencil between his teeth.

She sipped tea. Last night was fucking crazy. She was only unconscious for a moment before Kirsty found her and took her inside. She insisted on checking for signs of concussion. Hannah assumed that a retired astronaut had basic first aid.

She felt calmer as she sipped her tea, watched two woodpigeons chase each other across the branches of an oak, their mating dance shuddering the leaves.

'Hey.'

She jumped, tea scalding her hand as it spilled. Indy came into the kitchen and headed for the fridge.

'What are you doing home?' Hannah said.

Indy's head was inside the fridge. 'Forgot my lunch.'

Hannah breathed deep, imagined running out the door or diving out the window.

Indy closed the fridge holding a Tupperware box and looked over. She blinked and stepped forward. 'What the hell happened to you?'

'An accident.' Hannah's trembling hand went to her forehead.

Indy dropped her Tupperware on the counter and turned Hannah's face towards the light from the window. She lifted her chin, and Hannah thought of Kirsty touching her face last night.

'Accident, my arse.'

Hannah took Indy's hand and explained as plainly as she could, setting the cameras, having a drink in the kitchen, the cameras triggering, the brick, the chase, the plank in the face.

'Holy shit, why didn't you wake me last night? You could've been concussed.'

'Kirsty said I was fine.'

'Oh, well, if Kirsty said.'

Hannah hated the tone of Indy's voice, but she would've been exactly the same the other way round. 'She's medically trained.'

'I don't think she is. You still should've gone to A&E.'

Hannah gave Indy's hand a squeeze. 'I'd still be there now, with the waiting times.'

'Christ, Han, I thought you were better at self-care these days.'

A reference to her self-harm when she was younger, or at least her lack of self-regard. But she was better these days, or so she thought.

'Have you spoken to Thomas?'

Hannah looked out of the window, avoiding Indy's gaze. 'Not yet.'

'But you're going to, right?'

Hannah hugged her mug to her chest. 'The police won't do anything, you know that.'

Indy raised her eyebrows. 'This is assault, Han, if you don't report it, I will.'

Hannah's stomach tightened but she didn't speak.

Indy ran her tongue around her mouth before she spoke again. 'You have footage of this guy, right? Presumably the police can rustle up a list of names from Kirsty's trolls.'

Hannah thought about that. Kirsty and Mina didn't think Police Scotland had their best interests at heart, and Hannah got that. If you were anything other than mainstream, it was easy to believe the police would always think of you more as a perpetrator than a victim.

'I'll speak to Thomas.'

'And you have to drop the case.'

Hannah's back stiffened. 'They asked me to help, I'm going to help.'

'It's not safe.'

'I'm fine.'

Indy shook her head. 'I'm allowed to worry about you, you know.'

'I'd be pissed off if you didn't.'

Indy touched Hannah's arm. Hannah smiled and felt sick at the same time.

'There's something else.'

The tone of her voice was enough to make Indy look worried again.

Hannah sipped tea then cleared her throat. 'Kirsty kind of kissed me last night.'

'What the fuck?'

Hannah held a hand out as if to stop the wave crashing into her. 'It was crazy, she did it out of nowhere. I pulled away, made it clear she had the wrong idea.'

Indy narrowed her eyes. 'Han, why would she get the idea it was OK in the first place?'

Hannah's cheeks flushed, neck muscles tight. 'Crossed wires. She said she got a signal, I swear to God there was no signal.'

'Were you high?'

Hannah swallowed. 'We had a joint. Kirsty said they had an open relationship, she thought I was interested. I told her where to go.'

'Really?'

'Indy, please.' Hannah put her tea down and grabbed Indy's elbow, pulled her closer. Lowered her face and looked up, a joke version of coy, like an anime character. 'Of course. You don't think I'm interested in her, do you?'

Indy's eyes widened. 'You mean apart from the fact she's beautiful and charismatic and has been to fucking space, which was your childhood dream?' She frowned but her face softened as she shook her head. 'This case is bad juju.'

'It's just a case.'

'For a sexy astronaut who's totally into you.'

'I'm a grown woman, I told her I'm not interested.'

Hannah risked a kiss, and felt sick with relief when Indy kissed her back. She felt Indy's hands on her back, smelled her shampoo, the taste of her lips. But an image of Kirsty flashed in her mind, then the plank coming towards her face, and she waited for the pain.

30

JENNY

She pulled the van onto the verge of the Aberlady road. She'd driven round the grounds of Longcraig House and every entrance had a gate with security cameras. But across the road, the surrounding wall was partially tumbledown, thanks to what looked like a recent car accident, judging by the flimsy police tape fluttering between trees.

She got out and strode across the road then through the gap in the stonework. In the woods on the other side were yew and beech trees, and a worn path to a loch. There were reeds around the loch, two punts tied to a quay, a spread of wooded islands in the middle. It didn't look like they had any space for habitation.

This was pointless, but a hunch was a hunch, and she'd been chewing over what Bill Porterhouse said last night. He was happy for her to search the house, which meant Stella wasn't there. But he had acres of land, plenty of room to hide. Looking at the satellite pictures online, much of it was fields and parkland, exposed areas where it would be easy to spot someone. But these woods provided cover that might be useful if you didn't want to be found.

She wandered around the edge of the loch, expecting a groundskeeper to appear, brandishing his spade and shouting for her to beat it. But all she saw were rabbits in the long grass, blackbirds and ravens in the branches overhead. The sun flickered through the leaves and she wondered if this was what it felt like to be at peace. She passed the punts and thought about jumping into one, heading to an island.

She walked east, crossed over a gravel path that definitely wasn't on the online maps, into more woods, the going heavier. The dampness of recent rain gave the air an earthy tang, patches of mud around. She emerged through a copse of poplars into a clearing.

Up ahead was the mausoleum, a thirty-feet-high granite pyramid with Doric columns in front, a gateway flanked by marble statues. She admired how daft it was as she walked through the gate, staring at the naked figures towering over her, tiny cocks pointing at the tomb. She went inside, saw a stone sarcophagus sculpted in the shape of a knight, arms crossed over his chest in eternal peace. It was cool and clammy in here, pigeon shit covered the ground, the bluster of their wings in the eaves. She imagined the fifth marquess rising from his tomb to shoo them away. Or a giant door slamming behind her, like Indiana Jones. But it was just her in a pyramid in East Lothian with an old dead guy.

She stayed in there for a while, breathing the damp air, thinking about her dad. She imagined they'd built a massive stone pyramid in their back garden, entombed him inside. She could sit with him every day, tell him how fucked up she'd been since he died, how she felt like a ship without a rudder since his heart attack. She just missed him like fuck, that's all.

She left the mausoleum and headed further away from the house. More woods, a burn with a small bridge, grassy paths big enough for a vehicle. Someone must be maintaining the grounds, but she hadn't found storage sheds or gardening equipment.

She heard a woodpecker rat-tatting on a tree trunk then something else like an animal noise. She tilted her head, tried to get a direction. Trees rustling in the breeze, chirrup of sparrows, the burble of the burn behind her. Then the noise again, a snuffle and grunt to her right.

She walked that way through tightly packed trees, then suddenly there was a clearing. She stood behind an oak and stared.

A Range Rover was parked in the middle of the clearing, windows down, two people in the back seats. A woman's head stuck out the rear window as someone took her from behind. Her hair was over her face, so Jenny couldn't see if it was Stella. The rear windscreen was steamed up and four men stood around the car watching, trousers at their ankles as they played with themselves. They were arranged around the car to get a decent view of the action. Two of them were facing Jenny but she couldn't see their faces because they wore animal masks, a fox and a rabbit. The two with their backs to her looked as if they wore badger and deer masks.

She felt the rough bark of the tree under her fingers as she leaned against the trunk and breathed. The woman threw her hair around like a porn star, then reached out to grab the dick nearest her. Jenny caught a glimpse of her face, it wasn't Stella. Younger and cuter. One of the other men stepped forward and came into the open window, and Jenny wondered about the upholstery. Some poor bastard would have to clean that up.

The man in the rabbit mask was staring at her, cock in hand. Slowly, he pushed the mask to the top of his head. It was Bill Porterhouse, smiling at her with his eyebrows raised in invitation.

Jenny turned and left.

31

DOROTHY

The remains of the burnt-out camper were still there like a congealed cooking disaster. Scorched metal, melted plastic, burnt wood. The other caravans and campers formed a horseshoe around the space, and sunshine had brought many occupants into the central area. Two little girls kicked a football while a woman Dorothy didn't recognise sipped tea and kept an eye on them. Two young men had a pushbike upturned and a box of tools alongside.

Dorothy spotted Fara on a foldout chair at the other side, knitting in her lap. Fara saw her and waved, and Dorothy walked over, taking in the various vehicles and people. She thought about Webster and Low at the station, confirming Fara's impression that the police didn't give a shit about them.

'Hey,' she said, sitting next to Fara.

Fara held up her knitting, a jumper in red-and-black stripes. 'What do you think?'

'Better than anything I could do.'

'You learn to be resourceful. Got a bunch of free wool and *voilà*.'

One of the girls playing football lost her balance and fell over in a patch of dirt. She looked at her mum, who wasn't watching. She thought about crying, making a fuss. In the end she stood up, wiped the dirt from her leg, then kicked the ball to her friend.

'How did it go with the police?' Fara said.

They'd talked about it this morning, when Dorothy came to find Parker. The idea that Parker was dealing, whether it was reliable. Neither could think of a reason Ferguson would make it up, except maybe just to fuck with them. Fara didn't know Parker was involved in that shit, at least that's what she'd told Dorothy. Maybe she was hiding something too. There was plenty of weed in the camp, but heroin and bennies were not something Fara wanted. Having said that, she was in favour of decriminalising all drugs, and Dorothy saw her point. Imagine the bottom fell out the market, how that would affect organised crime. And the tax on drugs could be used to set up addiction treatment centres. Illegal drugs were just another way of othering a section of society.

Dorothy realised she hadn't answered the question. 'Not great. I spoke to Webster and Low again.'

Fara made a face as her knitting needles clacked. 'I told you they don't care.'

'Maybe they're just under-resourced.'

Fara paused her knitting. 'Maybe they hate us.' She saw the look on Dorothy's face. 'I know I sound paranoid but it comes from painful experience. The authorities are not our friends, and the police fuck with us. All they need are a few spurious complaints from locals to move us on, often without legal authority.'

Dorothy nodded at Parker's caravan. 'Is Parker around yet?'

Fara shook her head. 'I haven't seen him since yesterday. Billie and Ruby are in though.'

'How well do you know him? Do you trust him with Billie and Ruby?'

Fara placed her knitting needles in her lap. 'Hundred percent.'

'He's a little old for them.'

'They're adults, they make their own choices.'

'Come on, there's a power imbalance with a man in his late twenties and a teenage woman.'

'Only if the guy is a dickhead.'

As if on cue, the door to Parker's caravan opened and Billie stood there blinking. She was in shorts and a strappy vest top which had *Babe!* on the front in sequins. She spotted Fara and Dorothy, walked over, bare feet in the dirt as she pulled up a chair and rubbed her eyes. Her hair was in a loose bun, face pale, a Hello Kitty tattoo on her shoulder.

'Hey,' she said, stretching like a cat.

Fara started knitting again, the clack-clack of the needles like distant gunfire.

'Fara and I spoke to the Muirhouse boys last night,' Dorothy said.

'Uh-huh,' Billie said, cricking her neck. 'What about?'

'Your camper.'

'And?'

'They said they had nothing to do with it.'

'Well, they would.' There was something about Billie's nonchalant manner that unsettled Dorothy.

'But they mentioned Parker.'

Billie widened her eyes at that. 'Why?'

'They said they buy drugs from him.'

'Bullshit.'

'And maybe he's mixed up in something.'

'Parker takes care of us.'

Fara had her head down, pretending she wasn't listening. Billie glanced at her.

Dorothy brushed some dirt from her lap. 'Are you sure he's not shifting drugs? That might explain why someone would burn a camper here. As a message.'

Billie arched her back. 'It doesn't explain anything. Why burn our place and not Parker's?'

There was something going on under Billie's bravado, but Dorothy couldn't figure it out. Was Parker their pimp? Or was it something else? Maybe it was all about Ruby. Where was he anyway?

Dorothy nodded at the caravan. 'Where is Parker?'

Billie pushed herself out of her seat. 'Fuck's sake, we don't keep tabs on each other.'

Dorothy held her hands out. 'I'm just trying to help.'

'It wasn't to do with Parker, OK? I'm fucking telling you.'

She seemed so sure of herself, Dorothy wondered about that. 'It sounds like you know what it *is* about.'

'What?'

'It sounds like you know something you're not telling me.'

Billie looked at Parker's caravan, then stared at Fara, who avoided her gaze. 'I don't know anything, but I know Parker. He wouldn't be involved in anything dodgy. Maybe we should just forget about the fire, it was a pile of shit anyway. Me and Ruby are happier at Parker's.' She rubbed her chin. 'I need to get dressed.'

Dorothy watched her walk away, messing with her hair. She slammed the door behind her.

Dorothy looked at Fara, who'd stopped knitting. Fara raised her eyebrows, but like everything in this case, Dorothy wasn't sure what it meant.

32

HANNAH

Hannah stared at the computer screen, at the LaTeX thesis document she was tinkering with. She hadn't made any progress in weeks, just messing around with equations and graphs, trying to make it look pretty. She was supposed to be near the end of her PhD, but she was going to miss the deadline. Almost no one submitted their thesis in the allotted three years, but it still irritated her. She had her data set, had done the analysis, but was struggling to put together a narrative. Most physics PhDs are part of a much bigger piece of research, in her case, cataloguing exoplanets around distant stars could go on forever. Over five thousand were now identified and characterised – hot Jupiters, super-Earths, mini-Neptunes, ice giants. And of course the rocky planets in their star's Habitable Zone, the best candidates for extraterrestrial life. There was no evidence of that yet, but the next generation of telescopes might detect the chemical signifiers of biology on the surface. But that revelation always felt just over the event horizon.

Maybe she'd just had enough of her studies, doing a doctorate was a war of attrition. But she did feel proud of the exoplanets she'd discovered and categorised. She'd added a tiny bit to the mass of human knowledge, a miniscule addition to our communal experience.

She looked around the empty office, just a bare room for hot-desking, somewhere to crank out a few more words. The real number crunching happened in the lab down the corridor. She gazed out of the window at the incredible view. The dusty peak of Blackford Hill straight ahead, the yellow gorse of the Braids to her left, Pentlands in the distance. To her right was the city, sloping up to the castle. Her own flat was in there somewhere, and Indy working away at the Skelfs, helping the bereaved, caring for the deceased.

'Hey.'

Hannah spun round in her chair, knocking her notebook off the desk.

Mina stood there, big sunglasses on her head, hair and makeup impeccable, in a chunky sweater, very expensive jeans and strappy heels. Effortless chic that Hannah could never manage.

She picked up the notebook and threw it on the desk, tried to recover her composure. She recalled the intruder last night, the chase down the street, the piece of scaffolding to the head. Her hand went to her temple.

'How are you doing?' Mina said, sitting in an adjacent chair. She swung side to side like a kid. It made her seem younger, maybe that was the point. 'Kirsty told me about last night, showed me the footage. Terrifying.'

'I'm OK.' Hannah resisted the urge to touch her forehead again.

'This is what happens when you're doxxed. All these armchair weirdos are emboldened. I feel like we should move out for a while, but also, fuck those guys, they win if we do that.'

Hannah tried to take in Mina's energy. She was hyperactive, maybe just over-caffeinated.

'What were you up to last night?' Hannah tried to keep her voice even, but her tone wavered.

Mina stopped swinging on her chair and stared at Hannah. 'You think I had something to do with it?'

'I never said that.'

'You didn't have to say it. I saw the footage, it wasn't me, obviously.'

'It wasn't clear whether it was a man or a woman.'

Mina's eyes went wide. 'You are way out of line. You think I'd endanger my wife like that? You think I'd assault you?'

Hannah felt suddenly tired. 'I just...'

'Fucking hell.'

Hannah felt a headache spread across her face and closed her eyes. 'I'm just a bit out of it.'

'Why didn't you go to the hospital?'

'You sound like my wife.'

'And you sound like mine,' Mina said, a smile in her voice that made Hannah look up. 'She doesn't like fuss either. That's why she's let things get to the stage of bricks through the window.' Mina shifted her weight in the chair. 'You and her are very similar, you know. Interested in the big questions.'

'Surely everyone's interested in the big questions.'

Mina shook her head. 'Honestly, I can't think of anything worse than spending months in a tin can floating through space. I like my creature comforts. But I bet you would drop everything to become an astronaut.'

A few years ago, Hannah would've said yes. Now she wasn't so sure. 'Maybe.'

'It takes dedication and selfishness.'

Hannah couldn't help the surprise registering on her face, and Mina acknowledged it.

'She's the love of my life, but she's not perfect,' Mina said. 'Not by a long way.'

Hannah thought again about the brick through the window.

Mina narrowed her eyes. 'But that doesn't mean I would harm her.'

'OK.'

Mina stood up quickly and her chair spun from the momentum. 'She told me about you two last night, we don't keep secrets.'

The blood rushed to Hannah's face. 'I'm sorry...'

Mina held up a hand. 'Please. We're both free to pursue other interests. Sometimes together, if you know what I mean. We were kind of hoping ... but I understand. Indy's quite the wife.'

'She is.'

'And monogamy is fine for some.' Mina sighed. 'Anyway, I didn't come here for this.'

Hannah's hand went to her temple again, felt the bruise. 'Why did you come?'

'Yuri has disappeared.'

Hannah shook her head. 'What?'

'Our cat never normally misses a meal, but neither of us have seen him since last night.'

'Since the attack?'

'Exactly.'

'You think?'

Mina put her sunglasses back on. 'That's what we want you to find out.'

33

JENNY

One of the first things Jenny realised as a PI was that if you need to get the inside scoop, go to the pub. Booze loosens tongues, people reveal all the gossip after a few drinks. So here she was in The Longniddry Arms, a mile up the road from Longcraig House.

After stumbling on Sir Bill's sexcapade in the woods earlier, Jenny retreated to the van. She was sure the woman wasn't Stella, but then started to second-guess herself. There was something about voyeurism that gave her a frisson, despite herself. Maybe it was just the idea of breaking society's rules. When she was young, she saw herself as part of an alternative to the mainstream, proudly fucked plenty of men and a few women as a student. But that was a lifetime ago. Now she was a middle-aged woman with a job, she lived with her mum and was a mother herself. Maybe she was a mainstream bitch all along, playing at student rebellion. She knew plenty of folk from back then who became bankers and lawyers.

She'd Googled 'Longcraig House' and 'dogging', the only thing she came up with was that Longniddry Bents, the seaside bay down the road, was an infamous site thanks to unlit car parks and a remote location. But that was open to the public, a different story to Bill's private gathering. She wondered if she was being a prude, they all seemed like consenting adults. She kept coming back to the masks, what's the turn on with that? Maybe all this had nothing to do with Stella.

She sat at the bar of The Longniddry Arms and sipped her double gin and tonic. It was a converted steading with a restaurant through the way and this more humble bar for the locals. She got up and went round the groups of middle-aged and old men with a picture of Stella, but no one had seen her. She watched them carefully as they spoke, looking for signs of bullshit. She sat back at the bar and chatted to the young barman, who said the same. He had a big blond afro that would've got him a kicking at Jenny's school in the eighties. She wondered if he was bullied, or if things were easier now.

A bald, boxy man in his fifties came in and ordered a pint of IPA, sat on the stool next to her.

'This lady is looking for someone,' the barman said.

The man regarded Jenny over his pint. He had a drinker's nose, burst blood veins under the skin. His head was luminous in the bar spotlight, a boiled egg waiting to be cracked open and scooped out.

She showed him the picture on her phone. He shook his head.

'Stella McNamara,' Jenny said, watching him. 'She used to go out with the guy in the big house, William Porterhouse.'

It was only a moment, but the man glanced at the kid behind the bar. He recovered well, but there was something behind his eyes. 'Haven't seen her.'

Jenny took a slow drink, ice clinking in her glass. 'But you know Sir William, right?'

It was his turn to drink slow, buy himself thinking time. 'A lot of folk round here know Bill. He throws casual work to the locals, we're pretty grateful.'

'What kind of work?'

'Labouring, decorating, grunt work mostly.'

Jenny waved at the barman. 'Another pint of IPA for this gentleman, and the same again for me.'

It was a wafer-thin gesture, a free beer, but some guys will spill for less.

'Have you ever worked over there?'

'Not for a while.'

She could almost see the veins in his nose pulsing. 'What did you do?'

'Just some tree felling, clearing out the woods.' He finished his pint as the replacement arrived.

Jenny paid and stirred her gin. 'Have you been in the woods recently?'

'What sort of question is that?'

She looked at his clothes, saggy-arsed jeans, green plaid shirt, and tried to think if she'd seen them before. She tried to imagine him with an animal mask, cock in hand.

He cleared his throat. 'Bill is good for this community, his money filters into the village. If you're looking to rubbish the guy, you've come to the wrong place.'

'I was in the woods earlier.'

'Sounds like trespassing.'

'Maybe. But I saw something.'

He put his pint down and placed his hands together. 'Anything Bill does on his own land is up to him. As long as it's not illegal. It sounds like you were the one breaking the law.'

Jenny drank her gin and felt the buzz. She loved the confrontation, it made her feel young again.

'I'm not trying to rubbish him,' she said, holding out her phone. 'I'm just trying to find her.'

He took the phone from her, held it at arm's length to focus better. 'She doesn't look like the kind of woman he'd be interested in.'

'Why not?'

'Not his type.'

Jenny took her phone back. 'You mean she's not the kind of person to put on a show fucking in the back of a car in the woods?'

The guy took a few long gulps of IPA, then sighed as he lowered the glass. 'You're barking up the wrong tree.'

'Which tree should I be barking up?'

He drained his pint, stood and walked away. She sat there with the picture of Stella looking up at her, the taste of gin on her tongue, a deep darkness pushing at the corner of her mind.

34

DOROTHY

The Caves were quintessential Edinburgh. Derelict and hidden for hundreds of years in the vaults under South Bridge, the venue was gloomy and damp, centuries of ghosts haunting the mouldy walls and arched ceiling. The place was jumping, two hundred folk dancing, holding drinks and phones in the air. Dorothy played a tight, funky shuffle on the borrowed Ludwig kit. It wasn't her beloved Gretsch, but it was still lovely, smaller toms and a thin-body snare making it more bouncy and light.

The Multiverse were near the end of their set, rocking through an upbeat version of Brittany Howard's 'Stay High', the refugee choir swaying with big smiles on their faces. Dorothy grinned at Zack on bass. These shared moments on stage were something she would never tire of, this time with a teenage boy not yet out of school. Love of music made strange bedfellows, she'd learned that playing in countless bands.

They finished the song and went straight into 'Do You Realize??' by The Flaming Lips, the lyrics – about everyone you know dying – putting smiles on faces, choir, bandmates and crowd alike. The drumming wasn't hard, but it was unusually disjointed through the verses. The song built to the key change, then exploded into full-on, anthemic rock. Then it was time for the breakdown, before the final rousing climax. Maria added synth flourishes all over, Gillian played trumpet licks, Dorothy boomed round the toms, probably filling too much space.

The women in the choir waved Ukrainian flags as they shifted their hips to Dorothy's beat. This gig was a fundraiser for refugees, a tiny drop in the ocean, but these women knew what it was like to be displaced. To have to run away from your home, trek for hundreds, thousands of miles, wind up somewhere strange and new, afraid and alone.

The song finished and they soaked up the applause with wide smiles. Katy at the front of the choir thanked everyone and introduced their final song, a cover of Ivor Cutler's 'Women of the World', a plea for women to take over. The eighties original was weird and low-key but oddly prescient, more relevant now than ever. The Multiverse started slow, repetitive vocals underpinned by subtle kick drum and hi-hats. They built the thing with each iteration, the harmonies spreading around the cavernous room, bouncing off the walls, soaking into the grinning audience. The music filled the space, louder guitars, more trumpet. Dorothy got lost in it, throwing complex fills around the toms and snare, spilling over to the next bar like she couldn't be contained, as if the women of the world really *did* need to take over, or there wouldn't be a world left.

There was no fixed ending to the song, they just rode it until it felt right, depending on the energy in the room. The call was Dorothy's and she let it run longer than usual, feeling the audience willing them on. Eventually she glanced at Will and Zack, who nodded back, and they brought it crashing down, the choir holding the final note as long as they could, guitar feeding back, synth swathes swirling around. Dorothy felt herself float to the ceiling and look down. She thought about their protest, how the world fucked us all, the whole system needed a reboot, capitalism and consumerism and war and famine were beatable, all it took was a billion displays of willpower like this.

She stood and came to the front, took a bow with the rest of the band, high with adrenaline, soaked in sweat and good vibes.

✻

A cool breeze dried the sweat on her arms as she stood on the cobbled street outside the venue. The familiar mix of hyperactivity and weariness buzzed her brain, excited and tired at the same time.

Niddrie Street South was a dead-end lane, the back doors of apartments, hipster offices, a boarded-up frontage, probably more centuries-worth of history shut inside somewhere. Down the road was Bannerman's where she'd played in an indie-rock band in the eighties. She'd rehearsed in the practice rooms up the street, which were closed down now. More ghosts locked in there. Edinburgh was a crazy city in many ways, layers on top of each other, crowded and cramped, damp and dirty, full of life and death.

'That was amazing!'

She turned to see Brodie coming out of the venue. He hesitated, looked like he might hug her, then didn't.

'Thanks.'

He stood with his hands at his side. 'You guys are incredible.'

He wore a Sigur Rós T-shirt, an old one Dorothy recognised with an angel foetus on it.

'Hey, Mum,' Jenny said, stumbling out of the venue, Archie behind.

'Great set, Dorothy,' he said, smiling. 'Such a good band.'

Dorothy smiled. She used to be uncomfortable with compliments, but fuck it, she was in her eighth decade, if she couldn't take them now, then when?

Some of the girls from the choir were down the lane, laughing and hugging, passing a joint around. Dorothy smelled the weed and felt an unusual craving, the idea of coming down from her adrenaline rush was tempting.

Jenny was a little drunk as she chatted to Brodie. Dorothy realised she hadn't asked Jenny about Brodie staying with them, that was inconsiderate.

'Brodie,' she said. 'I heard you had a good day at work.'

He grinned. 'Honestly, I can't thank you enough.' He turned to Archie. 'And you, I already feel at home.'

'Just don't get too cosy in the studio,' Jenny said.

It felt like she meant it as a joke but it fell flat. Brodie glanced at Dorothy.

She touched his arm. 'Stay as long as you like.'

Jenny looked at Dorothy and Brodie. 'Yeah, yeah, sorry, I was just being a dick. You're welcome in our humble home.'

Well, at least she realised she was being a dick.

Dorothy remembered something. 'Brodie, I might have another job for you.'

He perked up at that. 'Oh yeah?'

The night air raised goosebumps on Dorothy's arms. 'I spoke to Natalya at the council today and got it confirmed, we've got the contract for the unclaimed funerals.'

'This is the lonely-funeral thing you were talking about.'

'I wondered if you'd like to organise the first one. It's just logistics, liaising with the council, paperwork, some publicity.'

Jenny slapped Brodie on the shoulder too hard. 'Hey, you've only been here a day and you're taking over.'

Brodie looked bashful. 'Hardly.'

'Are you interested?' Dorothy said.

He didn't even pretend to think about it. 'I'd love to. But I was thinking, the Lonely Funeral Project doesn't sound right. I don't think these people should feel lonely.'

'I agree.'

Jenny laughed. 'I can see why you hired him, Mum, he's a mini-version of you.'

Brodie looked nervous every time Jenny spoke. She had that effect on some men. It had its advantages but could also be destructive.

'I thought we could call it the Communal Funeral Project. How about that?'

Dorothy smiled. 'That sounds perfect.'

35

HANNAH

They were five minutes from Kirsty and Mina's place, walking in uncomfortable silence. Hannah glanced at Indy, thought about it from her point of view. Her wife was assaulted last night and kissed another woman, now they were heading back to the scene of both crimes. Hannah wanted Indy here, so everything was out in the open. She chewed over her conversation with Mina earlier. Maybe the stuff with the cat was just diverting attention from what had happened last night. Cats go missing all the time, right?

Her phone buzzed in her pocket and she took it out, stopped walking.

'It's Billie from Cramond.' She looked at Indy, who raised her eyebrows.

She answered. 'Hey.' Crying down the line. She put it on speaker and held her phone out. 'Are you OK?'

They stood under a streetlight, Victorian brickwork and large hedges at the edge of the light. Billie's life in Cramond was just a few miles from Kirsty in Cluny Drive, but it might as well be a different planet.

'I just wanted to hear a voice,' Billie said.

'Where are you?'

'The island.'

'Cramond? Are you trapped, is the tide in?'

'No.' There was a rustle of trees, Billie breathless, her voice catching. 'I can't find her.'

'Who?'

'Ruby, she's supposed to be here, she DMed me.'

Indy narrowed her eyes, concerned face.

'Are you high?' Hannah said.

'She said to meet at the old barracks.'

'It doesn't sound safe, head back to the caravans. I'm sure she'll show up.'

'I need to find her.'

'Billie, what have you taken?'

'I'm fine.'

'Maybe I should call the police.'

Billie snorted with laughter. 'No police.'

'I know a good guy, he can help.'

'No cops.'

Hannah looked at Indy and lifted her shoulders.

Indy leaned towards the phone. 'We'll come and get you. Stay on the line, OK?'

'My battery is low,' Billie said, then squealed.

Hannah jumped. 'What?'

'Fucking rat, I think. On my foot. I need to go.'

'No, stay on the line.'

'Save my battery.'

And she was gone.

❦

Crossing onto a tidal island in the middle of the night – what could go wrong?

Hannah heard the clanks of boat masts anchored in the Almond and chatter from the handful of people behind her – Fara had rustled up half a dozen for the search party.

Hannah stuck to her word, no cops. She spent the drive here trying to call Dorothy and Jenny, got voicemails. Gran was at the charity gig tonight, she didn't know about Mum. She tried calling Billie a few times, no answer. No sign of Ruby or Parker at the camp.

Their phone torches danced around the causeway as they

hurried across. They reached the island quicker than she expected, pushed by adrenaline. There were eight of them in total and they split into pairs. One to the gun turret on the right, another round the coast to the left. Fara and a friend took the low road through the woods, Hannah and Indy on the higher path. The interior was criss-crossed with paths and clearings amongst the trees, and Hannah could see Fara's torch between branches, heard Billie's name being called out. She phoned again, no answer. All she could hear was the rush of waves, the shouts of Billie's name. They came out of the trees at the north of the island, saw the lights of Dalgety Bay across the water.

She could make out a spread of crumbling concrete ruins ahead, blocky buildings linked by broken paths. No light from any of them. Out on the water, oil tankers sat, orange deck lights shimmering.

Indy came out of the first building and shook her head. She pointed her torch at the next one.

'I'll go this way,' Hannah said, pointing west.

'We stick together.'

'I'll just be over here, you'll see my torch.'

Indy lowered her torch. 'No. We stick together.'

Hannah followed her into the second building, empty except for the remains of a campfire and a sodden sleeping bag. The next building had more of the same, a pile of concrete rubble in the corner, a handful of floor mats, soaked and buckled by the elements. The wind whistled through the doorway of the next building as they entered. Hannah kept imagining some *Blair Witch* shit, but it was another derelict room, rusted metal rails set into the floor, windows long gone, just a shell covered in graffiti.

They walked down the slope to the next building, shouting Billie's and Ruby's names, Hannah feeling sick. She pointed her torch at the entrance, a silhouette of a cartoon ghost alongside a symbol of interlocked curves. She took a moment to place it, the biohazard sign from *28 Days Later*. She imagined a horde of zombies spilling from the doorway, braced herself against the on-slaught.

She went inside, played the beam around the walls, spotted something in the corner near the window frame. A dark shape.

'Billie.'

She ran over, saw Billie on her side, touched her arm, no response. She pulled her onto her back and pointed the torch at her face.

Her eyes were open, neck red and bruised. Hannah dropped her phone and shook her, heard the scuff of Indy's feet behind her.

Billie stared at nothing and flopped in Hannah's arms, her head lolling to the side to show off more bruises on her neck.

36

JENNY

Nobody had slept, and the frazzled energy in the room was palpable. Jenny poured boiling water into the large cafetiere and stuck the lid on, took it over to the kitchen table. But all the coffee in the world wasn't going to make this better.

Dorothy sat at the table with Schrödinger on her lap. That cat had softened over the years. He used to swipe at Jenny constantly, but since his dog pal Einstein died protecting Dorothy, Schrödinger had become a comforting presence in the house. He still brought dead mice and birds as presents, but he let himself be stroked and spoiled.

Indy sat across from Dorothy checking her phone for online chatter about last night. Thomas was next to her, on the phone to the station, getting the latest. Hannah stood at the window watching the sun peak over Salisbury Crags and spread its fingers across the wet grass of the Links.

Jenny walked over and wrapped her arms around Hannah from behind. She felt self-conscious, couldn't remember the last time she hugged her daughter, which made her feel guilty. What kind of mother doesn't jump at every opportunity to hug her child? She placed her forehead against Hannah's back, squeezed her waist. She was surprised when Hannah turned and hugged her back, burying her face in Jenny's shoulder, squeezing hard, body trembling.

After a long time, Hannah pulled away and her eyes were wet. Jenny tucked a strand of Hannah's hair behind her ear and put on a smile.

Last night, she and Dorothy got in from the gig and found

umpteen messages from Hannah and Thomas explaining that Billie's dead body had been found on Cramond Island. They drove down and met Hannah and Indy on the mainland, the police having escorted the search party from the island and cordoned it off. Forensics were at the scene while the cops searched the island in the two hours before high tide, but found no one. But the island was big enough to hide from some incompetent uniforms. Jenny wasn't at all sure the cops knew what they were doing. Billie was murdered under their noses while they were investigating her arson case.

Jenny sobered up quick on the drive to the island, hearing that Hannah had found the body. She'd spent so much of her life running away from emotional shit like that, drinking to avoid feelings. The fact she hadn't had an urge for a morning dram to cope made her feel proud. This time last year she would've been wasted or hungover already.

Thomas ended his call and the women looked at him in expectation. What must it be like to be him, always having to explain what the cops were up to with all the shit the Skelfs got embroiled in. He must wish for an easier life, but maybe Dorothy was worth it. Jenny liked that idea.

'Preliminary examination suggests Billie was strangled to death,' Thomas said, looking at Hannah. 'Just as you thought.'

Indy got up and came to her, rubbed her back and touched her cheek.

'And there's something else,' Thomas said. 'Signs of recent sexual activity.'

Silence hung heavy for a long moment before Dorothy spoke. 'Rape?'

'They can't say for sure yet.' Thomas sighed and rubbed his forehead. 'The searching officers haven't turned up anything. The coastguard have been patrolling the water around the island since last night. No sign of Parker or Ruby, no one at the camp has heard from them.'

'What does that mean?' Jenny said, walking to the table and plunging the coffee. She filled the cups on the table and took a big swig.

'Just what I said.'

'Come on, this isn't a press conference. You can speculate with us.'

Dorothy breathed deeply and looked at Thomas. 'There are a few possibilities, right? The first is that Parker or Ruby, or both of them, killed Billie.'

Hannah flinched at her words.

Jenny thought about Billie, younger than Hannah, but there would be no more adventures, no life of anarchy and rebellion, or settling down to a normal life, or whatever she wanted. Those choices had been taken from her.

Dorothy held up her fingers. 'Second option is that whoever killed Billie has done something to Parker and Ruby. Third option is that they're scared and have gone on the run. I guess a fourth possibility is that they're innocent and don't even know about Billie yet.'

Jenny shook her head. It was too much with no sleep and a headache at the base of her skull. Parker was drug-dealing and she knew from her student days that the guys who dealt always had hardnuts higher up. That could get scary. Enough for arson and murder, though? Maybe it was simpler. Hannah told her years ago about Occam's razor, the simplest answer is the most likely one.

She thought about Occam's razor for Stella. Jenny was hung up on the pervy ex-boyfriend on a country estate, maybe that was a wild-goose chase. What was the simplest explanation? She was living off-grid somewhere, like Fara at Cramond. But how do you stay completely off-grid, surely you leave some trace?

Hannah's sigh brought Jenny from her thoughts. She wanted to hug her daughter again and never let go. Seeing dead bodies was what they did here, but the violence of murder was different. And it wasn't the first time Hannah had been exposed. Jenny wanted to help, wanted to be a mother, but wasn't sure how.

Dorothy's phone buzzed and they all jumped. She looked at the screen. 'Fara.'

She answered, nodded, looked around the room. 'Ruby turned up.'

37

DOROTHY

She parked the van at the end of the jetty and touched Hannah's hand. She recognised the forensic team's grey people carrier sitting next to a police car along the road. Forensic investigators don't advertise themselves, just scientists doing their jobs.

Both women got out of the van and Dorothy smelled salty air. She wanted to walk to the island, see where Hannah had found Billie's body, but she wouldn't be allowed onto the crime scene. In any case, the real action was here with the campers.

Hannah stared at the island and hugged herself. Dorothy wrapped an arm around her and felt her shiver. She would give anything to swap places, be the one who found Billie. We do everything to take the pain from the ones we love.

'Come on.'

Dorothy walked towards the circle of campervans and caravans and Hannah followed. They stepped between vehicles into the circle, and Dorothy saw Webster and Low coming out of Fara's campervan. Fara followed them with her arms crossed, listening as they spoke. The body language was hostile from all three. Webster was talking, Low nodding, looking around until he caught Dorothy's eye and stared. He nudged Webster, who turned. He said goodbye to Fara and they strolled over to Dorothy and Hannah, stepping around a campfire of ash.

'Fancy seeing you here.' Webster made a show of looking beyond them. 'Boyfriend not with you?'

Dorothy didn't rise to it. 'How's Ruby?'

'Not saying much.'

'Where was she last night?'

Webster narrowed his eyes, smiled at Low. 'We're about to check her story.'

Hannah scratched her head. 'You're not arresting her, though?'

Webster shook his head. 'I got your statement from Olsson, Ms Skelf.' He made the 'Ms' sound dirty. 'It should really have been given to myself and DS Low.'

Dorothy straightened her shoulders. 'We did what we thought was correct. Hannah was in shock.'

'This is our investigation, please don't get in our way.'

Dorothy had fire in her belly. 'Who's getting in the way? We want to solve this as much as you. More, probably.'

Webster spat on the ground. 'Fucking amateurs. Did it ever occur to you that you might make things worse? Maybe your snooping around is the reason Billie's dead.'

Hannah blinked heavily. 'Fuck off.'

Dorothy almost laughed at Webster's face, fuming at his authority being questioned. Some police needed a course in empathy, or just basic manners. They were supposed to help the public, not fuck with them.

Webster eventually smiled. 'I could have you arrested for obstructing the investigation.'

'Go ahead,' Hannah said.

Webster scoped her up and down.

'Come on,' he said to Low, and they walked to the squad car and left.

'Fucking arsehole,' Hannah said.

Fara was still at the doorway of her camper, and raised her eyebrows as they approached. She stepped down and hugged Dorothy then moved on to Hannah. She held on for a long time then separated.

'How are you doing?' she said, still touching Hannah's arm.

'OK.'

'I can't imagine what it was like.'

Dorothy felt the sun on her face, incongruous warmth. 'How are you?'

Fara looked like she might crumple. 'Terrible, to be honest. I can't believe it.'

'And Ruby?'

Fara nodded at the camper and slid the door open. 'Come in.'

They followed her inside, where Ruby was sitting on the bed, face red and puffy, hair in a straggly pony. She wore Docs, a short skirt and a loose Guns N' Roses T-shirt. She scratched at her arm absent-mindedly, and Dorothy imagined her tiger tattoo writhing beneath her touch.

'Hey.' Dorothy joined her on the bed. There was a low bench across the van space, and Hannah and Fara sat there, hands in their laps.

Ruby sniffled, her breath ragged. 'I can't.'

Dorothy held her hand and she burst into tears, put her other hand over her mouth and sobbed. Dorothy rubbed her fingers for a long time. She glanced at Hannah, who had her head down. This wasn't healthy for anyone, but they had to live through it, that's the only thing to do with death.

Ruby eventually got her breath back. 'I can't believe she's dead.' She nodded at Fara then Hannah. 'Fara said you found her.'

Hannah fiddled with her hands. 'Yeah.'

Ruby looked like she was going to speak but didn't. Tears rolled down her face and she wiped them away.

Hannah looked up. 'She said you'd arranged to meet her there.'

Ruby looked at her like she was an alien and pulled on her earlobe. 'No, I never said that.'

Hannah leaned forward and Dorothy wondered what she was up to.

'They'll check the phone records,' Hannah said. 'They'll find out if you spoke to her or messaged her last night.'

Ruby's eyes went wide, and Dorothy wondered how she hadn't realised that already. 'No.'

'Yes,' Hannah said, leaning back. 'So why not start telling the truth?'

There was a steeliness to her voice that Dorothy hadn't heard before. Maybe finding dead bodies does that to you.

Fara looked at the three women, her gaze landing on Ruby rubbing her neck. 'Ruby?'

Ruby tried to steady her breath, her bottom lip wobbling. 'OK, I did message her to meet me there.'

Fara raised her eyebrows.

'Why?' Hannah said.

'It's not what you think.'

Dorothy wanted to hug her but she couldn't get in the way of this.

Ruby wiped her nose. 'We just wanted her out the way for a bit. She hung around us like a bad smell.'

Dorothy was beginning to get it. 'Who, you and Parker?'

Ruby took a long time, then gave a tiny nod.

'You were fucking Parker behind Billie's back,' Hannah said.

Fara spoke up. 'She's not on trial here, she's already been through it with the cops.'

'Did you tell them this?' Dorothy said.

A shake of the head. 'They wouldn't understand.'

Fara looked confused. 'But you weren't at Parker's place when we went to search for her.'

Ruby lowered her head. 'We were in the woods. You know.'

'Christ,' Hannah said. 'While your best friend was being murdered, you were fucking her boyfriend in the woods.'

'Han,' Dorothy said. 'Enough.'

Hannah pressed her lips together.

Dorothy wanted to reach out and touch Ruby's hand, but was worried the girl would bolt like a frightened deer.

'By the time we got back,' Ruby said, 'everyone was gone. We didn't know where. It was all a mistake, we just wanted to be alone...'

Dorothy wanted to believe, her grief seemed authentic. Was this really just teenage sexual melodrama gone wrong? 'So, where's Parker now?'

Ruby touched her hair. 'He ran. When we saw the police and ambulance, we panicked. He's scared of the cops, with good reason.'

'Because of the drugs?' Hannah said.

Ruby lowered her head. 'I'm so sorry, I'm so, so sorry.'

38

HANNAH

She missed the sea and was surprised by that. After Mum and Dad divorced when she was ten, she lived in a flat on Marlborough Street with Jenny until she moved in with Indy. Those were her formative years, teenage angst amongst the sixties tower block of the old Porty High School. And the beach bonfires, fumbling in the dark with boys, then girls, the crackle and spit of burning wood, the sound of the sea as a backdrop. She had a sudden rush now, walking away from Cramond along Silverknowes Prom, realising how much it all meant to her.

She smelled fishy decay amongst the flotsam strewn across the rocky beach below. Silverknowes wasn't as picturesque as Porty, rougher and more rugged. From Cramond to Granton Harbour there wasn't much sandy beach, just a few houses set back up an escarpment, a spread of industrial buildings with razor wire and security cameras.

She walked past the turn-off for Marine Drive and the esplanade widened, thick woods to her right. She wondered if that was where Ruby and Parker fucked last night. She imagined their pale bodies grunting in the moonlight while she stumbled onto Billie's body.

Now there were bright-blue skies, a fresh breeze, sharp views of Fife in the distance. Occasional joggers, the odd inquisitive dog followed by its owner. As if someone hadn't just been killed on the island behind her.

As she walked, the giant skeleton of the Granton Gasholder came into view. It was a four-storey blue cylinder of criss-crossed metal struts and supports which used to house a giant gas tank.

The tank was long gone, and there were plans to renovate the remaining structure, turn it into a community space.

She walked past a burnt-out bin and a pile of scorched wooden pallets, then saw the caravans ahead. The Traveller community, with some irony, had settled on a sliver of grass called Gypsy Brae. Hannah had read the local news about them – complaints, disturbances, mess. She treated it with disdain. Up the hill, the road had been blocked by huge concrete bollards across the tarmac. But Hannah could see the grass by the side of the road, dug up by deep caravan tracks where the Travellers had driven around them.

She approached the nearest caravan. These were newer vehicles than the ones at Cramond. Mobile homes with ariels on roofs, a few works vans for plumbers and joiners parked amongst them, one pine-panelled thing like a two-storey house on wheels. There were planters outside some of the vehicles, flowers blooming. Kids rode on pushbikes on the adjacent path, a gaggle of teenage boys stood around two scramblers near the trees. She wondered if there was any connection between these guys and the Muirhouse gang. Or any connection between the Travellers and the caravaners at Fara's place. That's what she was banking on.

Dorothy had gone back to the house after they spoke to Ruby, to prep for a cremation. Hannah said she would hang around to clear her head, but this was the plan all along – talk to the Travellers, see what they knew about Parker Ford.

A middle-aged couple sat on deckchairs outside one of the bigger vehicles, sipping green cans of Monster.

'Hey, missy,' the woman said. She had curly red hair, tiny pencil eyebrows and a lot of laughter lines. She was in pink shorts a size too small and a white vest top. Her skin was very brown and wrinkled. 'Can we help you?'

Hannah stood awkwardly. 'I hope so, I'm trying to find someone.'

The woman smiled at her, one of her teeth shining gold in the sun. 'Well, we know everyone around here.'

The man swigged from his can. 'Pretty girl like you can get any man she wants, I'd wager.'

'Leave her alone, Harry,' the woman said, banging his elbow so much he spilled his drink.

'Fuck, Barb.' He held his dripping hand out, shook off the juice.

'I'm a lesbian,' Hannah said.

He didn't flinch. 'Any woman then. Good on you.'

Hannah nodded down the road at Cramond. 'Did you hear about last night on the island?'

'The young lass found dead?' Barb said. 'Terrible business.'

'What did you hear?'

'Just that,' Harry said. 'She was found in the old wartime buildings.'

'Who told you?'

Barb shrugged. 'Not much goes on around here we don't know about.'

'I'm looking for Parker Ford.'

Harry and Barb looked at each other and Hannah wasn't sure what it meant.

'Six foot, skinny, emo-looking, black curly hair,' Hannah said. 'Looks like he might blow over in a light breeze.'

Barb pursed her lips and Harry shook his head. 'I don't think so, love.'

'Maybe he had some drugs on him, apparently he deals to the lads in Muirhouse. Maybe he deals around here as well.'

She was expecting some puritan bullshit but Harry put his can down and levered himself out of his deckchair. Hannah took a step back but Harry held his hands out in front of him like he was trying to calm a scared animal.

'Who are you?'

'I'm Hannah Skelf. I'm a private investigator looking into Billie's death.'

Barb got out of her seat too. 'That was her name?'

'Seventeen years old.'

Barb sucked her teeth. 'Christ almighty.'

Hannah turned to Harry. 'Well?'

Harry looked at Barb then back at Hannah.

'We know Parker,' he said. 'But this doesn't go any further. No cops.'

'The police won't bother you.'

'He has done business round here.'

'What about last night?'

Barb cleared her throat. 'He turned up in a state. Said he needed somewhere to stay. We could see the police lights down the road. We don't need that kind of attention.'

'So?'

Harry nodded. 'He went on his way. He wasn't happy but we gave him a few quid to tide him over.'

Barb frowned. 'We didn't know about the girl then. Do you think he did it?'

Hannah shrugged.

Harry took a swig from his can. 'He was proper scared last night, I can tell you that.'

'What of?'

Harry looked at her. 'Well, that's what you need to find out, isn't it?'

39
JENNY

'Larger than life' applied to Eric Banks, metaphorically and literally. Jenny sat at the back of Seafield Crem chapel and listened as relatives and friends of Big Eric regaled the congregation with tales about him. His spell in the army, an ill-judged investment in a racehorse, the time he got arrested for hitting Margaret Thatcher with an egg from an impressive distance. He was an old socialist and the life and soul of the party, apparently, always an open house and always an eye for helping those in need. Jenny would've loved to have a drink with the old rogue. The fact that all four of his ex-wives, along with his widow, were here, suggested the guy had plenty of charm.

She looked at the oversized coffin on the plinth. It wasn't obvious to those not in the industry that it was bigger than usual, but she could spot it. They used outsized coffins more and more these days as obesity rose, and she knew Eric would take a little longer to burn than most. But he would end up ashes all the same.

Dorothy sat next to her on the pew, fiddling with the order of service. Jenny wondered about all this stuff with Billie. Arson, now murder. She knew Dorothy wouldn't let this lie. It's always young women who get fucked, that's what Jenny had learned over the decades. Women were always at the receiving end of violence and pain.

She tried not to get het up about it. It was easy to fall back into destructive, angry thought patterns but she was trying fucking hard to keep her shit together.

Eric's coffin slowly lowered into the plinth and down into the pits of hell. It was a weird set-up here at Seafield, that the coffin descended out of sight, but the cremation oven was downstairs, so it made sense. She'd seen television dramas where the coffin rolled behind a curtain and you got a glimpse of flames, but that was unrealistic. The heat from the oven would blast the mourners.

She liked the idea of the resomator back at the house. The bereaved could watch the body dissolve, why not? The funeral business needed more transparency, shrouding death in mystery was for a bygone age. She hadn't thought about it growing up because she'd been so used to it, but other people were really frightened of death. Conversations with Mum, Hannah and Indy made her realise that other cultures had much healthier attitudes to death than here. More honesty could only be a good thing.

Dorothy threw Jenny a smile as they stood and waited for the mourners to leave. The widow did the line-up, shaking hands and hugging everyone, including the ex-wives. Big Eric must've been some guy.

Outside, there were two funeral cars to take Eric's family. Brodie and Archie were in their suits, holding doors open. Now they had Brodie working for them, they didn't have to hire random drivers from the agency. Dorothy once had to take over when a hired guy came back from a walk around the graveyard reeking of weed.

Jenny had a sinking feeling as the cars drove away, funerals always left an emptiness. Eric was gone, everyone else had to move on. She shared a sad smile with Dorothy.

'Hello there.'

It was Peter, the council guy who ran the crem. He was tall and pencil thin, cadaverous but friendly, as if Death was your mate.

'How's the death business?' Dorothy said, a running joke.

'Same old.' Peter pointed to his left. 'We've had problems in the garden of rest, people coming over the wall from the path. Found beer cans, roaches, even condoms.'

Jenny didn't have a problem with kids fucking in the memorial garden. Big Eric might've liked to see young love alongside his roses. The garden of rest was a nice idea, growing flowers and trees from the scattered ashes of the cremated, life from death. Maybe having a beer and a joint and getting frisky was part of that.

'It's maybe kids from the camp down the road,' Peter said.

'What?' Jenny said.

Peter pointed towards the crem entrance. 'The other side of Seafield Road, all that wasteland. It used to be where the railway stored old track and locomotives.'

Directly across the road from Seafield was the sewage works, a giant industrial plant that stank during summer. She always wondered what mourners thought of that, two kinds of disposal next to each other. But it also meant the abandoned land round about wasn't prime real estate.

'They've been there for ages, off Marine Esplanade, near the trees. Maybe it's not them, it could be kids from Craigentinny or Restalrig. Either way, it's irritating.'

Jenny thought about Stella and her van. She'd presumed Stella had stayed alone, using her rich ex's hiding place. But maybe she found a community just like Fara, or the guys on Gypsy Brae.

'That's a strange coincidence,' Dorothy said, and Jenny raised her eyebrows.

'Why?'

Dorothy smiled. 'Come on, I'll show you.'

40

DOROTHY

They stood at the junction waiting to cross Seafield Road. It was the main artery for the northeast of the city, a lot of construction trucks heading to the industrial parts of Leith. The road had recently been resurfaced but was already crumbling, potholes making cars weave around. Dorothy looked at the chimney for the cremation oven, then the Shed Centre where she bought a Christmas tree every year.

She and Jenny crossed the road, the tang from the sewage works in her throat. They walked over the defunct level crossing, tall weeds sprouting between railway tracks. There were cheap signs pointing to the right, Leith Business Centre, Edinburgh Scientific Services. The sewage works was straight ahead, a sprawl of buildings, pipes and structures that looked straight out of a 1970s science-fiction movie. It was actually called a wastewater treatment works and was run by an anonymous private company called Veolia, presumably because calling it a human shit factory was not good PR.

They turned left, Dorothy enjoying the quizzical looks from Jenny as they walked along the road, bundles of razor wire along the top of the fence for the sewage plant. Who would try to break into a place like that?

On their left, they passed mossy warehouses, skips, shipping containers and piles of wooden pallets. Then the fence ended and there was half a square mile of open dirt and scrubby grass.

'Where are we going?' Jenny said.

Dorothy climbed the low ridge at the edge of the site and went down the other side. It would take a lot of work, for sure, but she could picture it, one day, maybe after she'd gone.

She stood next to a puddle, felt the mud under her feet, and turned with her arms out. 'Welcome to our new green burial site.'

Jenny looked confused. 'We don't have a green burial site.'

'We do now.' Dorothy could see a shopping trolley in a ditch, sodden mattresses in a stack. No matter, it would all be fixed.

'Since when?'

'I've been negotiating with Natalya at the council. She's the one who gave us the unclaimed funerals. I sounded her out about buying some land from them. Obviously, we couldn't afford anything in the city centre. But there's no demand for land next to a sewage plant.'

'And you did all this without consulting us?'

Dorothy did feel bad about that. 'I didn't know if it would come off, so I didn't see any point mentioning it until it was real. I only got the call this morning that it's approved, if we want it.'

'Do we?'

'I think so.'

She had a good feeling about this. They buried Archie's mother two years ago in Binning Memorial Wood in East Lothian, the only green burial site in this part of Scotland. It seemed crazy that there weren't more options like that, especially in Scotland's capital city. This was part of the plan to lower their carbon footprint. Stop burning people and releasing carbon dioxide. Stop filling bodies with chemicals and sticking them in the ground. The resomator was a great step forward but Dorothy wanted more. Turn this derelict space into a peaceful woodland, somewhere to bury your loved ones, without chemicals. A way to get back in touch with grieving, to feel connected to the dead and the earth.

She'd gone along with conventional funeral practices for decades without thinking about it. There was so much less awareness of environmental issues even a few years ago. People got cremated or buried because that's what they'd always done, but the worst excuse for anything is 'we've always done it that way'.

Traditions are important, but they need to be updated. That was overdue in the funeral business.

Jenny waved at the empty space. 'It's a hell of a lot of work, look at this place.'

'Archie thinks we can do it.'

Jenny tilted her head. 'Oh, so you spoke to Archie about it.'

'He'll manage the site, the council will help with manpower, digging the ground, planting trees.'

Jenny raised her eyebrows. 'You really must've sweet-talked them, I've never known the council to help anyone.'

Dorothy looked around. There was a clear view of the back of Arthur's Seat and Salisbury Crags, silhouettes against the skyline. The other way was the grey expanse of the Firth of Forth. Edinburgh was defined by these landmarks, a few hundred thousand people nestled between hills and sea, eking out a living here for thousands of years. The Skelfs were just adding their tiny drop of life to the ocean of existence.

Jenny looked to the right. 'You're not buying the whole site, right?'

'No, only a quarter, at this end.'

Jenny nodded to the distance. 'Because I wouldn't fancy shifting those caravans.'

Dorothy had seen them on previous trips to the site, in the distance next to the trees by the derelict railway. But she welcomed neighbours of any kind.

Jenny held up a hand to shade her eyes, stared at the caravans for a long time.

All Dorothy could think about was how beautiful this place would be a hundred years from now, when she would be buried here along with countless others, helping the forest grow.

41

HANNAH

She stood outside Kirsty's house and calmed her breath. She didn't know why she was here, except Kirsty sounded frantic on the phone. Hannah couldn't get Billie's dead gaze out of her mind. She thought about what the Travellers said about Parker, that he was scared. And she thought about Ruby at the camp. Her best friend just died and she felt guilty, but there was something more than that. Now, amongst the million-pound houses of Blackford, she felt a million miles away from caravans by the beach.

She rang the doorbell. She'd been besotted with Kirsty a week ago, a heroine for all she'd done. But this case felt weird now, something happening she couldn't get a handle on. She'd hoped to clear the air with Kirsty about the kiss but had been sidetracked by the Cramond case. A murder was more important than a missing cat, or whatever was happening now, and she wasn't sure she could hold both things in her head. Sometimes you just overload.

The door opened and Kirsty grabbed Hannah into a hug. She smelled of weed and red wine and Hannah felt her tremble. The hug went on too long, Kirsty sniffling through ragged breaths. The whole thing was uncomfortably similar to the stalker Hannah had a year ago. Eventually she prised herself away and stood back. Kirsty's eyes were red.

'Yuri's dead.' Kirsty took her hand. 'Come.'

She led her to the kitchen and Hannah remembered Mina standing here saying she thought Kirsty had come back wrong from space.

'Look.' Kirsty pointed to the far end of the kitchen island and Hannah saw Yuri.

She approached slowly, half expecting the cat to leap up and hiss at her, arch his back and jump to the floor. But he just lay there on the island, tail flat. As Hannah got closer she saw discolouration around his mouth, dried blood and grey foam on his whiskers.

'The vet said he was poisoned,' Kirsty said, placing two fingers on the cat's ribs, like she might feel a heartbeat. 'What kind of sick bastard would do that?'

'It could've been an accident, like rat poison.'

Kirsty shook her head. 'This was deliberate. His body was lying on the back step earlier. It's a message, like the brick.'

Kirsty reached for a half-empty bottle of red wine and poured some into a glass already stained with dregs.

'I'm not sure that's helping,' Hannah said.

'You don't have pets, do you?'

Hannah thought of Schrödinger, indifferent and aloof. 'I just don't think you should jump to conclusions.'

She watched Kirsty glug wine.

'Wait,' Hannah said. 'You said he was found on the back step. Like, on the patio?'

Kirsty nodded.

'There should be camera footage.' She pulled her phone out, took a moment to navigate the app. 'When did you find him?'

'When I came down for breakfast, nine-thirty.'

Hannah tracked through the footage. The first recording prior to nine-thirty was at 5am, a minute of footage. She walked over to Kirsty, who gripped her wine glass like a bomb, and pressed play.

It was dark in the back garden, but the security light threw a glow a few yards over the grass. A figure emerged from the gloom carrying Yuri by the tail, as if they might swing him around their head. The person was dressed in black, balaclava on.

'That's the same person as the other night,' Hannah said, touching her forehead. 'At least, it looks like it.'

The figure looked female, but she wasn't entirely sure. Hannah thought again about Mina. It was too obvious, right? And why the hell would she be doing this?

The person kept their head down, aware of the camera, then threw Yuri's body onto the patio. They stood for a moment, then pointed at the camera, before moving to the side out of range.

'Jesus Christ,' Kirsty said, finished her wine.

'Was Mina with you last night?'

Kirsty looked confused, and Hannah wondered if it genuinely hadn't occurred to her.

'Was she in bed with you at 5am last night?'

'I was asleep, but of course she was there.'

'How do you know?'

'I'm a very light sleeper, I would know if she was sneaking out and ... anyway, she fucking loves Yuri, the idea she would do anything to him is crazy. This isn't her.'

Hannah raised her eyebrows.

'It wasn't Mina,' Kirsty said. 'I would recognise her walk.'

'Unless she was trying to hide it.'

Kirsty slammed her glass on the worktop. Hannah was surprised the stem didn't snap.

'It wasn't Mina, end of discussion.'

Hannah took a step back.

'Please,' Kirsty said. 'Just find out who did this.'

Hannah put her phone away.

Kirsty's face softened as she touched Hannah's elbow. 'You don't have to go right now, do you? Stay for a bit, I don't want to be alone.'

Hannah didn't want to hang around, but Kirsty was barely hanging on.

'OK,' Hannah said, nodding at the glass. 'But no more wine or weed.'

Kirsty swallowed and nodded.

Hannah looked at her for a long time, then moved around the kitchen island, giving Yuri's body a wide berth. 'How about I put the kettle on?'

42
DOROTHY

She didn't eat much red meat these days, but you couldn't beat a good steak. She swiped the last piece of sirloin around the plate, soaking up the chimichurri, and popped it in her mouth. She glanced at Thomas still eating his. She'd always been a fast eater, always wanted to just get on with it.

She took a sip of Rioja and looked round. They were in The Chop House, just a few minutes from home. It was a little hipstery for Dorothy – for some reason they had *Nothing To See Here* in large letters across the front window – but the food was great. They sat in a red-leather booth looking over Bruntsfield Links, and the busy street and peaceful park beyond reminded Dorothy how close together everything was here. She grew up in Pismo Beach, a small seaside town up the coast from Los Angeles, but even there in the fifties and sixties, the tendency was to spread out, drive everywhere. It harked back to the frontier spirit of colonisation, spreading yourself across the land, taking whatever you wanted and settling, claiming as much land as possible from the people who'd lived there for thousands of years before you. It was a shock when she first came to Scotland in 1970. Many didn't have cars and most walked around the city.

Thomas finished his steak and dabbed his mouth with a napkin as Dorothy ran her fingers along the stem of her glass.

'So, any further with Billie?'

They hadn't talked about it so far, Dorothy sensing tension. Instead she'd talked about the new green-funeral plans, Thomas listening attentively. It was a cliché to say a man was a good listener, but they were hard to find, and she appreciated it. But more recently, she craved more openness from him, especially about work. She thought about his struggles as a black police officer. He'd had it bad, of course, microaggressions and abuse that she could only guess at. But he was high up now, so much of that shit would've stopped or at least reduced. Were things really better now than decades ago? Not by enough, never enough.

Thomas drank some Sauvignon Blanc. 'Webster and Low are doing all they can.'

Dorothy cleared her throat. 'Are you sure they're the right guys for this?'

Thomas narrowed his eyes. 'How do you mean?' He knew what she meant, but wanted her to say it.

'I mean, maybe for an arson case, but this is murder now. Billie deserves better.'

'I know they rub people the wrong way, but they're good.'

'Rubbing people the wrong way is an understatement.'

'How so?'

'They were assholes this morning. At least, Webster was, Low doesn't seem to have any personality of his own.'

'What did Webster say?'

Dorothy sighed. She and Thomas were familiar with police officers who looked backward rather than forward, who loved their privilege. White guys strutting about, enjoying the power they had over others. Dorothy was used to that arrogance from back home fifty years ago. And from everything she'd seen in the news, it had only gotten worse over there. But there was less of that culture over here, at least she'd thought so. Maybe the right-wing, militarised bullshit of the US police had encouraged a certain type of Scottish officer to act the same.

'He doesn't seem sympathetic to the campers,' Dorothy said. 'Maybe he's good at his job, but isn't empathy essential for a cop?'

Thomas sighed. They'd been over this so often.

'It's not up to me who's on the case, it comes from higher up.'

'Can't you have a word?'

Thomas rubbed his chin. There was stubble there, white amongst the black. He was normally clean-shaven, but she liked it.

'Because my girlfriend says so? How would that look.'

Dorothy snorted. '*Girlfriend.*'

He reached for her hand. 'Aren't you?'

'I suppose. Your seventy-three-year-old girlfriend.'

'Age is just a number.'

'A number that's going up all the time.'

'Dorothy, don't.'

It was a gentle rebuke, but he meant it. She never felt her age anyway, it was uncharacteristic to mention it. If you thought about the future, acted young, it went a long way to feeling young. She'd seen plenty of people in their later years deteriorating fast when they fixated on the past. But she'd always been forward-looking, propelling herself into the future.

'But where's the investigation at, do you at least know that?'

It was unfair to use him for inside knowledge. She wondered if that made him insecure, if he worried that it was the only reason she was with him. But she was the insecure one. He was fifteen years younger, what did he see in her?

'They still haven't found the Parker kid,' he said. 'They've spoken to the Ferguson boys, asked about drugs, but haven't got any further with Parker's supplier.'

'You think he did it?'

'I don't know.'

Dorothy gave him a look. 'I didn't ask what you know. You have thirty years of experience as a cop, what do you think?'

'Hunches are not how the police work. He's our prime suspect, that's all. If you go missing when your girlfriend is murdered, that's suspicious.'

'But Hannah said he was petrified.'

'Maybe petrified of getting caught.'

Dorothy shook her head. Parker was the obvious suspect and

she wished he hadn't run away. But there was something about this that didn't feel right.

'Maybe we're all scared of being caught,' she said. She didn't know why, but it felt true.

43

HANNAH

She finished the dregs of her tea and wondered why she'd hung around. She'd been in awe of Kirsty a week ago. The first Scottish female astronaut, for God's sake, if that wasn't something to hold up as an example to others, then what was? But the scales had fallen from her eyes. Kirsty was just trying to get along, whatever gets you through the night, same as everyone else. Maybe it was harder for her, she'd had this overview effect up in space, this life-changing, eye-opening experience up there. That perspective shift, inspiring awe at the complexity of life on Earth. Then she had to come back down to earth, literally. How do you go shopping for milk when you've been to space? How do you sort out car insurance or bin collection, all the million other mundane things in your life, with what you'd seen?

One of Hannah's pet hates had always been when a musician got successful, their next album was about how hard it was to be a successful musician on the road. Or authors who moaned about how hard it was that their book was a success, the endless book tours, saying the same things every night. But Kirsty's experience was similar, right? She was seen as exceptional because of what she'd done, yet she just wanted to be normal. Instead, someone was throwing bricks through her window and killing her cat. Yuri was still in the kitchen, while Kirsty and Hannah sat in the living room.

'How are you doing?' Kirsty said.

She felt a little queasy, maybe just uneasy about being here. 'I'm OK.' Her mouth felt weird, like she wasn't used to speaking.

Kirsty looked out the window. 'I don't think I can stay here with Yuri through there, knowing there could be a knock on the door.'

'You should tell the police.'

'Do you think they'll do anything?'

'Maybe.' Hannah didn't really think so. The police were overstretched and didn't exactly bend over backward for harassment cases.

Kirsty shook her head. 'Can we go for a walk?'

Hannah stood up, felt a rush of blood to her head and touched the arm of the sofa to steady herself.

'Come on,' Kirsty said, ushering her out the front door and into the dark street.

They walked east and Hannah saw the black expanse of Blackford Hill ahead. Kirsty had her arm through hers, and Hannah thought about the kiss. They turned up Midmar Drive. Across the road were allotments in the shadow of the hill, and Hannah thought about what was growing there, the network of roots from plants, flowers and trees beyond. She'd read somewhere that plants warned each other about threats through their root systems, not just plants of the same species. They were looking out for each other, they knew they needed each other for the ecosystem to work. Millions of years had brought them to this point.

A car drove past and Hannah winced at its shimmering headlights.

They reached the top of the road.

'Want to go up the hill?'

Hannah remembered last year, when a black jaguar was spotted around here. But it was long gone, surely.

'OK.'

She touched a fence post as they headed for Blackford Hill, felt the roughness of the wood and pictured the life the tree had long ago. She frowned, blinked heavily.

There was a gentle slope through grassland, then over an old stone dyke into trees. The slope steepened, rocky outcrops and gorse bushes clinging to the ledges.

Hannah's mouth was dry and sticky and she tried to swallow. Kirsty ahead of her turned to wait. Of course a retired astronaut was fitter than her. Kirsty seemed to glow in the dark, defying the laws of optics, of energy conservation. Where was her halo coming from? Hannah heard a car in the distance, the rustle of leaves on the trees, the wind whistling over their heads like a message from God.

'Come on,' Kirsty said.

She led Hannah up the last bit of path to the top of the hill, the radio-transmitter aerial looming in the darkness as they headed left to the summit, dusty earth underfoot at the exposed peak.

Hannah was panting as they reached the trig point, but Kirsty seemed like she hadn't exerted herself.

'Look.' Kirsty swept an arm around the view of the city.

Hannah had been up here at night before, but it never felt like this. Thousands of streetlights and houses, cars moving between like blood cells, it was overwhelming. They were all interconnected in a miasma of life, and she felt overpowering love towards them all, just trying to stay alive, become part of something bigger. And the trees in between, stalwarts amongst us that we never notice. Millions of insects and birds and mammals, germs and bacteria and microscopic organisms living their best lives. And above them, clouds with their burden of rain, beyond that countless asteroids and meteors and moons and planets and stars and supernovae and black holes, dancing to gravity's beat, dark matter underpinning it all, dark energy flowing from galaxy to galaxy, the exoplanets she'd found, the International Space Station Kirsty had floated in, all of it painfully connected in a way she'd never seen before.

She turned to Kirsty. 'What did you put in my tea?'

In the gloom, Kirsty's smile seemed to shift across her face, take on a life of its own.

'You wanted to know what the overview effect felt like,' Kirsty said, her words escaping from her mouth like mist then dissipating into the cosmos.

'What was it?'

'Just a small dose of psilocybin. I took some too. Magic mushrooms. Psychedelics open your mind, like what happened to me up there.'

She threw a thumb in the air, and Hannah saw tracers emerge from it and wind their way into the sky. She watched them go, then turned back.

'You can't just drug people.'

Kirsty looked sorry. 'Would you have agreed if I'd asked?'

'Fuck no.'

Kirsty held out her hands as if this was explanation enough. 'Besides, it's better not to have any expectations. I knew the trip was coming and began to second-guess it on the way up the hill. It's better to just let go, empty your mind.'

Hannah looked at the sky. Thin clouds were dancing east, choreographed in a zigzag she couldn't decode. They weren't obeying classical Newtonian physics, it was all chaos theory.

'Coronal mass ejections,' Kirsty said.

Hannah held a hand in front of her face and watched tracers float from her fingertips. 'What?'

'Sun storms. They happen all the time, and the Earth's magnetic field protects us. But there was one while I was in the ISS. It knocked out the station's electronics for a few hours, millions of charged particles passing through our bodies that whole time. I didn't feel it of course, at least not to begin with. But as I was up there, no systems working, not knowing if we were going to die, I began to feel warmed by them. A gift from the sun to me, spreading its energy through the universe. Connecting me to the cosmos, to everything that had ever happened.'

Hannah realised she hadn't breathed in the last few seconds, and gulped in air. She remembered something. 'You came back wrong.'

Kirsty laughed. 'Maybe, but not the way that stupid trope means.' She shook her head. 'This must sound crazy to you.'

Hannah stared at Kirsty's face and body shimmering and squirming in an impossible way. She looked beyond her at the glimmering city, the throbbing darkness of Arthur's Seat, the ebbing and flowing Forth.

'No, I get it. I totally fucking get it.'

44

JENNY

Jenny parked on Marine Esplanade beyond the sewage works. A patch of waste ground alongside had been used as a fly-tipping site – broken chairs, two fridge-freezers, a stained sofa. In the forgotten parts of town, no CCTV meant it was easy to get away with this shit.

She got out and locked the van. It didn't feel safe. The wash of the sea to her right calmed her as she headed west, away from the Skelfs' new burial site towards the spread of caravans and campers off Albert Road.

This had nagged at her all day. The idea that there were groups of transient people living amongst us felt weird. She was ashamed she'd never given these people much thought before, never considered the hassle they got, the hardship of the itinerant lifestyle. But the whole thing with Fara and Billie had opened her eyes. And now the search for Stella.

She'd spent a few hours on online chat forums trying to find out the latest movements of transient people in Edinburgh. Mostly it was just local Facebook groups moaning about folk in their areas. With that reaction, no wonder some people had come here. Their only neighbours were an empty field and run-down factories, an industrial estate and transport companies at Leith Docks.

Stella shouldn't be within a thousand miles of Edinburgh, but there was something that made Jenny think she might stick around. Craig loved the city, it had defined him, maybe Stella would respect that. She wouldn't take his body to the middle of nowhere.

Jenny got to the end of Marine Esplanade and saw a low, burnt-out building, window frames blackened and walls graffitied. She thought about their house in Bruntsfield, how Stella had almost burned the place down.

She thrust her hand in her pocket and pulled out the *netsuke* Archie made for her. It was a talisman, even though she didn't believe in luck. You make your own luck. But she rubbed the fox's nose anyway, reassured by the smooth wood against her fingers.

She crossed the road and walked into the rubble-strewn field, switching on her phone torch. She passed the burnt-out building, strode across the dirt towards the lights at the far side of the field, flickering by the trees. She crossed over the defunct railway sidings, saw a huddle of rusted rolling stock to her left. On the right was a private waste site beyond razor-wire fences.

She reached the first caravan. There was a campfire in the middle of the vehicles, just like at Cramond. Three women Jenny's age sat around it. She stepped towards them, past a kid's bike and a clothesline strung between campers. The vehicles had smiley suns painted on them, the old CND logo, the Extinction Rebellion symbol. Maybe these were women from the Faslane nuclear sub base. Women had campaigned for decades outside it, until it became a way of life. That desire to do the right thing turned into a found family.

The women heard her footsteps and turned. One of them lifted a baseball bat that leaned against her chair. She had a purple quiff, large hoop earrings, green bomber jacket, jeans and Docs. The others were less militant-looking, down jackets and jeans, beanie hats. Jenny switched her torch off but scanned their faces in the firelight, no Stella.

'Hi,' she said, hands awkward by her side.

'What do you want?' Quiff said. 'Fucking weird time to be visiting.'

'My name is Jenny Skelf, sorry to both you.'

One of the others tilted her head. 'Like the funerals?'

'Exactly.'

'No one dead here,' Quiff said. 'At least not yet.'

Jenny held her hands out, palms up. 'I'm trying to find someone.'

Quiff snorted. 'Why?'

The usual question at this stage was who, but Jenny understood their wariness. As Cramond had proven, these people were vulnerable. But why *was* she looking for Stella, really? A year ago she would've said revenge, justice. But since Violet died, she'd been driven by something else. Maybe decency, closure. Wanting to do the right thing, whatever that was.

'She went missing a year ago,' Jenny said. 'She's my ex-sister-in-law, and her mother just died. I thought she should know.'

Some softening of the faces around the fire.

She waited for someone to say something, but they didn't. 'Her name's Stella McNamara.'

She watched their faces and rubbed the *netsuke* in her pocket. She didn't see signs of recognition. Quiff stood, the baseball bat swinging loose at her side.

'Not many here use real names,' she said.

'I understand.'

Quiff glanced over Jenny's shoulder.

She turned and saw Stella coming out of a campervan. She realised it was the van she'd had at the Skelf house that night, converted into a camper, with a new paint job.

'Jenny,' she said, walking over. She seemed unsurprised, as if her past was always going to catch up with her. 'How did you find me?'

How to explain the serendipity of the universe? You make your own luck. 'I got lucky.'

Stella nodded. 'Why are you here?'

Compared to last time Jenny saw her, Stella was a ghost. She'd been furious about her brother, angry at the world. Now she seemed like a piece of flotsam moving with the tides.

'Your mum.'

Stella stared at Jenny. She was leaner than a year ago but stronger looking, as if the world had toughened her up. She had shorter hair, was wearing a long-sleeve top and jeans, tattoo on her neck. She had a flicker of Craig's mannerisms, the way she walked, the lopsided mouth. Her eyes looked wet in the firelight.

'She's dead,' Stella said flatly.

Jenny nodded and waited for what would happen next.

45

DOROTHY

She lay in bed and stared at the ceiling. As she got older, sleep was harder to come by. She felt drained and needed to re-energise somehow, all this took its toll. The funerals obviously, but she was used to that. But the other stuff – Billie's death, Stella missing, Hannah's astronaut, responsibility for this new kid Brodie – all made her anxious. Then there was the perennial worry about Jenny and Hannah, the price you paid for a family, fretting that everything would be OK with them. She pictured herself at their new burial site, standing at Jenny and Hannah's open graves, and felt sick. She couldn't bear it if either of them died before her.

Thomas made a noise next to her. He was facing her and she felt his breath on her arm. She envied what a deep sleeper he was. She ran a finger up his arm, touched his earlobe. Earlier tonight he'd seemed unsatisfied in a way she hadn't seen before. The world grinds us all down, the secret is finding the tiny moments of joy.

The doorbell rang downstairs and she looked at Thomas, but he didn't stir. She felt a knot in her gut as she threw on a kimono over her pyjamas. She was halfway down the stairs when the bell went again, and she glanced up at Jenny's bedroom, saw the door was open. Maybe she'd forgotten her keys. It was almost three in the morning.

She reached the door and opened it.

Parker stood shifting his weight, rubbing the back of his neck. He looked at Dorothy, his pupils too small to be natural. He towered over her but was almost emaciated. He wore a leather biker's jacket to look bulkier, but the effect was the opposite, like a little boy dressing up. Torn black jeans, black Converse, Damned

T-shirt, two gold chains. He looked like someone's idea of a gang member from a dystopian eighties movie.

'Fara said I could trust you,' he said, looking at the ground.

She opened the door wider. 'Come in.'

He smelled of sweat and beer as he walked past, something chemical too. By the time she'd closed the door and turned he was lighting a joint.

'Can I smoke?'

Dorothy glanced upstairs then pointed to one of the discreet grieving rooms. 'Through here.'

He followed her and she put on a lamp. He sat on the low sofa and she emptied a dish of potpourri onto the coffee table and slid it over as an ashtray. She sat in an armchair, perched forward with her hands in her lap.

'Fara's right, you can trust me.'

'But your boyfriend's a cop.'

'Correct.' She couldn't help her eyes going to the ceiling.

'He's upstairs now?'

'He's asleep. And I won't say anything you don't want me to.'

He sucked on the joint and exhaled out the side of his mouth. Dorothy thought about the molecules of cannabis clinging to the curtains, the paintings on the wall, soaking into the wallpaper.

He smoked hungrily, trying to calm down. His eyes were pinholes, his movements jerky. 'I can't believe Billie's dead.'

Dorothy had been in this room countless times with the bereaved. There was nothing to say that helped, really. Just being here was what mattered.

'I can't fucking believe it.' Parker shook his head hard. 'First the fire, now this.' He took another toke.

'I spoke to Ruby,' Dorothy said eventually.

He stared at her. 'What did she say?'

Dorothy gave him a look which he understood.

'So you know.'

'Ruby was distraught.'

'Yeah, we were all tight.'

Dorothy didn't speak, but maybe her energy gave her away. Or maybe Parker was projecting his own guilt.

'I love Billie,' he said, between puffs. 'I mean I "loved" her, I guess. Fuck.'

'So what was going on with Ruby?'

He shook his head as if he wanted it to fall off and roll across the room. 'Fucking stupid, just following my dick. Grass is always greener. I was loaded, we both were, we weren't thinking.'

So much heartbreak was caused by people not thinking of others. Dorothy had an affair so long ago it felt like she was a different person in a different universe. But she'd wanted to escape, was fed up with the everyday shit of life, sucked in by the promise of something exotic.

'Why did you run?' she said.

Parker offered her the joint. She looked at it for a long moment, then shook her head.

'Why do you think?' he said. 'I'm the drug-dealing boyfriend, prime fucking suspect, any idiot knows that.'

'But you and Ruby have each other as an alibi.'

'You think the cops will believe that?'

'Why not?'

Parker barked a laugh and pointed at the ceiling. 'I don't know what your boyfriend's like, but most cops don't give a shit about the truth. If I present them with this, they won't think too hard about what really happened.'

'I know they can be...' Dorothy couldn't think how to finish the sentence.

'Cunts?' Parker said.

'They need evidence, and if there's no evidence against you, you'll be fine.'

Parker took another toke, the joint was almost finished. The room was hazy with weed smoke. He lowered his head.

'There will be evidence of ... contact,' he said. 'Sex. We did it a few hours before.'

'Before you were with Ruby?'

'I get it, I'm a piece of shit.'

'Was it consensual?'

He looked shocked by the accusation. 'Of course, what the fuck? I would never do anything like that, Jesus. That's just ... You have no idea what those girls went through.'

Dorothy stayed silent.

Parker stubbed the roach out in the ashtray, jamming it into the ceramic. 'They were groomed up in Peterhead as kids. By Billie's dad and uncle. Plus some others. Raping them for years before they got up the guts to tell Billie's mum. She didn't believe them, so they left.'

His eyes were red and he blinked through the hash smoke in the room.

'I just tried to look after them, you know? OK, it became sexual, but not at the start. I just helped them out, hooked them up with the van, got them in with Fara. We were mates, right? And when things developed with Billie ... it was good, you know? She had issues, of course. But she was kind and caring and I loved her.'

He shook his head and glanced at Dorothy. 'I know, I fucking know. The thing with Ruby, you don't have to say anything. I already feel guilty as fuck. Nothing you say will make me feel any worse.'

He was close to tears, and swallowed hard.

Dorothy narrowed her eyes as she watched him. 'So what do *you* think happened to Billie?'

'Fucked if I know.'

'What about the guys you get drugs from?'

Parker chewed his lip. 'They're not good guys, of course, but there's no problem there. Pretty slick business, to be honest.'

He sat on his hands.

'You should tell all this to the police,' Dorothy said.

He laughed and fixed a stare on her. 'You really think I can trust those clowns to do the right thing?'

46

JENNY

She stared at the flames flicking and spitting into a night sky sprayed with stars. Small motes of ash floated up like released spirits, spiralling skyward to meet their maker.

Jenny watched Stella reassure the other women as they retired to their vans. She balled her fists at her sides. The last time she'd seen Stella, the woman set fire to their house. Stella walked back to the campfire and gestured for her to take a seat. The foldout chair was low and looked difficult to get out of, hard to make a quick exit.

'I'll stand,' Jenny said.

'I need to sit down.'

Stella's energy was not at all what Jenny expected. But then she'd just been told her mother was dead. Your parents dying was part of getting older, but it didn't make it any less devastating. Both of their dads were dead, and now Stella was parentless.

Stella stared at her hands. 'Tell me how she died.'

She seemed harmless but Jenny had been fooled before. 'Motor neurone disease.'

'What the hell? She was fine a year ago.'

'Was she?' Jenny remembered Violet shellshocked from identifying Craig's body. She pictured a rattling teacup as Violet passed it over in the hotel lobby.

'I had no idea.'

Stella swallowed hard through trembling breath. Her hands covered her face and she began sobbing, animal noises from her gut. She howled, made a couple of camper doors open, the women checking on her. She cried and cried and Jenny didn't know what to do.

Stella wiped her cheeks and sniffed, burbled then breathed deeply.

'She hired me to find you,' Jenny said.

'What?'

'She wanted to see you before...'

'Jesus, you're not making this any better.'

'You deserve the truth. I met her five days ago, but she must've been closer than she realised. She died the next night.'

'How was she?'

Jenny pressed her lips together. 'She could hardly speak or swallow.'

'Christ.' Stella started crying again, flickering flames reflecting on her face. 'I am the worst daughter on the planet.'

Jenny felt awkward to be still standing. Stella wasn't in any condition to do anything except cry. Jenny sat on the chair alongside her, but stayed perched forward.

'There's a lot of competition for that title,' she said in a flat voice.

Stella looked up. 'What have you done to Dorothy?'

'Been a fuck-up for years, never got my shit together. Lost it over Craig more than once.'

Stella flinched at the mention of her brother, and Jenny shut up.

A log on the fire snapped and Jenny jumped. She looked at the caravans and campers with their lights on. Beyond that, empty darkness. Behind her was the sea, the same stretch of water where she'd set Craig adrift on a burning boat. Up above, the stars that had shone over all this bullshit for millennia. She found that reassuring. No matter what they were up to down here, stars didn't give a fuck. She saw the appeal of astrophysics for Hannah.

Stella dried her tears. 'How did you find me?'

'Tried various leads. I chased down that posh ex of yours, Porterhouse.'

'Bill? How is he?'

Jenny pictured him in a rabbit mask, jerking off over the couple in the car. 'Getting by.'

'He was a bit of a perv, to be honest.'

A look passed between them, but neither followed it up.

'Another case Mum's working is for some campers in Cramond. That got me thinking about living off-grid. Then Peter from Seafield Crem mentioned there were people here.'

'I couldn't go too far from Mum. I always thought I'd make everything right, turn up on her doorstep and give her a cuddle.'

Deep sobs this time, tears falling onto the dirt.

Jenny had expected confrontation, violence. But maybe living like this changed you. Time to contemplate. Jenny could do with a year out of her life to contemplate. But she'd go mad without all the bullshit to distract her.

Eventually Stella settled down. The firelight gave her a shape-shifting quality, and Jenny struggled to make sense of her face.

'I'm so sorry,' Stella said, sniffling and wiping her nose.

Jenny stayed silent, something she learned from Mum.

'I swear, I didn't know anyone was inside your house when I set it on fire.'

Rage swelled inside Jenny as she remembered Hannah and Indy trapped in the embalming room.

Stella struggled for breath. 'I saw it in the news, that they were inside. There were no lights on, I just wanted you to have a taste of...'

'You nearly killed my daughter.'

Stella put her head in her hands. 'I know. I was fucking crazy. We both were. It feels like Craig had some supernatural hold over us, right? We were fighting over his dead body. Why, after every-thing he did?'

'I thought you didn't believe he was capable of that stuff.'

Stella shook her head. 'I was delusional. I know that now.'

'Why not give yourself up?'

Stella stared at the fire. 'I couldn't put Mum through that. I didn't know how to square it. She'd already lost Dad and Craig. I thought it would kill her...' She realised where that sentence was heading and stopped.

Jenny was surprised to feel sorry for her. Here she was at a campfire with another woman whose life was ruined by Craig. His ripples were still being felt, they always would be, out in the oceans, into the cosmos, flowing over the uncaring stars.

'You know what I have to ask,' Jenny said.

Stella nodded but didn't speak. The fire crackled and spat.

'Where is he, Stella? Where's Craig?'

47

HANNAH

Pain pounded at the base of her skull, and her mouth was like cotton. She smacked her lips, tried to work up some saliva. It was still pre-dawn as she walked down Marchmont Road, half-light buzzing at the edge of her vision. Her body fizzed in time with her footsteps, and she sensed the tenements leaning in to listen to her. She'd taken magic mushrooms a few times before but not for years, and had forgotten the extent of the comedown. A bus trundled towards the Meadows and she felt sucked in by the slipstream, as if she might surf along behind it. She giggled and it sounded like someone else, a happier Hannah, more in tune with herself.

She walked along Marchmont Crescent and Sciennes Road to Argyle Place. The streets were mostly empty, just a few shift workers. She felt empathy for them all, imagined what their jobs were like, their home lives, husbands or wives, boyfriends or girlfriends, kids or grandparents needing to be cared for. Happy or sad.

She reached the bottom of the road and looked at her stairwell door. Then turned to the trees in the Meadows across the road. Stood staring at the leaves for a long time, tried to decode their fundamental message. She looked down Middle Meadow Walk, the overarching branches made it look like a tunnel to another dimension, a portal to a different Edinburgh where everyone worked in harmony.

She jumped when a van honked its horn at a car in front. She watched them both drive away then went upstairs, thinking about the pint of water she was about to drink.

She walked into the kitchen and Indy was there in her work suit, looking at her phone.

'Jesus, Han, where have you been?'

Hannah tried to shake the brain fog, could only feel the pounding in her neck. 'Sorry, babes.' She walked towards the cupboard, took out a glass and filled it at the sink. 'I was with Kirsty.'

Indy's eyes widened as Hannah glugged water and felt the coolness down her throat. She pictured her spongy brain soaking it up, springing back to life.

'The woman you kissed two nights ago? What the actual fuck?'

Hannah shook her head. 'It's nothing like that, sorry, I should've called.'

'You think? You can't just stay out all night and expect me not to worry. Maybe you should answer your phone, for fuck's sake.'

Hannah took her phone from her pocket. Five missed calls, ten texts, all from Indy, curious then angry then panicked. Hannah took another big drink of water, her mouth was already dry again. She stepped towards Indy, who backed away.

'I lost track of time.'

Indy laughed under her breath. 'Lost track of a whole fucking night. With a woman who wants to sleep with you.'

'Nothing happened.' Hannah hated the sound of her voice, she sounded pathetic. 'I don't have any feelings for her, not like that.'

'Then what?'

Hannah took another step forward and Indy again backed away. Hannah felt the heat of her anger and wanted to cry. She'd felt so much in the last eight hours, so much that was positive in the universe, and now here was the woman she loved hating her.

'We were up Blackford Hill, we watched the city and talked.'

Indy narrowed her gaze and Hannah clutched her glass tighter.

'Are you high right now?' Indy said.

Hannah could see the veins in Indy's neck pulsing, wondered about the blood cells flowing there.

'I didn't mean to be,' Hannah said. 'She put psilocybin in my tea—'

'She fucking what?' Indy had her arms out wide. 'She drugged you?'

Hannah put her glass down on the counter and held her hand out. 'It's fine.'

'It's not fine, Han. She drugged you without your knowledge, that is not OK. She's a maniac. Her and her weird-ass wife have been nothing but trouble since we met.'

'Her cat was killed.' Even to Hannah's ears that sounded stupid.

'Her cat? Are you serious?'

'She didn't want to be alone.'

Indy poked her tongue between her teeth, controlling her rage. 'That is the oldest trick in the book, Han, and you know it. We've both had girlfriends we've broken up with who tried that. Shit, I've done it myself. "Don't leave, I can't be alone." Then there's wine and weed and you're in each other's pants for one last fumble, except it never is. She's so obviously into you, her and Mina want you as their fuckbunny.'

Hannah wanted to explain, but she didn't know if she had an explanation that made sense. She wanted to tell Indy what she'd felt on Blackford Hill, looking over the interconnected city. The overview effect Kirsty had talked about, the perspective that changes how you feel about everything, from the smallest microbe to the largest supernova. She imagined a coronal mass ejection, a solar storm splurging energy and particles through her and Indy and everyone else in Edinburgh, making them feel part of something bigger.

'I wish you'd been there,' she said weakly.

'Up a fucking hill, tripping balls with your MILF? No thanks.' Indy looked out of the window, seething.

Hannah just stood there. She hated the silence but didn't want to speak.

Eventually Indy turned back. 'I thought you dropped this case,' she said under her breath. 'That's what we were going to do when you got the call from Billie, remember? What happened to that?'

'I went there to do it,' Hannah said. 'But then the cat, the footage.'

'What footage?'

Hannah struggled to focus. 'The cameras around the house. Yuri was killed, they dumped his body on the patio as a message.'

Indy ran her tongue around her teeth. 'This whole thing is fucking toxic, Han. Get out of it, now. First you were attacked by some lunatic, then the same arsehole killed their cat? It never ends with a dead pet.'

Hannah held her hands out. 'Then Kirsty and Mina are in danger, they need our help.'

'They need the police's help.'

Hannah rubbed at her arm. 'The police won't do anything, not enough manpower.'

'I don't have time for this,' Indy said, putting her jacket on and checking her phone. 'I have to get to work, there's a viewing in twenty minutes. Han, promise you'll drop this case.'

Hannah remembered all the streetlights shimmering from the top of Blackford Hill. The oneness she'd felt up there, the desire to help others.

Indy stared at her. 'Han, promise.'

Hannah took a long time to speak. 'I promise.'

48

DOROTHY

She tried to be present for the sake of Margaret Khan and her loved ones, but she kept chewing over last night with Parker, Billie's ghost haunting them. She felt guilty that she didn't mention Parker's late-night visit to Thomas over breakfast. She thought about that, and her conversation with Thomas about the police. So many people didn't trust them and Dorothy understood that attitude, even if she didn't entirely share it.

Dorothy and Indy stood at the back of the viewing room as Margaret's family and friends came and went. Margaret was white and Christian, had married Mohammed and taken his name but not his religion. The mourners were a mix of cultures brought together in grief. It must've be hard, forming a partnership like that. But Mohammed and Margaret had done all right, judging by the number of people here for the viewing. She was only fifty-two, heart attack while walking the dog. Lots more women died from heart attacks than people thought, because the public focus was on men. The symptoms of heart attack are different in women and they often go untreated for hours. So many died when they could've been saved.

The Skelfs mostly did Christian or non-religious funerals, but not exclusively. Dorothy would've liked broader appeal, but Muslims, Jews and Hindus tended to bury or cremate their own. All three religions normally had their funerals very soon after death unless there was a specific reason not to. In comparison, Christians seemed to take ages, as if they didn't want to admit the deceased was gone.

Everything Indy and Hannah said about the future of funerals made sense. Anything that brought us closer to natural grief and mourning was a good thing. She looked at Indy now, who'd been in a foul mood since she got here.

The viewing room briefly emptied, and Dorothy touched her arm.

'Are you OK?'

'Fine.'

'Is it Hannah?'

Indy glowered. 'She's fine.'

Dorothy took the hint and waved at Margaret's coffin. 'If you've got this...'

Indy waved her away and Dorothy went to reception. Brodie was supposed to be answering the phones but the desk was empty. Dorothy checked the other rooms. She walked to the business end of the building where Archie was tinkering with someone in the embalming room. They should really call it a preparation room from now on, since they were trying not to embalm. It was hard, years of tradition upended since Jim died. But Dorothy wasn't stuck in the past, she hated fake nostalgia for some imaginary bygone era when everything had supposedly been perfect. Life in the past was shit for most people.

'Archie, have you seen Brodie?'

'He's not at reception?'

Dorothy sucked her teeth and walked back to reception, then out the front door. She saw the charred stump of the old pine tree, new shoots rising from it. Just another hundred years and it would be back to normal.

Then she saw Brodie in the wind phone, the handset at his mouth, his body bowed as if in prayer. His shoulders shook and she realised he was crying. Two of Margaret's cousins were smoking by the hedge, glancing at the phone box. Dorothy remembered having to queue for a phone box years ago. That seemed like a different lifetime. How could so much of life just dissolve like that?

She nodded at the two middle-aged women smoking and waited. Turned her face to the sun, listened to sparrows in the bushes, heard the traffic noise over the wall. Tried to live in the moment, but Billie and Parker crowded into her thoughts.

Eventually Brodie left the wind phone, straightening his shirt and tie, looking flushed. He saw Dorothy and came over.

'Sorry I left reception,' he said, rubbing his palm.

Dorothy saw one of the cousins go into the wind phone and pick up the handset, put it to her mouth and ear.

'Don't worry,' Dorothy said. 'How are you?'

Brodie glanced at the box. 'I just needed ... to talk.'

Dorothy waited but he didn't say more. 'How are you getting on with Johnny Sullivan?'

This was the first of the unclaimed deceased they were doing.

'Scheduled for two days' time at the house.'

They would do all the communal funerals in the resomator until they had the green-burial site up and running, then they might mix it up.

'I put info on all our socials.'

'We don't have socials.'

'We do now. Best way to get news out. I also placed ads in the *Evening News* and *Scotsman*, don't worry, I paid for it myself.'

Dorothy shook her head. 'Don't be stupid, we'll cover that.'

'The *News* picked up on it, ran a wee article. I hope you don't mind, I gave a quote.'

'You think people will come?'

'I hope so.'

Dorothy touched his arm. 'Thank you.' She glanced at the wind phone. 'And if you ever need to talk...'

Brodie swallowed and looked at the ground.

The sound of footsteps on gravel made Dorothy turn. Jenny and Hannah were coming up the path, both still in the same clothes as yesterday. Jenny looked wired and Hannah trailed behind, face pale.

'I need to speak to you and Han together,' Jenny said.

'What is it?'

Jenny glanced at Brodie then pointed at the house. 'Inside.'

49

JENNY

She watched Hannah and Dorothy sit at the kitchen table and re-membered Stella's face lit by the campfire. She stared at the huge map on the wall, all the veins and arteries bringing life to the city. Countless dead beneath their feet.

'What is this?' Dorothy said.

Hannah looked exhausted.

Jenny sighed. 'I found Stella.'

Hannah sat up and blinked too much. 'Where?'

Jenny walked to the map and pressed her finger against Marine Esplanade, imagined smudging out Stella and her van friends. The expanse of blue to the north was in sharp contrast to the crazy clutter of streets and lanes, vennels and nooks that made up the ancient city. Jenny peered at the map and saw two craggy outcrops just beyond the East Sands of Leith, called Middle Craigs and Eastern Craigs. They sat just north of where Stella was. She laughed to herself – his name was there all along. His name was all over this city – Craigleith, Craigentinny, Craigmillar, Craigour, Craiglockhart, Craighall, Craigroyston. Shit, there's must be a hundred streets with his name in it. He was everywhere, always had been.

She turned. 'Marine Esplanade.'

Dorothy raised her eyebrows. 'In one of the vans at the other end from our burial site.'

Jenny nodded.

Hannah shook her head. 'Burial site?'

It didn't happen often that Jenny knew more than her daughter. She threw a thumb at Dorothy. 'Mum bought a piece of land at Seafield, across from the crem. She's building a green-burial site.'

Hannah pushed a hand through her hair like she wanted to dig into her skull. 'What's this got to do with Stella?'

'Nothing,' Jenny said. 'Total fucking coincidence. Mum took me to the site yesterday, and I went to talk to the campers last night. Stella has been there all along.'

'For the last year?' Dorothy said.

'A community of a dozen women and a few kids.'

'How has she been living?' Hannah said, sitting forward. 'She never accessed her bank account or benefits.'

Jenny lifted her shoulders. 'Seasonal work picking fruit in the summer, tatties in the autumn. Making things and selling them, trading stuff for food. There's a whole grey economy out there. Also, some of the other women come from independent wealth and share. A dead husband or a sold house is enough to live off for a long time, according to Stella.'

'Did you tell her Violet's dead?' Dorothy said.

Jenny looked out of the window, imagined all the dead of the city rising up and looking for breakfast. 'She guessed.'

'Was she angry?'

'More resigned. I think life has been tough for the last year, and now to find this out...'

Dorothy pushed her chair back and stood. Schrödinger raised his head from the armchair by the window, then slouched over to her and nuzzled her leg. She picked him up and stroked his neck. Jenny heard a low purr.

'Do you think she'll run?' Dorothy said.

'I don't think so.'

'She's wanted for arson and attempted murder.'

They both looked at Hannah. It had been a coincidence that she and Indy were trapped in the embalming room by an obsessed stalker, right when Stella tried to torch the house.

Hannah looked empty, unable to process.

Jenny sat down and held her hand, which was cold. 'She says she thought the house was empty.'

'Do you believe her?'

Jenny thought back to that night. Stella was obsessed with what she was doing to the house, her revenge. 'I do.'

Hannah sucked her teeth. 'I do too.'

Dorothy let Schrödinger down. 'She still tried to burn down our family home.'

'I don't think she was in her right mind,' Jenny said.

Dorothy stared at her. 'Jen, I didn't expect this from you.'

'What do you mean?'

Dorothy waved a hand around, as if including the entire cosmos. 'Forgiveness. Calm. They haven't been your defining characteristics in the past.'

Jenny chewed that over. 'Maybe I've had enough of being angry. It's hard when you're in that place to see it, but it was killing me.'

She saw tears in her mum's eyes and swallowed. She pushed her chair back and hugged her, felt her warmth, tried to remember when they'd last held each other.

Dorothy sniffed and blinked away tears. 'Christ.'

Jenny rubbed her arm, then turned to Hannah. 'There's another reason I don't think she'll run. She won't leave Craig.'

'What do you mean?'

Jenny rubbed her neck. 'She buried him in the trees by the disused railway. Next to Marine Esplanade.'

Hannah lowered her head and Jenny went back to the table. This was Hannah's father, his charred and waterlogged body, in a shallow grave on derelict ground half an hour across town. He'd killed Hannah's friend Mel, tried to kill Jenny and Dorothy, but he was still her dad. Jenny couldn't fathom what that felt like. She wrapped her arms around her daughter and held on, feeling her chest rise and fall. Eventually she let go. Hannah's eyes were wet and Jenny wanted to wipe the tears away.

'So, what should we do?' Dorothy said. 'She's still wanted by the police.'

'Don't tell Thomas,' Hannah said, rubbing her forehead.

Dorothy nodded and Jenny wondered about that.

Indy appeared in the doorway. She glanced at Hannah, then looked at her watch and spoke to Dorothy. 'We should head to Billie's memorial.'

Dorothy looked around the room. 'Come on, we're all going.'

50

HANNAH

The glitching techno sent judders through Hannah's body, and she imagined her constituent quarks shaking themselves loose, floating into the ether. She didn't mind, felt happy to disintegrate. Parts of her floating into the sea and sky, up into space past the ISS, through the energy streams bursting from the sun, beyond the gas clouds and debris into the cold nothingness between galaxies.

'Here.' Fara held out a beer to her. She took it, felt the condensation on the bottle, took a long swig, her body yearning for liquid.

Fara narrowed her eyes. 'Are you tripping?'

Hannah smiled. 'Not anymore. Last night, mushrooms.'

Fara touched Hannah's wrist. 'Were you with someone you trust? A safe environment is important on shrooms.'

Hannah took a drink of lager. 'No, I wasn't.'

There were fifteen people milling around the campfire, some dancing, others swaying to the beat. Dorothy was talking to an older guy Hannah didn't recognise. Jenny glugged a beer on her own. Indy was talking to Ruby, their heads close. Hannah imagined them kissing, stripping and getting down to it in the dirt. Indy was right to feel jealous of Hannah and Kirsty, Hannah would feel the same. It was hard to explain why she had nothing to worry about. Hannah had promised to quit the case and she would, right after this.

Indy and Ruby hugged hard, then Indy tucked Ruby's hair behind her ear. She held her shoulders in a gesture of support, then Ruby walked to two teenage boys at the other side of the fire.

Hannah gazed through the flames to see if Parker was one of them, but they were younger and shorter, nervous around Ruby.

'Hey.' Indy had sneaked up on her.

Hannah drank. 'I saw you with Ruby.'

'She's struggling.'

'Looked like you were a comfort.' It was a stupid thing to say, but sometimes you just want to say something stupid.

Indy pulled her head back in surprise. 'Fuck you, Han. I was making sure she was OK after her best friend was murdered.'

Hannah waved her beer bottle around. 'I know, Jesus, I'm sorry. I'm all over the fucking place, OK? I haven't slept.'

'Whose fault is that?'

'Mine.'

'No, it's Kirsty's.'

Hannah welcomed the softening in her voice. 'Urgh, I hate it when we fight.'

Indy touched Hannah's cheek. Hannah leaned into it like a puppy and didn't give a shit.

'Of course you do,' Indy said, 'otherwise it wouldn't be a fight. But it doesn't mean we're any less solid, OK?'

Hannah took Indy's hand and kissed it. 'I love you.'

Indy gave her a look. 'And you're dropping the case, right?'

'I said I would.'

The music had become more chilled. Hannah recognised it as something Gran drummed along to sometimes, Sufjan Stevens. Delicate voice, big orchestral sound. Folk swayed their heads, hands in the air, the clink of beer bottles.

Dorothy left the older guy and walked round the fire, stopped to talk to Fara. She was so graceful in her movements, an air of calm. Hannah had seen that façade crack when Grandpa died, but she was amazed that this woman in her eighth decade was so together. She hoped she and Indy had a fraction of Dorothy's cool when they were her age. If they made it that far.

'How's Ruby coping?' Hannah said eventually. She looked for

Ruby but couldn't see her, just the two teenage boys jostling and joking.

'She isn't,' Indy said. 'We both know it takes a long time to get your shit together after someone dies. Even then, it never leaves you, right?'

Grief had brought them together. They first met after Indy came to the Skelfs to arrange her parents' funeral. Dorothy spotted a lost soul and gave Indy a job. When Hannah met her at the house, it felt like Indy was the missing jigsaw piece that made her sky complete.

Since then Grandpa had died, then Melanie, then Dad. She and Indy could've died last year too. And here they were at a memorial for another murdered young woman. Maybe they were cursed.

Dorothy joined them. 'Fara says this could go on all night.'

Indy shook her head. 'What about the bastard responsible?'

'I don't think the police are any further forward.'

Indy shook her head and Hannah took a drink. She was still coming down off the mushrooms, her mind making connections, thoughts firing out like a coronal mass ejection, her desire to be part of something bigger thrumming in her belly.

Dorothy looked at the mourners dancing around the fire.

'We'll just have to solve it ourselves,' she said.

51

JENNY

The music faded as Jenny walked away from Cramond along the prom. The sky was full of stars and the wind rustled the trees. Ruby was a hundred yards ahead, walking hesitantly. Jenny couldn't decide if she was drunk, stoned or grief-stricken, maybe all three. That's how Jenny had coped in the past.

Ruby glanced over her shoulder and Jenny ducked beneath the bow of an oak tree overhanging the path. Ruby looked back to the memorial, a beacon of light in the distance. She kept walking and Jenny followed.

She'd watched Ruby at Billie's memorial for a while. Ruby talked to a few people but seemed distracted, kept checking her phone. Not unusual for a teenage girl but something about her body language made Jenny pay attention. She kept looking round and Jenny wondered if Parker was messaging her to meet up. Then Ruby excused herself and slipped away from the camp. Jenny decided to follow.

The prom curved one way then the other, the trees on the right thinning to reveal a hilly field. On the left, the Firth of Forth was implacable in the dark. The Forth would always be associated with Craig's death for Jenny. She thought about Stella, surprised she wasn't more angry. She didn't feel bad for killing Craig but she felt for Stella, alone in the world.

Ruby glanced over her shoulder again, face lit up by her phone screen. She stumbled a little. Jenny stood in the dark, listened to the waves. Ruby kept going. There were trees again on the right, the land sloping upward. The prom crossed a thin burn and Jenny heard water burbling over stones.

She lost Ruby round a bend, then spotted her again. Ruby was on the path up the hill at the edge of the trees. Near the top, she cut into the woods.

Jenny walked up the hill, listening, and reached the point where Ruby had disappeared. She looked round. She could make out the shadowy rump of Cramond Island in the distance. The tide was in, it was isolated. She wondered about Billie's body, if forensics found anything. She saw the fire of the memorial on the shore, figures shifting in the shadows, the drift of music on the breeze. It seemed a million miles away.

She heard a noise from the trees and turned. She picked up a hefty branch and brandished it as she walked into the woods, tentative steps on the dusty path. Darkness swallowed her and she thought about using her phone torch, but decided against throwing out a beacon. She stepped over stones and exposed tree roots into a hollow then up the other side. She saw movement in a clearing to the left. She walked to the edge of the clearing and stopped.

There was a car parked with its headlights pointing away, all four doors open. Jenny saw a gate from a field up the slope, how they must've got in. In the headlight beam, Ruby was on her knees in the dirt, surrounded by three men with their trousers at their ankles. One gripped her hair as she sucked his cock. The other two men stroked themselves as they watched. A fourth man stood by the driver's door, filming it on his phone.

The first guy came, legs quivering. He shoved Ruby over to the next guy. Ruby flinched and shook her head. The second guy slapped her and the first one spoke in a low growl, pointing at the guy filming. Ruby eventually took the second guy in her mouth.

Jenny felt ashamed. She should stop this, but there were four men against her and Ruby. She wondered about getting help, but it would take too long. Eventually, Ruby finished off the second guy, then the third, the others laughing and encouraging him until he came. The first guy leaned over Ruby and spoke to her, then spat in her face. Ruby was crying.

The men turned to the car and Jenny got a clear view of two of them in the headlights. She didn't recognise them.

Ruby sat in the dirt as the car doors closed and the engine revved. The car drove through the gate and away.

Jenny ran to Ruby, who'd taken her top off and was using it to wipe her face.

'Ruby.'

She recoiled and scuttling backward.

'It's Jenny, from the Skelfs.'

Ruby looked beyond Jenny, then over her shoulder where the car had disappeared.

'What the fuck?' Jenny said.

Ruby burst into tears.

52

DOROTHY

The memorial was winding down. Hannah and Indy had gone uptown, and Dorothy wandered the burnt-out remains of Billie and Ruby's campervan. She kicked a scorched wheel rim then the tyre, melted into the ground.

'Mum.'

She turned to see Jenny with her arm round Ruby. Their body language said trouble.

'Is there somewhere we can go?' Jenny said.

Ruby sniffled into her hands, avoided eye contact.

'My place,' Fara said, appearing like a magician.

They walked to Fara's camper. She opened the door and held it as they went in. A comedown groove was playing outside, laidback beats and electric piano. It faded as Fara closed the door and put a lamp on. Dorothy sat on the sofa with Ruby while Jenny stood with her fists at her sides.

Fara poured a large glass of water at the sink and handed it to Ruby, who held it in both hands, drops spilling from her trembling hands.

'What's this about?' Fara said.

Ruby glanced at Jenny, who raised her eyebrows and waited. Ruby lowered her head.

'Are you OK?' Dorothy said, touching Ruby's back. She wore a short black skirt and no tights, filthy bra-top.

'She's not OK,' Jenny said.

'Maybe let her answer.' Dorothy turned to Ruby. 'There's no rush.'

Jenny looked out of the window as if marauders were coming over the horizon with AK47s.

Fara kneeled down and placed a hand on Ruby's knee. Dorothy saw they were grazed red, grit stuck to the raw skin. She wanted to get an antiseptic wipe and a plaster.

'Rubes, it's OK,' Fara said. 'You're with friends.'

Ruby shook her head, hair falling over her face. She pushed her hair behind her ear and looked around.

'It's not safe,' she said, looking at Jenny. 'Nowhere is safe.'

Fara looked at Jenny.

Dorothy held her silence.

'It's OK,' Fara said.

'Tell them what happened.' This was Jenny, shaking her head.

'Jen, please.' Dorothy didn't understand the anger, but there must be a reason, Jenny had been on such an even keel lately.

Ruby took a long sip of water, breathed with a shudder and clutched the glass too hard.

'It's not what you think,' she said, glancing at Jenny. 'I wanted to.'

Dorothy worried that Jenny was going to explode, she'd seen that rage before. But Jenny's face softened and she unclenched her fists.

'Ruby.' Her voice was so low Dorothy could hardly hear. 'Come on. I saw.'

Ruby's lip trembled. She suddenly seemed younger than eighteen.

Ruby rubbed at her skirt. 'They said if I didn't...'

'What happened?' Fara said, still kneeling at Ruby's feet.

Ruby looked at Jenny again. Dorothy could feel sparks in the air, tracers trying to find somewhere to land.

'You tell them,' Ruby said to Jenny.

Jenny cleared her throat, then seemed hesitant. She looked at Ruby for a long time. 'I just saw Ruby in the woods by Silverknowes Beach. With four men. They were forcing her ... to give them blowjobs. They raped her.'

Ruby flinched. 'It wasn't rape.'

Jenny shook her head, wide-eyed. 'I saw, Ruby. They raped you.'

'Who was it?' Dorothy said.

'I saw two of them clearly, but I didn't recognise them.'

Ruby rubbed at her skirt again, took a drink of water. 'It was the cops, the ones investigating Billie.'

'Webster and Low,' Dorothy said. A weight descended on the van and she felt crushed. A picture was coalescing out of the darkness. 'You said they threatened you.'

Ruby sniffed, her breath ragged.

'Breathe,' Fara said, placing a hand on hers.

Ruby swallowed. 'They said if I didn't do it, I would end up like her.'

The electricity in the air connected to Dorothy and she felt sick. She leaned towards Ruby. 'Did they say they killed her?'

Ruby started crying, touching her hair, the glass of water spilling on her lap. 'They didn't need to.'

'What do you mean?'

'They were doing the same thing to her before,' Ruby said. 'For a long time. They liked her, that's what they said. She told me one time when she was high, made me swear not to tell. She didn't want Parker to know, in case he thought she was a slut. Or in case he tried to fight them. They're cops, they always win.'

'Why did she do it?'

Ruby sniffed and shook her head. 'They groomed her. Got her drunk and high, told her she was pretty. Then, the first time, they filmed her. Told her it would be on Pornhub in minutes if she didn't come back for more. Told her they would do the same to me if she didn't go along with it. Or worse. They had her.'

Christ almighty, Dorothy thought.

Fara slumped on the floor. 'Were all four of them police?'

Ruby nodded.

Jenny stretched her neck, veins visible at her collarbone. 'Could you identify them?'

Ruby's lip went out again, but she gave a firmer head nod. 'Yeah, but...'

'You have to report this.' Jenny angled her head, kindness in her eyes that surprised Dorothy again. 'They're not above the law.'

'But they'll fuck me up.' Ruby was crying again. 'You saw what happened to Billie.'

Dorothy shook her head. 'You think they killed Billie.'

Ruby stared at her. 'Don't you?'

Jenny leaned closer, like a confessional. 'Did they tell you that?'

Ruby looked gutted out. 'No.'

'But why kill her?' Dorothy said.

Ruby shrugged and looked around at the women. Dorothy followed her gaze, they looked like a painting of crisis, like an old master.

'Because they could,' Ruby said.

53

HANNAH

Hannah had left most of her pancakes and maple syrup. She felt sick after hearing Jenny talk about what happened to Ruby. They were at the kitchen table with Dorothy and Indy in heavy silence. Hannah wrapped her hands around her mug of tea, felt the heat enter her skin, thought about the first law of thermodynamics – that energy cannot be created or destroyed, only converted from one form to another. Everything in the universe obeyed that law, from the mug in her hands to the death of her dad to a supernova exploding.

Indy finally broke the silence. 'And she won't go to the police?'

Jenny raised her eyebrows at Dorothy, handing her the floor.

'She wouldn't last night, but Fara called me half an hour ago. She stayed up most of the night talking to her, and she's persuaded her to go to the station. I've spoken to Thomas, made sure a friendly female officer will take her statement.'

'It's horrible,' Hannah said, and felt the weakness of those words. Horrible didn't come close.

'Not just the rape,' Jenny said. 'The implication of Billie's murder.'

Hannah was surprised at her mum's tone. She had the bit between her teeth, but she was also calm, together. Something in her had changed.

Dorothy frowned. 'Let's not get ahead of ourselves. Webster and Low will argue the sex was consensual—'

'It wasn't,' Jenny said.

'They'll say it was. But even so, they're compromised in the investigation.'

Jenny shook her head. 'Compromised? They're murderers.'

Hannah took a sip of tea. 'What did Thomas say?'

'We only talked briefly about that,' Dorothy said. 'I was mainly concerned with getting Ruby to the station, otherwise, none of this can happen.'

'I was a witness,' Jenny said.

Dorothy pressed her lips together. 'Without Ruby, there's nothing.'

Indy stood up and went to the whiteboards. On the PI board, Billie's name was surrounded by others – Parker, Fara, Ruby and the Ferguson boys. Indy added Webster and Low, then wrote *Cop 3* and *Cop 4*.

She turned back. 'We don't know who these guys are?'

Hannah felt her heart swell as Indy tapped the marker pen against her cheek. she was officially just a funeral director but it seemed natural she would step into investigations too. And these breakfasts were essential for the businesses, but they were much more than that, a way to stay grounded in each other's lives.

Dorothy shook her head. 'Ruby reckons she could identify them in a line-up.'

'Do you think that'll happen?' Jenny said.

Hannah took another sip of tea. 'How do you mean?'

'Cops tend to circle the wagons, protect their own. There are hundreds of sexual-assault complaints against officers being "investigated".' She did the air quotes. 'No one has been sacked, let alone prosecuted. The most they get is a few weeks of paid suspension, then they're back.'

Indy tapped the whiteboard. 'But this is more serious. They're now suspected of murder and arson.'

Jenny nodded. 'But they'll be lawyered up. Unless there's proper evidence, I'm not convinced. And even if there is, it's hard to build a case for murder, a hundred times harder if the suspects are cops. Are their colleagues going to investigate it properly?'

Dorothy went to Indy at the whiteboard. 'Thomas will try his best to ensure they do.'

Jenny ran a hand through her hair. 'He's only one guy, Mum. And he's not in charge, there are plenty above him. It's not exactly the most progressive organisation.'

Hannah sighed. 'So what are you suggesting?'

Jenny shrugged. 'We do it by the book, of course. Ruby gives a statement, I'll give a statement. I presume Webster and Low will be removed from the case and investigated. After that, who knows?'

'That's pretty unsatisfying,' Hannah said.

Jenny chewed her lip. 'For sure.'

Dorothy took the pen from Indy and circled Ruby's name. 'Let's just see. I'm meeting Ruby and Fara at St Leonard's. I'll report back.'

Hannah looked at Jenny, then at the whiteboard. 'And what about Stella?'

Jenny sucked her teeth. 'I'm giving her a ride to Pitlochry later. Violet has already been cremated, Stella missed the funeral. We're going to collect the ashes.'

'And what about Craig?' Indy said.

'I'm going to speak to her about him on the way up the road.'

Dorothy turned to Hannah. 'What about your astronaut?'

Hannah shared a look with Indy. 'We're dropping the case.'

Jenny looked surprised. 'Why?'

Hannah shook her head. 'They're a weird couple. To be honest, I don't feel a hundred percent safe.'

'Really?' Dorothy said.

Hannah wondered if Indy would say something about the attack, the drugs, the kiss. But she stayed silent.

'I tried to quit last night,' Hannah said. 'Went round there, but there was no one in. I've messaged them both, but they're ghosting me. Maybe they've decided to drop it.'

'Good riddance,' Indy said, a smile softening her tone.

Dorothy looked at the funeral whiteboard, then turned to Indy. 'And we have Michelle Murata's funeral later, right?'

Indy nodded. The death business never stopped.

54
DOROTHY

She waited in Thomas's office. He was downstairs with DS Griffiths, taking Ruby's statement, Fara in the room for support. Dorothy knew Griffiths in passing, had dealt with her over a couple of cases. She was young and keen, Dorothy got good vibes from her. She wouldn't cover for rapists and murderers, even if they were colleagues.

Dorothy played with the stationery on Thomas's desk, unravelling paperclips, clicking the stapler. It was anachronistic, having these things in a twenty-first-century office. There were filing cabinets behind her, and she wondered if they would always have a paper trail in the police. Maybe that was for the best.

She glanced at the door, then walked to the cabinet nearest the window. Found the drawer for open cases, checked under M for McNamara. Files for both Craig and Stella. Craig's case wasn't really still open, except his body was missing. But it had been examined by Graham at the mortuary before Stella removed it, which confirmed Jenny's story of self-defence. Dorothy thought of the ripples of Craig's actions. Melanie Cheng's family and friends would always grieve, the female prison guard he seduced had lost her career and marriage. Fiona would always carry the scars of Sophia's abduction. Jenny and Dorothy had their own scars from fights with Craig. And poor Hannah, carrying the weight that her dad was a murderer.

Hannah had mentioned once that she worried it was genetic. She might inherit his traits, she had his poison running through her veins. But it didn't work like that, people broke the chains of their heritage all the time. Sons of alcoholic fathers becoming teetotal, daughters of abusive mothers refusing to pass that bullshit to their own kids. You had to be strong but you also needed support.

Dorothy flicked through the files for Stella and Craig, but there was nothing she didn't know already. She realised how it would look if Thomas opened the door. She closed the folders and placed them back in the drawer.

She looked out of the window at Salisbury Crags. The sharp morning light made the grass look crisp, the crevices of the cliff jagged and dangerous, gorse pulsing yellow. The sky was pale blue, two jet trails crossing over the Forth, where the planes approached the airport.

The door opened and Thomas came in, mouth turned down.

'How did it go?' Dorothy said.

'She got through it.'

Dorothy liked that his first response was to think of it from Ruby's perspective. 'Where is she now?'

'Fara took her for the forensic examination.'

'Do you think they'll get much?'

'Even if they do, Webster will claim she consented.'

'They hit her.'

'If there's any sign of that they'll pass it off as roughhousing, you know how it goes.' He looked defeated.

'You sound like you've given up.'

He came round the desk. 'I'm just being realistic. You know the system.'

Dorothy gritted her teeth. 'That's not good enough.'

Thomas shrugged.

'Did she identify the other two?'

'Not yet, it all takes time.'

'But Webster and Low are suspended?'

Thomas looked at his hands. He had bags under his eyes, lines on his forehead, as if he'd aged overnight. 'They're off the murder case.'

'But still working?'

'Until we get more evidence.'

'Jesus, Thomas.'

'We can't suspend every officer who's had a complaint against him, we wouldn't have anyone left.'

She stared at him long and hard, and he understood. 'Doesn't that tell you something about the officers you're employing?'

'*I'm* not employing anyone, Dorothy, come on, we've talked about this.'

'You know what I mean.'

'I do.' He rubbed the back of his neck.

'So that's it? They can just act like nothing happened?'

Thomas held his hands out. 'We have to do it by the book.'

'The system is fucked, Thomas. You know, there's an episode of *The Simpsons* where Marge says to Chief Wiggum, "I thought you said the law was powerless". He says, "powerless to help you, not punish you". I used to think that was a joke.'

She knew it wasn't his fault, but she was so angry.

'What do you want me to do, beat them up, arrest them? Anything I do at this stage will only result in them getting away.'

Dorothy watched a couple at the top of Salisbury Crags looking over the city, all of this bullshit. She turned back. 'What about forensics from Billie's murder?'

'We've taken DNA samples from Webster and Low.'

'Was there DNA at the scene?'

'They're still working on that.'

'Jesus, how long does it take?'

'Everyone is trying their best, Dorothy.'

Dorothy pictured Billie alone on Cramond Island, Ruby scared in the woods.

'It's not enough,' she said, and left without looking back.

55
JENNY

She walked with Archie past the Hermitage and alongside the Braid Burn. The water was low, not enough rain recently. They started fast, both burning energy, but gradually relaxed thanks to the burbling burn, rustling trees and birdsong. Fresh air and exercise, it wasn't rocket science.

Jenny had spent the last fifteen minutes ranting about Ruby, Webster and the rest. It seemed insane that those pricks weren't locked up already. She knew in her heart they killed Billie, and it made her teeth itch to think they weren't already suffering. But she agreed with Dorothy – they had to do it by the book, otherwise the cunts might walk.

They strolled past a woman walking two retrievers, swapped smiles and hellos.

Jenny breathed deeply. 'You didn't tell me about Mum's green-funeral plans.'

Archie's clambered over some thick tree roots. The path was dusty and he kicked up a little cloud. 'It wasn't my place, Jen, sorry.'

'I thought we were friends.' She was joking and hoped her tone was clear.

He caught her smile and threw it back at her. 'Fuck off.'

'I just would've liked a heads-up.'

'It's Dorothy's business at the end of the day.'

Jenny nodded. More dog walkers, then a young dad with two toddlers splashing in the burn in their wellies.

'And how do you feel about it?' she said.

'I like a challenge.'

Jenny shook her head. 'You've got all this expertise in embalming. Are you just going to throw that away?'

Archie sucked his teeth. 'Ach, I like the idea of a green future for the funeral business. We've done enough damage to the world.'

Jenny gave him a sideways look. 'And you've got a bunch of land-management experience, yeah?'

He smiled. 'Dorothy wouldn't ask me if she didn't think I could do it. She knows folk better than they know themselves. If she offers you something, you say yes.'

'You love her, don't you?'

Archie didn't blink. 'Of course, she saved me.'

Mum did a lot of saving people. Archie, Indy, Schrödinger and now Brodie. And all the countless bereaved families over the decades. Some legacy – what did Jenny have in comparison?

The path reached a crossroads, a bridge over the burn heading to Howe Dean and the Braids, towards the observatory in the other direction. Straight on was the back of King's Buildings, Craigmillar Park golf course where the police found Hannah's friend Melanie, the murder that exposed Craig for what he was. They headed left up the hill through the trees.

'So how's Stella?' Archie said.

She'd told him all about it. He was easy to talk to, never judged. And he was an outsider, it felt different from talking to Mum or Hannah.

Jenny checked her watch. 'I'm about to head to Pitlochry with her, collect Violet's ashes.'

He just nodded.

'She's...' Jenny didn't know what to say. Resigned, defeated? Aren't we all.

'And how are you?' Archie said.

The weight of the question was more than the words could hold. They walked out of the trees into fresh air, a breeze scooting over Blackford Hill into their faces. Jenny breathed it in like she'd been stuck at the bottom of the ocean for a week.

'Honestly? I think I'm OK.'

※

She gazed down the Forth as they drove over the Queensferry Crossing. The central struts strobed the sunlight coming up the firth, and Jenny shielded her eyes as she stared at the two bridges alongside. She remembered crossing this bridge two years ago, on her way to uncovering Craig in Elie.

Jenny looked at Stella behind the wheel of her campervan. It seemed pretty roadworthy, given it'd been parked in waste ground for a year. Jenny turned up earlier with a can of petrol, enough to get them to a station, where she filled up the van and paid. She realised then the sacrifices Stella made to stay off the radar.

'OK?' Stella asked now.

Jenny's instincts said Stella was not dangerous. But her instincts had been fucking terrible so often. She sometimes thought the only constant in her life was her ability to make dreadful decisions. But this felt good. Helping her ex-sister-in-law pick up her dead mother's ashes. Why not?

'Yeah,' she said. 'You?'

Stella nodded as they drove into Fife. Jenny listened to the inane burble of local daytime radio. They were held up at Perth roadworks, then took the A9 to Pitlochry. Stella knew the way to the funeral directors, parked outside.

'Do you want me to come with you?' Jenny said.

Stella scrunched her face then went inside. They'd parked just off the main road, a quaint Victorian high street straight off a chocolate box. This was Tory country for the most part and Jenny felt like an interloper. She longed to get back to the unpredictable energy of Edinburgh.

Stella came out holding a carrier bag with something heavy in it. She opened the van door and got in, pulled a plain wooden box from the bag. Jenny wondered how many people went to Violet's funeral, all shaking their heads at her misfortune – a dead husband, a dead son, a missing daughter, motor neurone disease. Life is pain, and all that.

'Take this.' Stella handed the box to Jenny then put her seatbelt on and started the engine.

Jenny half expected her to pull something crazy. But this version of Stella was more than just a year older.

They drove in the opposite direction to Edinburgh.

'Where are we going?' Jenny said, her grip on the box tightening.

'Just a quick stop.'

Stella headed up the hill, away from the river. The houses here were large and grand. They took a right turn. They were high enough now that Jenny could see the hills on the other side of the River Tummel, a high bank of trees, velvety green.

Stella pulled into the driveway of a big, whitewashed Victorian house, parked out front. Two storeys, big windows, long stretch of grass and flowerbeds to either side. She looked at the front door for a long time.

'This your mum's place?' Jenny said, glancing at the box of ashes.

'Mine now. I spoke to the family solicitor yesterday, after you found me. As well as informing me I'd missed Mum's funeral, he explained I'm the sole beneficiary.' She gave Jenny a look. 'If I don't go to prison for arson and attempted murder.'

Jenny nodded. There was a time she would've given anything to have this control over Stella, to get closure on this McNamara bullshit. But sitting outside the house Stella and Craig grew up in, holding what remained of Violet, made her feel differently. 'Do you want to go inside?'

Stella looked close to tears. 'Not really.'

'It might help.'

'It might send me over the edge.'

'I've been over the edge a few times. It's not as bad as you think.'

Stella switched the engine off and Jenny heard birds in the trees.
'Come on,' Stella said, then looked at the ashes. 'Leave her here.'

She went to the house and Jenny followed. Stella pulled out keys
and opened the front door, walked around the ground floor.
Everything was neat and orderly. There was a hospital bed in the
large room on the ground floor, medical equipment and a wheelchair in the corner. Stella ran a hand over the back of the wheelchair.

'I never knew any of this.'

She went to the kitchen, pristine. The fridge was virtually
empty, just some protein drinks. A line of pans hung above the
stove.

Jenny thought about Craig growing up here. Out in the garden
with Stella, playing cops and robbers. What a lie that was – good
versus evil. It was all inside all of us, waiting to come out, the good
and the bad.

Stella opened the doors to the garden. She stood there in the
breeze. 'You're thinking about him, aren't you?'

'Yes.'

'His room is a guest bedroom now. Same with mine. I guess
parents hold on to that stuff for a while, until it's clear the kids are
not coming back. They have to get used to it, right?'

Jenny thought about Hannah. 'I suppose.'

'There were no clues, you know.'

Jenny stared at her. The sunlight cast her face in darkness, and
Jenny couldn't get a sense of her meaning. 'About what?'

'Reasons why Craig turned out the way he did. He wasn't some
vicious little bastard, torturing animals or bullying at school. There
weren't any signs. He was happy here, we both were.' She looked
around the room and out to the garden. 'We all were.'

She looked over the glen to the hills on the other side. She
must've seen this view thousands of times. She smiled at it and
breathed deeply, then turned to Jenny.

'I think it's time to dig up the past,' she said.

56

HANNAH

Hannah sat in the kitchen watching Schrödinger sniff his way around the skirting board. She'd managed to waste most of the day in here already, drinking tea, checking her phone, reading an old Octavia Butler novel she had in her bag, playing with the cat. Not thinking about Kirsty and Mina.

Indy, Archie and Brodie were downstairs, and she found that comforting. She felt connected through the floorboards. The memories of this house were a congregation of ghosts passing through her. You were never truly alone, that's what physics taught you. In fact, there was no 'you', no definitive self, unconnected from the universe.

That whole thing with Schrödinger's cat, the famous quantum physics thought experiment that showed how crazy the universe was. According to quantum theory, a cat inside a closed box is *both alive and dead* until someone opens it and looks. But that theory really does describe the universe. That means the act of observing an event actually changes the outcome of the event. That was profound. The idea of an impartial, unconnected observer watching the world was totally wrong. We're all up to our necks in the universe, we can't be separated from it.

She decided she couldn't hide in this kitchen for the rest of the day, she had to get out and engage with the universe. Time to do some work.

She said goodbye to the cat and to Brodie downstairs, then walked to her office at the astrophysics campus. Every driver or cyclist who passed, she thought of their lives, the countless connections to everyone else on the planet, even the most lonely person. She found it hard to stomach that the council had unclaimed dead bodies, people with no connection. But she loved the idea of the Communal Funeral Project. *They* would be the community for these people, they would celebrate their lives, notice their passing.

The wind was fresh as she walked down Kilgraston Road onto Oswald Road, the folds of Blackford Hill framed by the tree-lined street. The radio antenna up there looked like a transmitter to heaven, and Hannah thought about the electromagnetic waves passing through us all the time. She thought of the millions of neutrinos screaming through her body every second. She thought of the coronal mass ejection Kirsty talked about, a message from the Sun God. The fluxing magnetic fields swirling around us that birds and animals use to navigate, that we have no awareness of. Humans were blinkered idiots, fumbling through the universe, searching for meaning.

Christ, that psilocybin had really done a number on her. She hated Kirsty for spiking her tea, but she kind of understood it too. She was experiencing something like the overview effect and she loved it. She wanted to wrap her arms around the planet and give it a hug. This was our home, we needed to look after it.

But Indy was right. Kirsty and Mina were trouble and she had to drop the case. She was glad they'd ghosted her, it made life easier. She remembered kissing Kirsty, the dead cat on the worktop, the brick through the window. She touched her temple where she was hit. But she still felt a glow when she thought of Kirsty, despite it all.

She crossed Charterhall Road into the park, then walked uphill towards campus. Kirsty and Mina's house was on the other side of the hill. The hill where she'd sat with Kirsty, her mind flooded with connections.

She felt a burn in her calves and sweat on her brow, then emerged from the trees at the campus entrance and spotted Mina, looking worried.

Hannah hesitated, looked behind her, then at Mina. They were connected, she needed something. This wasn't over.

Mina spotted her and ran over. As she got closer, Hannah saw tired eyes and puffy cheeks.

'Something's happened to Kirsty, she hasn't come home.'

Hannah narrowed her eyes. This felt like the missing cat all over again. But then, Yuri *did* turn up dead.

'Since when?'

'I last saw her yesterday morning, when she got in from being with you.'

'You guys have an open thing, right? Could it be that?'

'No.'

'Why not?'

Mina held her phone up. 'We keep tabs on the tracking app.'

Hannah shook her head. Two students walked past them into the campus. 'That doesn't sound very trusting.'

Mina put her hands on her hips. 'I don't need a fucking ethics lesson, I just need to find Kirsty.'

'And the app isn't working?'

'Her tracking is switched off. We never do that.'

'Never?'

'Never.'

'Have you gone to the police?'

Mina snorted a laugh. 'They didn't give a shit about Yuri. This will be no different.'

The mention of the cat reminded Hannah of something. 'The footage. I have access to the cameras at your house.'

She got her phone out and opened the app. There had been twelve activations in the last day and a half, all time stamped.

'When exactly did you last see her?'

'When I went to work yesterday, just after nine. She went to bed after being out all night.'

Hannah opened the first file stamped after that time, but it was just the postie shoving mail through their letterbox. The next was a neighbour's cat mooching around the patio. Then the next file showed someone coming to the door. A woman in her late twenties, hoodie hiding her face, jeans, trainers, hands in her pockets. She looked familiar but Hannah couldn't place her. She rang the doorbell and waited, looked around. Eventually the door opened. The woman spoke, presumably to Kirsty off screen. She looked calm. Then she produced a kitchen knife from down the back of her jeans and raised her face.

'Fuck,' Mina said. 'It's Nadia.'

Hannah remembered her. 'From the museum?'

57

DOROTHY

Morningside Cemetery was beautiful in the afternoon sun. A breeze funnelled down the central boulevard of tall pines and messed with the top layer of soil on the pile next to Michelle Murata's open grave. Her white coffin was covered in bouquets of chrysanthemums and lilies, placed there by mourners. Dorothy looked around the large crowd, from little kids to the very old. There was a host of different ethnicities, including many Japanese from Michelle's husband's side of the family, everyone in bright clothes. They were doing more funerals like this, celebrations that eschewed the standard black for something more joyous.

Michelle worked for a refugee charity for two decades, helping them with getting settled, asylum claims, benefits, accommodation, citizenship. Dorothy wondered about the ledger of her own life. She tried to do good, make tiny changes that helped people.

She looked to her left, where Thomas's wife's grave was. They sometimes visited Morag together, which Dorothy still felt weird about. But grief never left you, she understood that.

She glanced at a nearby gravestone. She always sought it out here, the inscription for the elderly man read: *At least he tried*. She wondered what they meant. That he tried, but failed? Or at least *he* tried, as opposed to someone else? Or maybe it was just sincere, at least he tried. That was something to celebrate.

Today's ceremony was humanist, the celebrant a young woman with her hair in braids, wearing red dungarees, a plaid shirt and Converse. She was good, and Dorothy made a note to remember her, in case other bereaved wanted a referral. Summing up a life was a tough job if you didn't know the person well, but some celebrants were naturals at putting people at ease.

Michelle's husband, Akira, had his head bowed and was crying, incongruous with his Hawaiian shirt and green trousers. Michelle had died from a simple fall down the steps outside her work, landing awkwardly on her head. A fractured skull and intracerebral haematoma, she was pronounced dead immediately. Life was so delicate, it was a miracle any of us were here at all.

Dorothy caught Archie's eye. He was waiting at the hearse and the family's car, Brodie alongside. Dorothy thought about how they'd both come to her by chance, grieving and damaged. Everyone she knew was carrying a weight. She, Jenny and Hannah all had Jim's death, and now Craig's. Archie's mum was dead, Brodie's son, Indy's parents. Stella's whole family. It was almost too much, the only thing that made it bearable was sharing the load.

The mourners lowered Michelle into the ground and each threw a clod of dirt on top. Akira joined in, body trembling. The celebrant finished with a poem by Keats and a Buddhist prayer of connection, then the mourners began drifting away. There was a wake at the Whale Arts Centre in Wester Hailes, with a huge spread courtesy of all the families Michelle had helped.

Archie and Brodie opened the car doors for Akira, Michelle's sister and her mother, and Dorothy felt a hand grab her arm.

'Let's go for a walk.'

Webster pushed her away from the funeral until they were amongst pine trees. She stumbled over a root and he pulled her up.

'Get your hands off me,' Dorothy said.

He glanced behind to check they were out of sight. 'Keep walking.'

Dorothy tried to pull away, but his grip was tight. 'What is this?'

'I just want a quiet word.'

'In secret?'

Webster pulled her harder so she stumbled again. 'You fucking women.'

The way he said it made Dorothy feel sick.

They walked until they were halfway along the boulevard, then Webster dragged her behind the biggest tree. She staggered over pinecones then he pinned her to the trunk. Rage in his eyes, but she didn't flinch.

'What the fuck are you bitches playing at?'

Dorothy blinked. 'What do you mean?'

'Don't play fucking innocent, I know you're behind this shit.'

'I don't know what you're talking about.'

He hit her cheek hard with the back of his hand. She felt tears in her eyes and thought about Thomas.

'I'm not fucking around,' he said. 'You're in danger.'

Dorothy managed a nod. 'Thanks for the warning.'

'Leave us alone.'

She wondered if she screamed now, whether Archie or Brodie would hear, if they would make it in time.

'You convinced that wee slut to complain about us.'

'You raped her.'

'She fucking wanted it. Begged for it. Some slags are just like that. Your daughter got the wrong end of the stick.'

The way he said 'daughter' made Dorothy think. He knew them all, it wasn't just about what he could do to Dorothy, or Ruby. Or what he did to Billie.

'I'm sure the truth will come out.'

Webster raised his fist then paused.

'Fucking right, and I'll sue you for defamation. You think you can go around accusing decent cops of murder?'

'I haven't accused anyone of anything.' She wanted to say so much more, but she was scared.

'When they find the real killer, you're going to be sorry.'

She stared him down. 'I'll be glad when the murderer is brought to justice.'

'You think your actions don't have consequences?'

'We all deserve the truth.' Her voice shook but she didn't care.

'Try telling that to Benny, in a fucking coma because of you.'

'What are you talking about?'

'As if you don't know.' He spat on the ground near her feet. 'Benny Low was attacked two hours ago by some cunt in a balaclava, a hundred yards from St Leonard's. They were waiting for him coming off shift.'

'I didn't know.'

'Like fuck,' Webster said. 'I bet it was your boyfriend. He's gone off the deep end over this, gave me and Benny the bollocking of our lives when he chucked us off the case. Had to be restrained.'

'Thomas?'

'If Benny doesn't come out of that coma, I'm coming for you. Understand?'

Dorothy stared at him and thought about Thomas, then nodded.

58
HANNAH

Hannah got the story from Mina as they drove across town to Regent Terrace. Kirsty and Mina met Nadia a year ago at the Museum of Scotland at some evening function. Champagne was flowing and the spotlit exhibits created a weird atmosphere, according to Mina. Drinking and flirting amongst the Persian sculptures and other stolen spoils of empire got them all feeling frisky. That and the MDMA they'd all taken. Mina kissed Nadia amongst the Japanese artefacts, pressing her against a full samurai outfit while Kirsty watched. Then Kirsty joined in, the three of them getting down to it amongst the sarcophagi in the Ancient Egypt room.

There followed an intense affair, mostly the three together, but sometimes just Mina or Kirsty at Nadia's tiny apartment on Regent Terrace, with views to the back of Salisbury Crags. Her flat was on the top floor and she had access to the roof. They were interrupted up there mid-fuck more than once by neighbours. When they weren't on the roof, they were fucking in Regent Gardens, a private park backing onto Regent Terrace, one of the hidden spaces just for the rich in the middle of the city.

Mina didn't hold back on details. It seemed she and Kirsty liked to use younger, impressionable women. It wasn't too different from the way powerful men had always abused their status. The power imbalance was the thing, not gender or sexuality, and it stuck in Hannah's craw.

Mina bounced her Porsche over the cobbles and swung into Regent Terrace. This was five minutes' walk from the top of Easter Road, but a very different kind of Edinburgh.

Mina pressed the buzzer at number eight. Georgian stonework, big wide door, shutters over the windows. She tried Kirsty's phone again, voicemail. Then she tried Nadia's number, the same.

Hannah couldn't work out Nadia's plan, or Mina's. She thought about contacting Thomas, or Indy. But Mina had been clear about the police, and Indy would just tell her to come home immediately. She wasn't wrong, but Hannah had to see how this ended.

Mina pressed the buzzer again. What was she expecting, Nadia to let them in? She stepped back and looked up, then pressed the doorbell of next door and waited. An old woman appeared at the window, then disappeared. Mina pressed again. The woman opened the door and poked her nose out. Cashmere jumper, string of pearls, cadaverous cheeks.

'Sorry to bother you,' Mina said, trying to sound charming. 'I'm looking for a friend, Nadia North, lives on the second floor.'

'I remember you, and your girlfriend.' She virtually spat the last word out.

Mina's smile tightened.

'You led that girl astray.'

'Please,' Mina said in a strained voice.

'She's never been the same.'

Mina glanced at Hannah as if to say, look what I have to put up with.

'Have you seen her,' Mina said. 'It's rather urgent.'

The woman glanced at Hannah. 'Got your talons into another young thing?'

Mina sighed. 'She's a friend, and we're trying to find Nadia. Have you seen her?'

The woman gave Mina a withering stare.

Hannah smiled. 'It would actually be super-helpful if you knew anything.'

The woman stood still for so long Hannah thought there was a glitch in the matrix.

'Watch yourself with this one,' the woman said to Hannah.

Mina rolled her eyes.

'I will,' Hannah said. 'But Nadia could be in trouble. We want to help her.'

The woman stuck her chin out and looked both ways along the road.

'She was here earlier, which was quite unusual. I mean, I don't normally watch people's comings and goings.'

Mina couldn't help herself. 'I'll bet.'

The woman scowled. She wore powdery foundation that had rubbed away at her neck. She would look better without, she had a strong face.

'She was supposed to be at work,' the woman said, eyeballing Mina, 'but she came back at lunchtime with your fancy woman.'

'Was Kirsty OK?' Mina looked at the second-floor windows. 'Are they still in there?'

The woman shook her head. 'They left soon after, with a bag.'

Hannah nodded. 'Did you get a chance to speak to them?'

'I happened to be out here sweeping the step.'

'Did you speak to them or not?' Mina snapped.

The woman spoke to Hannah. 'Nadia said she was going back to work.'

Hannah frowned. That didn't make any sense. Why abduct someone at knifepoint, then take them to a museum?

Mina's eyes widened. 'I know where they are.'

59

JENNY

Jenny stared at the flames dancing in the dusk. Hannah had told her once how energy was never lost, only converted, chemical energy stored in wood from photosynthesis turned into heat and light. That girl could bring physics into anything, even toasting marshmallows. Jenny wondered what she was doing just now. Whatever it was, it was surely better than this.

She looked at Stella, shadows flickering on her face.

'Are you sure about this?'

Stella nodded.

The rest of the women were in their campers and caravans. A cold wind blew from the north and Jenny thought of the Cramond camp sheltering from the same wind, huddled against the world.

Stella pushed out of her camp chair. She picked up two shovels and held one out. 'Come on.'

Jenny stood and took the shovel. She wondered how she'd got to this. She'd become friends with Fiona, bonding over their shared abuse by Craig. Maybe this was similar, Stella could join their recovery group, Women Damaged by Craig.

Stella walked towards the woods by the disused railway sidings, shovel over her shoulder. Jenny felt the heft of her own shovel, the weight of what they were about to do.

She followed Stella and caught up with her at the first trees, elm and beech. The trees were close together and Jenny was glad they still had their leaves, they needed the cover. She imagined a dog walker stumbling over them, having to explain. According to Stella, the woods were inaccessible from the other side, high fences to stop kids getting onto the railway tracks back in the day. So the only way in was past the campers, and Stella had told them to intercept anyone.

Stella looked around. Jenny got her phone out and switched on the torch, pointed it at Stella then the trees.

'Do you know where he is?'

'Of course.' But her face wasn't as confident as her voice. She turned, feet shuffling through moss and leaves. There were no signs of human activity, no empty cans or used condoms. There were plenty of remote woods and derelict places where kids went to drink and fuck. She thought of Bill dogging on his estate, Ruby abused at Silverknowes. The woods had always been used for pervy shit.

'This way,' Stella said, heading east.

Jenny heard traffic in the distance, presumably Seafield Road. To her left she glimpsed something, realised it was a train of old rusted carriages, sitting on buckled tracks, yoked together like cattle waiting for slaughter.

Stella stopped and stared at the ground.

Jenny played the torch around the thicket. This was a good place to bury something you didn't want found. 'Here?'

Stella looked at the trees, then at the ground, then at Jenny. 'Here.'

She placed the shovel blade against the ground and leaned on it, pushing it into the soil. The air was clammy, the ground damp, easier to dig.

Jenny heard the rip and squelch of the shovel through wet earth. She placed the torch in the crook of a tree branch then joined Stella. She started digging, pushing her weight on the shovel, levering soil, tossing it to the side. Her calves burned with the first shovelfuls, but that stopped as she got into a rhythm, as the pile of earth grew beside them.

Their breath billowed in the torch beam. Jenny smelled dampness and mulch, saw worms wriggling on her shovel, slaters and centipedes too. All the bugs that live in the shadows of the world.

She could still hear faint car noise to the right. It was mad that this was possible in the heart of the city.

They dug for longer than she expected. Stella must've made sure Craig was buried deep enough that foxes or badgers couldn't get him. The sweat on Jenny's brow cooled in the night air, her arms aching, back grumbling. She thought they would go on forever, then she heard something, a plastic ruffle.

Stella stopped digging, turned her shovel and began scraping dirt away. Jenny did the same and saw the black plastic body bag. Stella dropped the shovel and got on her knees, scraped dirt with her hands. Jenny copied. The shape of the bag became clear. Stella scraped more earth, Jenny likewise. The reek was powerful. Jenny found a corner of the bag and pulled, lifting the plastic away in a shower of soil. Stella did the same at her end. They looked at each other and heaved upwards, earth falling as they lifted the bag onto the ground alongside.

Jenny was surprised how light he was. She wondered if this was an elaborate set up, Stella luring her into the woods to kill her. Craig somehow alive, the whole thing a massive con designed to destroy her.

But then she looked at Stella's face. No tears, just sorrow.

They sat on their haunches for a long time looking at the bag, their breath puffing in the torchlight. Jenny felt the dampness under her.

'I need to see him,' she said eventually.

Stella looked at her flatly. 'I know.'

Jenny examined the bag. The zip was at her end, teeth clogged with dirt. She brushed it, held the zip in one hand, the end of the bag in the other, and pulled.

Nothing.

She jiggled it, brushed more earth away, tried again.

It slid down, jerkily at first, then smoother.

She zipped it halfway. Sat for a moment. Then pulled the bag open.

Craig.

He was badly decomposed and discoloured. One of his eyes was gone, the other collapsed. His face was all sorts of dead colours, black and purple, brown and dark green, one ear putrefied. His scalp had rotted away, some hairs still clinging on. His mouth was open as if he was about to speak. The skin around his mouth was decayed, most of his lips gone.

She felt her pulse in her throat. It was still him, the man she loved once, who ruined her. Who she obsessed about for years. Hannah's fucking dad. Violet's son. Stella's brother.

She imagined him blinking his half-eye, lifting a hand to grab her, his mouth forming that cute smile. She remembered their wedding day, how fucking happy she was, till death they do part.

She reached down and touched his cheek. Like wrinkled fingers after the bath has gone cold. We're all just haunted meat, waiting to die.

She took her hand away and looked at Stella. She stared at her brother's face, and Jenny couldn't guess what she was thinking. We never know other people, no matter how hard we try.

Eventually Stella caught her eye and nodded.

Jenny zipped up the bag. 'Let's get him up the road.'

60

DOROTHY

She recognised a couple of people in the crowd outside BrewDog on Lothian Road, looked amongst them for Thomas. She spotted Griffiths, the officer who took Ruby's statement.

She touched her elbow. 'Hey, Zara?'

Zara looked surprised. 'Dorothy, right?'

Glances between her off-duty colleagues. Some no doubt knew about her and Thomas, how dare this old woman snare their silver-fox boss?

'They said at the station you were all at a leaving do.'

It was like she was checking up on her boyfriend, and she felt her cheeks flush. She checked the crowd for Webster, didn't see him. Low was in the hospital, but what about the other two who raped Ruby? It could be any of these young men in their shirts, chinos and slip-on shoes.

Zara looked around. 'Thomas was here earlier but I guess he must've slipped out. He doesn't usually stay, doesn't like to get too chummy with the rank and file.'

'Any idea where he would've gone?'

She looked at the three women she was with, then something occurred to her. 'Maybe he's gone to check on Benny in hospital. Did you hear about that?'

'Webster told me.'

'When did you see Don?'

'Never mind.'

Dorothy wondered. It was crazy to think Thomas would hurt Low. But just pretend for a minute he had, wouldn't Webster be next on the list?

'Was Webster supposed to be here?'

Zara nodded. 'Said he would be.'

There was a burst of laughter from a group of men nearby. Dorothy turned and they were smirking at her. She refused to be intimidated by a bunch of babies, but it still niggled. She felt the bruises on her arms where Webster had pinned her against the tree. The lads staring at her might not be rapists or murderers, but their bullshit came from the same place.

She turned back to Zara. 'If you see Thomas, get him to call me?'

One of the women sniggered and Dorothy glared at her then left. She walked up Lothian Road but stopped across Festival Square. She called Thomas again. Voicemail.

'Call me, it's important.'

She looked up and down the road, then opened the Find My Phone app. She and Thomas had set it up as a joke ages ago, never used it. She wondered if he still had his switched on.

The map showed her own phone, then zoomed out to display the whole of Edinburgh, and there he was in Cramond. Must be talking to Ruby.

She called Ruby, no answer. Tried Fara, the same.

She heard laughter from BrewDog, just drunk fun but ominous in the darkness.

She stepped into the road and hailed a cab. 'Cramond, please.'

The driver turned along the Western Approach Road, cut through Dalry and round Murrayfield Stadium, lit up like an alien spaceship. They went over the hill and turned left at The Mary Erskine School, down through Ravelston. Behind the high wall to the left was Corstorphine Hill, and she thought of the funerals they'd performed at the cemetery on the other side. Over Queensferry Road, past Lauriston Castle, and Dorothy felt the weight of history. People had lived here for thousands of years, trying to stay connected.

She checked the app. The dot now showed Thomas's phone at the beach. She tried all of their numbers again, nothing.

Then they were in Cramond, down the winding road to the shore. They chugged along until the river was in view. Dorothy paid and jumped out, looked up and down. No people. She heard waves lapping, the clunk of sailing boats in the river.

She walked round the corner, saw the small circle of caravans and campers, a fire burning in the middle. She noticed something else as she approached – no other noise. No conversations, no music, nothing.

She stood in the middle of the circle, feeling the heat from the fire, listening to the crackle.

Fara's campervan door was open. She went over and looked inside. Empty. She checked the other vehicles, the same. It was like the rapture had taken everyone up to heaven.

She called Fara one more time. Then Ruby. Then Thomas.

Checked the app again. Thomas's phone had moved from the beach to the island.

She looked at the dark mass of the island, silhouetted against the lights of Fife.

The tide was out and she made a decision.

61

HANNAH

Mina drove like a lunatic through the roadworks on North Bridge. She ran a red light into Chambers Street then swerved onto the cobbles of West College Street. At the top of the road she bumped onto the wide pavement, the underpass to Potterrow student union ahead, Old College behind. Hannah knew this part of town well from her early student days, before science students got shipped out to the King's Buildings campus.

Mina jumped out and Hannah followed.

'I don't understand, the museum's closed now.'

Mina spoke over her shoulder 'Not if you know a secret way in.'

She stopped at a doorway covered in graffiti. The smell from nearby bins was rancid, decaying food and piss. The doorway had a keypad alongside. Mina flipped it open then stood thinking. She keyed in a four-digit number, the red light blinked. She tried again, same. Third time she got it, the light went green and Hannah heard a click.

Mina hauled the door open. It was heavier than it looked, thick metal.

'Lucky they haven't changed it.'

They were in a corridor of dark-grey walls that ran two ways, ahead and to the right.

'Where the hell are we going?' Hannah said.

Mina couldn't decide, looked both ways. 'Have you ever wondered how big this place is?'

'How do you mean?'

'The museum takes up half of Chambers Street, fills out the

whole block to Potterrow. The bit that's open to the public is only a tiny fraction, there are hundreds of nooks and crannies.' She gave Hannah a look. 'Perfect for a bit of privacy.'

Hannah shook her head. 'You mean this was your little fuckpad with this woman?'

'You make it sound sordid.'

'I'm not *making* it sound like anything.'

Mina decided and pointed. 'This way.'

Hannah followed through a rabbit warren of narrow corridors. They passed rooms full of filing cabinets, a storeroom of stacked paintings in ornate frames, then a room of heating pipes and air-con controls.

Mina headed up some stairs and Hannah lost her bearings. They passed lift doors and a sign for a fire exit. More stairs, they must be high up now, but there were no windows.

Another door, another keypad. Mina punched in the number again and they were into a long, glass-fronted room looking over George IV Bridge to Greyfriars Kirkyard. They were high enough to see over the tenements to the church beyond.

'This way,' Mina said, pushing at a glass door. They were out-doors on a balcony, traffic noise in Hannah's ears. She glimpsed tourists at Bobby's statue as she followed Mina along the balcony. At the end there was a gate with another keypad, but it was all the same code and Mina was through.

They turned into a secluded section of balcony at the corner of the building, and there were Nadia and Kirsty at a table with two glasses of white wine. Kirsty's arms were slumped in her lap, her head to the side, the kitchen knife sitting on the table. Nadia looked younger out of her museum uniform, hair in a pony, Kickers on her feet.

Nadia smiled at Mina then Hannah. 'You found me then.'

Mina stepped forward. 'Let her go.'

Nadia picked up the knife and pointed it at Mina. 'Stop.'

Hannah stared at Kirsty. She'd barely reacted to them arriving.

Hannah tried to see her face, but she just stared at her lap. Behind her and Nadia was an extraordinary view of Edinburgh Castle, lit up in the evening. Hannah wondered how many Old Town places had little gems like this balcony secreted away.

'What is this about, Nadia?' Mina said with her hands out.

Nadia took a slug of wine and waved the knife like a sushi chef. 'This is about us.'

'Put the knife down and we can talk.'

Nadia smiled. 'Yeah, no, I'm not gonna do that.' She had a manic energy, nothing to lose.

Hannah took a step to the side to see Kirsty's face. 'What have you done to her?'

Nadia stared at Mina for a long time. She flicked the knife towards Hannah, but spoke to Mina. 'So this is your new fuck-puppet.'

Hannah held a hand out. 'I'm just a friend.'

'Sure,' Nadia said with a pout. 'I believe you.'

She stood up and her chair scraped against the concrete. Mina jumped at the sound and Hannah stepped forward and to the side.

Mina shook her head. 'You didn't answer Hannah's question, what have you done to her?'

Kirsty still hadn't looked up.

'Just a little adventure. It's your favourite drug after all.'

Hannah swallowed. 'Psilocybin.'

Nadia nodded. 'So they drugged you too.' She pointed the knife at the stars. 'Expand your mind, the overview effect, get a bit of fucking perspective.'

Mina took a breath. 'The police are on their way, Nadia. This is over.'

Nadia put on a smile. 'The police are not on their way, because you wouldn't want me to tell them about all the times you drugged and raped me.'

Mina looked shocked. 'We never did that. We took drugs, all of us, and had fun.'

'Fun for you, maybe. Fucking trauma for me.'

Mina held her hands out. 'Nadia, please, you're misremembering. We went our separate ways, that's all.'

Nadia's voice turned hard. 'Don't tell me what I remember. You abused me, like you abused others. Like you're abusing this poor girl.' The knife-edge glinted at Hannah.

Kirsty raised her head and looked around. Her pupils were wide and black. She stared at the castle then turned. 'Mina?'

'Kirsty, it's OK, just hang on.'

Kirsty looked at her for a long time but didn't speak.

'I just wanted you to have a taste of your own medicine,' Nadia said. 'How many women have you coerced like me? And you always get away with it.'

'Nadia, you've got us wrong, we're just open to new experiences.'

Nadia laughed. 'Tell that to my flashbacks and PTSD.' She held out the second glass of wine to Mina. 'Drink this.'

Mina shook her head.

Nadia took a step towards Kirsty. 'Drink it, or I'll gut her.'

'What's in it?'

'Does it matter?'

Hannah had stepped closer to Nadia while they talked.

Nadia held the wine out, the knife a foot from Kirsty's chest.

Mina put her hands out in appeasement, blinked too much. 'Nadia, please.'

Hannah was looking for a chance but the knife was too close to Kirsty.

'Drink.' Nadia thrust the glass out, a little spilling on her hand.

Kirsty looked at the glass then at the knife. She put her hand out and pressed her palm against the knife point, pushed hard so that the blade passed quickly through her hand and out the other side, blood squirting from the wound as she slid her palm to meet the handle. Nadia turned, horrified at the mess, and stepped away but Kirsty stood up, wobbled on her feet and fell towards her. The two of them stumbled from the table towards the edge of the balcony.

Hannah bolted towards them, Mina behind. Kirsty held Nadia's arm with one hand, her other hand still had the knife lodged in it, pulsing blood all over Nadia's chest, the two of them staggering next to the low balcony wall. Nadia pulled the knife out of Kirsty's palm in a bloody spurt, then pointed it at her throat. Hannah reached them and brought her fist down on Nadia's wrist, making the knife clatter over the edge.

Mina grabbed Kirsty and dragged her away as Nadia gripped Hannah. Their momentum took them to the edge of the roof. Hannah saw panic in Nadia's eyes as she fell backward. Hannah grabbed her wrist and yanked hard, pulling Nadia away from the ledge so that they fell on top of each other on the balcony.

Hannah pushed Nadia off her and sat up.

Mina was holding Kirsty, who had her hand in front of her face, blood streaming down her arm from the massive hole in her palm.

'I think I've cut myself,' she said.

62

DOROTHY

She was three quarters of the way along the causeway when she realised the tide was coming in. Water sloshed across the concrete in small rivulets, splashing against her shoes. She had her phone torch on, the beam playing over her wet feet, then into the darkness of the firth. She looked back at the mainland, streetlights and houses. She wouldn't make it back over there in time. She turned to face the island. Thomas was here.

She splashed on, legs cold and wet, torch beam bobbing as she started to run, her breathing controlled, trying not to panic. It was still a hundred yards and the water was at her knees, Christ it came in fast. She pushed harder, the current trying to pull her into the dragon's teeth. She stumbled over a pothole in the concrete, righted herself, flexed her ankle then went on. The water was at her thighs and she was heaving through, muscles burning.

She was fifty yards from the island, wading slowly, saltwater spraying her face, torch beam haphazard. She stumbled again and fell, head underwater, her lungs shocked from the cold, one arm down to push up from the concrete, her phone in her hand plunging below the surface before she struggled back to standing. Waves jostled her as she heaved her legs forward, up the slope and finally clear. She slumped on the sand and tried to get her breath back.

She looked at her phone, just a black screen. She tried switching it off and on again, got a blank white screen. She shook it, tried again, nothing. Did it again and got her home screen, took a shaky breath. The wind made her wet clothes stick to her. She stood up, tried to make a call, couldn't get service. She stared at the mainland. She had no idea where the nearest phone mast was. She got a flicker of service and checked Find My Phone. It took ages to connect, then showed Thomas's phone on the other side of the island amongst the old war battlements. Where Billie was found.

She looked back at Cramond. Thought about the police standing outside BrewDog laughing. Wondered about Webster, not there. She thought about Ruby, Fara and the rest. Where were they?

She looked at her phone, but the screen had blacked out again. She sighed and walked up the slope to the middle of the island. There was enough moonlight to see the path and she was careful with her footing.

She took the right-hand path at a fork and went past the first military building, covered in ivy, windows gone, crumbling cement exposing metal girders underneath. She looked inside just in case, but this wasn't where Thomas's location dot had been. She went along the path, which followed the contours of the land to a second building, a gun placement with a collapsed roof. No one there.

She saw a couple more buildings up ahead. She looked over to Fife, imagined all the people cosy in their houses.

A noise on her left made her stop, then she heard an owl calling, another responding from the woods.

She reached the third dilapidated building, which contained the wet remnants of a party, a torn sleeping bag, beer cans, soggy ash.

The next building was down the slope to the north shore. She climbed down, checking her phone, but it was still blank. She felt the chill through her wet clothes, goose pimples in the breeze. Her shoes squelched as she walked.

She reached the doorway and stopped, listened. Could hear waves by the shore, the call of a curlew.

She stepped inside, saw a small electric lamp on the floor, the outline of someone leaning against a concrete pillar in the centre of the room. She stepped round and saw it was Thomas, bruised eyes and smashed nose, drool and blood hanging from his mouth, head to the side.

'Thomas?'

He moved his head but didn't open his eyes.

'Well, hello.'

Dorothy jumped at Webster's voice behind her. She spun round and saw him step from the corner with a gun.

'I did warn you,' he said, smiling.

63

JENNY

Stella opened the van door and they stared at Craig's muddy body bag for a while.

'We should get him in,' Jenny said.

She had a flashback to a year ago, the same van parked in the same driveway. Stella committed assault and arson. But Jenny understood what grief could do. The hold Craig had over women – wives, girlfriends, sisters, mothers, daughters.

They each took an end of the bag and carried it between them. They reached the embalming-room entrance and Jenny pressed the door button. As it opened, she saw Archie and Brodie standing over a deceased's body, obviously working late.

Archie looked Stella up and down. 'What's she doing here?'

Brodie looked confused.

'She's fine.' Jenny glanced at Stella, who had her head down.

Archie stroked his beard then pointed at the bag. 'Is that who I think it is?'

'Yeah.'

'Why is he here?'

'We're doing his funeral.'

Archie stepped closer. 'Looks like he's already been buried.'

'Not officially.'

Archie looked at her, then Stella. 'Right.'

Jenny's arms were tired and she shifted her weight. 'We need to put him in one of the fridges.'

Archie turned to the wall of fridge doors. 'Number eight.' He walked over and opened the door, slid a tray out.

Jenny and Stella carried Craig over, then hoisted him onto the shelf with a thud. Loose mud scattered on the floor.

Archie sucked his teeth. 'What sort of state is he in?'

Stella rested a hand on the shelf. 'Not great.'

Brodie was still standing at the other body. Jenny wanted to explain that it wasn't every day she brought dug-up corpses into the business.

Archie went to push the tray into the fridge but Stella stopped him.

'Just a minute.'

She rested a hand on the bag, dirt under her fingernails. She closed her eyes and breathed. 'OK.'

Archie slid the body away and closed the door. Wrote *Craig McNamara* on the little whiteboard on the door in black marker.

Jenny pointed to the door. 'Where's Mum?'

'I presumed she was with you or Thomas.'

Jenny got out her phone. Called Dorothy, voicemail. Thomas, same. She checked where Dorothy's phone was on the app, Cramond Island. Thought about Hannah finding Billie there. Imagined how dark it must be at this time of night. She called Fara then Ruby, no answer. Then Hannah.

She picked up eventually.

'Hey,' Jenny said. 'Have you heard from Gran?'

Conversations and bustle in the background. 'No.'

'Are you OK?'

'I'm at A&E.'

Jenny felt sick. 'Why?'

Hannah sighed. 'I'm fine. It's OK.'

'What happened? Is Indy with you?'

'Yeah, we're here with Kirsty.' A pause. 'It's a long story, and I don't feel like getting into it. She'll be OK. But I have to hang around to give a statement to the police.'

'What?'

'Like I said, long story. What's this about Gran?'

Jenny looked at the fridge door with Craig's name. Reached out and felt the cold metal. Hannah's dad inside. Something else they would have to get into, but not right now.

'Probably nothing,' Jenny said. She didn't want to add to Hannah's worries.

'Mum, you wouldn't be ringing if you thought it was nothing.'

Jenny ran a hand through her hair. 'I checked the app, her phone is in Cramond.'

'She's probably talking to Fara or Ruby.'

'No, on the island. And I can't get hold of Fara or Ruby.'

Silence.

'Maybe you should call the police,' Hannah said.

Jenny turned away from the others in the embalming room.

'Webster and Low are the police,' she said quietly.

More silence down the line, then Hannah spoke. 'I'll meet you there.'

'What about your astronaut?'

'This is more important. I'll be there as soon as I can.'

Hannah ended the call and Jenny looked round the room. 'Who wants to come to Cramond Island?'

64

DOROTHY

'This is over,' Dorothy said. She couldn't see much of Webster in the gloom, but she felt hate radiating from him. She wasn't sure what she meant by what she'd said. His career, his life, maybe hers too, and Thomas's. It would all be over soon one way or another. This too shall pass.

He strode forward and grabbed her hair, brought the butt of the gun down on her face. She tried to raise an arm to block it but pain seared across her cheek. Blood spurted from a cut at the corner of her eye and she was struggling to breathe. He brought the gun down again, this time on the side of her nose. She heard a crack and blood dripped into her mouth.

He yanked her hair so that she staggered and fell next to Thomas at the pillar. She raised her hands to her face. Touched her nose and it felt like a knife was slicing it. She laid a finger on the cut at her eye, so much blood. She tried to concentrate on something other than pain, the damp concrete under her, the metal taste of blood, the smell of seaweed and salt, the low buzz of the electric lamp.

'Thomas.' She reached out and touched his face. He leaned into her fingers. His face was bloody and beaten, a pulpy mess. 'It's OK.'

Webster laughed.

She turned.

He was on his haunches a couple of feet away, the gun in his hand like he didn't need it. She tried to see some compassion or reason in his face, but couldn't make anything out.

'It's not going to be OK,' Webster said eventually.

'There's still a way out of this for you.'

He put on a smile and waved the gun at Thomas. 'Oh, I know, it's just not the way out you want.'

Dorothy saw that Thomas's arms were behind his back around the pillar, secured by handcuffs. She looked at his body, no bullet holes or bleeding wounds, nothing obviously broken.

She wanted to say something to Webster. He was right, of course, the only way out for him now was to kill them both and cover it up.

'People are coming,' she said.

'We both know that's not true.'

He sat down across from her. She wondered at his confidence. She thought about lunging for the gun but he would shoot her easily. She was dizzy with pain, struggling to breathe.

'OK, I'll play along,' Webster said. 'Who's coming to save you?'

'The police.'

He laughed. 'I am the police, did you forget?'

Dorothy shook her head and regretted it as pain shot through her cheek. She wiped blood from her lip. 'There are good police officers. Thomas told them he was coming here. They'll be here soon.'

Webster faked a yawn. 'Thomas didn't tell anyone, I brought him here. And as for other police, I know they're not coming.'

'How?'

Webster shrugged. 'Because someone would let me know.'

'The other officers who raped Ruby.'

Webster's grip on the gun tightened. 'That wasn't fucking rape, how many times do I have to tell you?'

'You coerced Ruby into oral sex, that's rape.'

He backhanded her across the face. Tears sprang to her eyes and she felt her heart in her throat.

'Let's just agree to disagree. I'm sure the courts would see it my way, not that it'll ever come to that.'

Dorothy blinked away tears. 'That's why there's no one at the camp. Your partners rounded them up.'

Webster nodded in approval. 'You're smart for an old bird. Just routine enquiries into the murder of a vulnerable young woman.'

'You killed her.'

Webster placed the barrel of the gun against his cheek in contemplation, then wiggled it in the air. 'She was alive when we left her.'

'Bullshit.'

'It doesn't matter what you think. No one cares.'

'My family cares,' Dorothy said. 'They know I came here, they'll find me.'

Webster sighed and stood up, went to the window. 'I don't see anyone.' He cupped a hand to his mouth. 'Hello?'

His voice echoed around the walls as he mimicked listening for a reply.

He walked back to Dorothy and Thomas. 'Even if they did know you were here, and they were coming, how the fuck would they get on the island? The tide's in for the next six hours.'

Dorothy glanced at Thomas and tried to think. He needed medical attention, they both did. She still had her phone in her pocket, but it wasn't working properly. Maybe she could get it to work. But she still had to overpower Webster and that seemed impossible. But she and Thomas could hold on. As long as they stayed alive, there was hope. She needed to keep this going until she had an opening.

'Why?' she said softly.

He leaned down, pretending he hadn't heard. 'I beg your pardon?'

Dorothy pointed at Thomas. 'Why are you doing this to him?'

'Because he fucked my boy Benny.'

'He didn't do that.'

'Of course he did. Who else?'

'Thomas doesn't have a violent bone in his body.'

'Maybe that's what you see,' Webster said, kneeling down. 'But I see a vindictive, woke prick, obsessed with doing the right thing.

Always taking the criminals' side over his own force. Fucking sickens me, to be honest. He took us off Billie's case on the word of that fucking slag.'

'My daughter saw you with Ruby.'

'She loved it then changed her mind. Went running to our boss, put our jobs on the line.'

'This isn't about your jobs, this is about having power over others.'

Webster's eyes went wide. 'We are the fucking law, what is it you don't understand about that?'

'That doesn't mean you can do whatever you want.'

Webster roared with laughter. 'That's exactly what it means.'

Dorothy tried to keep her voice calm. 'Is that why you killed Billie?'

'Why the fuck should I tell you anything?'

'Why not? You said yourself, I'm not going anywhere.'

Webster looked round the room, considering this. He waved the gun. 'It just escalated. We were having fun with her, like Ruby, then she got cold feet, threatened to go to our boss. The fire was a warning, but that just made things worse. In the end, we had to deal with her.'

'By raping and murdering her.'

'You still don't understand how the world works, at your age. I feel sorry for you.'

'No, *I* feel sorry for *you*.'

Webster's smile faded. He leaned forward and shoved the gun muzzle into Dorothy's cheek. She could smell the cold metal.

'You don't get to feel sorry for me,' he said. 'Understand?'

His finger trembled on the trigger and for the first time since she got on the island, Dorothy thought she was going to die.

65

HANNAH

The taxi turned the corner at the shore and Hannah saw Jenny, Archie and Brodie standing by the hearse.

'Bit late for a funeral,' the driver said with a nervous laugh.

She paid and jumped out, ran to Mum and the others. They were by the water, waves lapping over the causeway. To their right, Fara's camp looked empty.

'No one there,' Archie said. 'We checked.'

Hannah frowned. 'How could they all be gone?'

Archie shrugged.

'Where's Gran?' Hannah looked at the causeway. Only the tops of the dragon's teeth were showing, which meant it was at least seven feet deep.

Jenny stared at her phone then pointed at the island. 'Over there, I think. The signal comes and goes.'

'She's not answering?'

Jenny shook her head.

'And no Thomas?'

Another head shake.

'How about the coastguard?'

Jenny mulled that over. 'They'll take too long to get here.'

Hannah kicked at the ground.

Brodie cleared his throat. 'We could steal a boat.'

Everyone stared at him.

He pointed at the sailing boats lined up on the other side of the estuary. 'Take one of those.'

'Do you know how to sail?' Jenny said.

'They've got motors,' Brodie said.

Jenny gave him a look and Archie smiled.

Hannah walked to the riverbank and the others followed.

'How do you steal one? Do you need keys, do they have security?'

Brodie stripped off his hoodie, trainers and jeans then dived into the water, his long body arching through the air. He surfaced and swam through the river until he was at the nearest boat. He grabbed the edge and pulled himself up, shoulder muscles tightening. He levered into the boat then searched in the back.

Hannah heard an engine splutter into life, then Brodie looked up with a grin and waved. He pressed some buttons on a box near the stern, then unwound the rope that was tying the boat to a metal cleat and threw it onto the deck. He grabbed the tiller and angled it, revved the engine and brought the boat over the estuary, expertly turning it alongside them. He gathered the rope and threw it ashore.

'Pull,' he said.

Archie pulled until the hull was next to the bank, then held it in place. Brodie put out a hand and Hannah handed him his clothes then skipped into the boat. Jenny followed more cautiously, then Archie did the same, bringing the loose rope with him.

'So we're stealing a boat,' Jenny said.

They left the shelter of the mainland and the wind whipped around them, Hannah pulling her jacket collar tight. She couldn't believe she was here. A couple of hours ago she was on a museum roof, trying to talk down a crazy woman. Then at the hospital with Kirsty, staring at the hole in her hand. She'd left Mina and Indy there, waiting while Kirsty was in surgery. Indy had protested at Hannah leaving, of course, but she'd insisted.

Brodie passed the tiller to Archie and gave him instructions while he pulled his clothes back on.

They approached the west side of the island, Jenny's face lit up by the app on her phone.

'Her signal's flickering on the northeast side.'

Hannah felt the cold whip through her. 'That's where I found Billie, in one of the ruined buildings.'

Jenny stared at her, then at Brodie. 'Quick as you can.'

He gunned the engine and they ploughed through the waves, rounded the northwest corner. They nearly ran straight into some weird outflow pipe, Brodie seeing it last minute in the dark and swerving so that they were thrown around.

Jenny pointed towards the cluster of buildings, visible as outlines against the sky. Brodie manoeuvred the boat towards shore but there were only rocks, no beach. Stone scraped along the hull and Brodie navigated away. Eventually Hannah spotted a gravel beach and Brodie headed for it. When he was close, Archie jumped out and waded ashore with the rope, tied it around a boulder. He pulled the rope until the boat ran aground on gravel, then the rest jumped into the wash, cold sending shivers through Hannah's body.

The four of them stood on the shore and looked up the slope. A huddle of small buildings, some with their roofs collapsed. A gnarly path split left and right.

'Which way?' Hannah said.

Jenny looked at her phone. 'Her signal's gone.'

'Let's go in pairs, we'll find her quicker if we split up.'

Jenny looked at the two men, then at Hannah. 'I don't like it.'

'It makes sense,' Archie said.

'Me and Brodie this way,' Hannah said. 'You take Archie.'

Brodie looked to Jenny for confirmation. Eventually she nodded.

'Let's go,' Hannah said, touching Brodie's arm.

66

DOROTHY

She held eye contact with him. Her heart was chaos in her chest, the gun muzzle pushed into her cheek, her body trembling. Webster's hands shook too, and she wondered if the gun would go off by mistake.

He closed his eyes and she thought about snatching the gun or knocking it from his hand. But before she had a chance to do anything he opened his eyes and sat back. She felt the ghost of the gun still against her cheek. Her hand went to her eye, the blood there had slowed. She touched her nose, ragged pain.

She turned to Thomas. He'd passed out and she wondered what internal injuries he might have. It didn't take much, the wrong knock to the head and it was over. Life can end fast, she'd learned that in the funeral business, we're all on a knife-edge the whole time.

'He was useless,' Webster said, pointing the gun at Thomas.

'What do you mean?'

'I wanted him to confess to assaulting Benny, but the cunt didn't say anything, just kept passing out from the pain. Low threshold, obviously. Should've guessed as much, from an old lefty like him. Never had to face the real world, never had to toughen up. Fuck knows how he became a cop.'

Dorothy looked between the two men. Both police officers, somehow.

Webster said he would be alerted if the police received a call about this. And someone had rounded up Fara and the rest. Who knows how far this went? Surely the young women officers outside BrewDog earlier couldn't be a part of this. And plenty of male officers must find this shit repulsive. But were they strong enough to stand up to it? Bullies get their way because they intimidate, because folk are scared. Same everywhere.

'How did you become a cop?' Dorothy said.

Webster stood up and wagged a finger. 'Don't be so fucking obvious.'

'What?'

'You're just trying to buy time.'

Dorothy tried to smile and her face hurt. 'So, indulge me, Don.'

The use of his first name made Webster suck his teeth. 'Fuck off, you don't get to analyse me. You think my abusive dad drove me to become a hardnut? I've seen the fucking cop dramas, I'm not an idiot. The cycle of abuse, blah, blah, blah, that shit is so reductive.'

Dorothy shifted her weight, stiff from sitting on concrete. Could she overpower a young man with a gun? She couldn't run, if she left Thomas behind, Webster would kill him.

'I only asked how you came into the force, that's all. Then you started talking about abuse.'

Webster grinned. 'I liked the uniforms, how about that? Why don't you tell me how you got into funerals?'

Dorothy made a show of thinking about it. She heard Thomas groan, then something else. It might've just been the wind outside, or a rat, or the waves on the shore. She thought about her phone still in her pocket. She traced Thomas, so maybe others had traced her. But that was a pipe dream, no one would miss her until morning. She had to do this herself.

'I try to help people,' she said, 'but that's not why I got into it. My husband inherited the company. Some things are just accidents.'

Webster hadn't been listening. He went to the window. 'Did you hear something?'

'No.'

He peered out the open window frame.

There was a noise behind Dorothy, footsteps on concrete.

She turned and saw Hannah, and her heart sank. The last thing she wanted was more people she loved in danger. Hannah had her finger to her lips and was creeping forward. Dorothy shook her head, but didn't speak. Webster was still leaning out the window, then Hannah stood on a leaf and the noise made him turn back.

Hannah ran at him but he ducked out the way and grabbed her, punched her hard in the stomach, then brought the gun down on the back of her head so that she crumpled to the floor.

He took a step back and stared at her. 'What the fuck? Did you arrive same time as your gran?'

He waved the gun around the room.

'What a parade of pathetic wankers. You think caring about other people's feelings will help you now? Maybe if one of you had learned self-defence or looked after your own interests, you wouldn't be in this fucking mess.'

Webster stepped towards them. Behind him, Dorothy saw two hands appear on the window ledge, then Brodie's face as he pulled himself onto the ledge. He crouched there taking in the scene.

'It's your own fault,' Webster said, pointing the gun at Dorothy.

Brodie jumped into the room and the sound made Webster turn. Brodie heaved his shoulder into the bigger man, knocking them both over. Webster tried to point the gun at Brodie's back but Brodie punched his stomach, making Webster double over. Dorothy pushed herself up from the floor and staggered towards them. She swung her boot at Webster's hand and connected with the gun, which skittered across the concrete.

Webster threw Brodie off and scuttled towards the gun, but Dorothy got there first and kicked it further away. Brodie ran and reached for it but Webster piled into him, shoving him against the wall and pinning his throat. Dorothy lunged for the gun and grabbed it, her hands shaking. She fired a warning shot into the wall and the bang rattled her brain.

Webster eased the pressure on Brodie and turned to Dorothy. She pointed the gun at him and he smiled.

'Well.' He took a step towards her.

'Stay where you are.'

He put his hands out as if to surrender but kept walking, one step, another.

'Stay there or I'll shoot.'

He smiled at her and lunged for the gun. She pulled the trigger and the noise was deafening. She'd closed her eyes but opened them now. Webster stood in front of her, his stomach a bleeding mess. He looked down and put a hand to it, which came away red. He stared at Dorothy in disbelief, then dropped to his knees.

67

HANNAH

The sight of Thomas in the hospital bed made Hannah feel sick. She couldn't imagine how it made Gran feel. Dorothy stared at him with a vacant look. Nothing was broken, just a lot of bruising and blood loss. They'd pumped him full of morphine, so he'd be out for a while. He looked old.

Webster had survived, but only just. Emergency surgery had patched up his stomach, and he was somewhere else in this building, starting the long road to recovery.

Webster aside, four of them had been admitted to hospital last night, thanks to the coastguard – Thomas, Dorothy, Hannah and Brodie. She and Brodie were released straight away, then gave statements to an incredulous DS Griffiths. Gran had shot a police officer, after all.

Archie and Jenny came to the ERI too, and Indy was still there with Kirsty and Mina. It seemed like half their lives were spent in hospitals and police stations. Hannah longed for a time when she could just study, help with the odd funeral, maybe take on a simple missing cat case or something. But nothing was ever simple for the Skelfs.

The others had gone home for sleep, but Dorothy insisted on staying with Thomas, and Hannah insisted on staying with Dorothy. Gran had had her nose reset and been given painkillers, plus a few butterfly stitches for the cut on her eye. Hannah wasn't worried about the physical scars.

It had helped their discussion with Griffiths that Thomas stayed conscious long enough to give his account. Webster forced him at gunpoint to the island, intent on killing him in revenge for Low, in the same place he and the others killed Billie. A power trip out of control, believing they were untouchable.

Dorothy had her eyes closed and started to sway. She reached out to the bed to steady herself.

Hannah went and held her. 'You're exhausted.'

'I'm fine.'

Hannah rubbed her arms, then pulled over a chair and made her sit. 'If you insist on staying, you can sleep here.'

Dorothy's smile was full of sadness. Hannah had seen that before, when Grandpa died.

'How did I get such a smart granddaughter?' Dorothy said, making herself comfortable.

'I learned from the best.'

'I hope you mean your mum.'

'And you.'

Dorothy rested her hand on Thomas's and closed her eyes. Hannah hoped she would sleep. If she did, Hannah hoped she didn't dream of Webster.

❦

She was spaced from lack of sleep but still buzzing with adrenaline. She watched Indy stir sugar into her latte. They needed sugar and caffeine to keep going. Hannah leaned her head on Indy's shoulder. She felt bad, putting Indy through all this. Hannah had been through two kinds of crazy shit in the last twenty-four hours, and her main concern was her wife's feelings.

'You OK?' Indy said.

'I will be.'

Hannah looked at the Söderberg breakfast crowd, all pastries and chatter. She gazed down Middle Meadow Walk and saw Kirsty and Mina coming towards them. The morning was clear and crisp, a sharp bite to the wind. Kirsty held on to Mina for support. Hannah thought of her and Indy, Dorothy and Jenny, always holding each other up.

Hannah waved for them to sit. Kirsty's hand was heavily bandaged and she placed it in her lap, as if ashamed. Mina rested her hand on top of it.

'Hey,' Indy said.

Mina nodded. 'Hi.'

Kirsty had her head down, no eye contact. Hannah wondered about her dosage. Hannah's own psylocibin trip had long aftereffects. Kirsty looked completely hollowed out.

'How are you?' she said to her.

Kirsty nodded but kept her head down.

A waitress came and asked for any orders, but Mina waved her away and cleared her throat. 'We wanted to say thank you.'

Hannah pressed her lips together and felt Indy squeeze her hand. 'OK.'

Mina glanced up and down the Walk. 'If it wasn't for you, God knows what would've happened.'

Indy leaned forward. 'And if it wasn't for you, my wife wouldn't have been in danger.'

Kirsty raised her head. Her eyes were bloodshot, pupils tiny. She looked around the table and settled on Hannah. 'I'm sorry.'

'You could've mentioned it,' Indy said. 'That you had a mad ex-girlfriend.'

'We didn't think...' Kirsty trailed off and lowered her head.

'How's your hand?' Hannah said.

Kirsty frowned. 'Sore.'

Mina looked at her. 'They gave her something in hospital to help her come down, but said it could take a while. Nadia wouldn't say how much she gave her. But I'll take care of her.'

Hannah touched her ear. 'What about Nadia?'

'Awaiting psychiatric assessment.'

'Was it all her? The online trolling too?'

Mina shook her head. 'Just the stuff at the house. When we were seeing her, she never knew where we lived, we always met at her place or the museum. She didn't take it well when we finished it.

Then, when we got doxxed, she started the harassment campaign. Just wanted to make us sweat, I think, especially Kirsty. She was obsessed with her astronaut girlfriend, thought she had a piece of celebrity or something. Then it just escalated, classic stalker stuff.'

'Why?'

Mina swallowed heavily. 'You heard her, she's not well, needs help.'

Hannah wondered about that. This surely must've warned them about treating other women like shit.

'What about her accusations?' Hannah said.

Mina stared at her. 'We never did anything like that. I swear to God.'

Hannah wondered if Nadia had any evidence, how it might play out. 'Really?'

Mina stared at her for a long time, but Hannah didn't flinch. 'Really.'

Hannah thought about how they'd groomed her in similar fashion, what Nadia had said on the rooftop.

'What will they charge her with?'

Mina shook her head. 'To be honest, I wasn't listening. I just want this to go away, I want to get back to normal.'

Hannah wondered what 'normal' meant for these two. She looked at Kirsty, staring at her bandaged hand like a lost child.

'We'd better go,' Mina said, touching Kirsty's arm. Kirsty flinched. Mina turned to Hannah. 'Thank you. I mean it.'

Hannah spoke to Kirsty as she stood up. 'Take care, Kirsty.'

The look in her eyes made Hannah squirm. Spaced out but more than that. All this shit about the overview effect, some sense of wonder, a feeling you were part of an interconnected universe, cosmic rays and neutrinos, solar bursts and supernovae, dark matter and black holes, animals and plants and mountains and caves and oceans and dirt. Hannah already felt connected to all that without going into space. It was all right here.

Kirsty smiled weakly and let herself be led away.

68

JENNY

Another day, another funeral. But this wasn't just anyone, this was the final goodbye to the man who dominated her life for years.

Jenny looked around the chapel extension. There were six of them standing in a circle around the resomator and Craig's body on the gurney. Hannah looked wiped out. This was her dad, after all. Jenny felt her heart break as she looked at her daughter struggle. It was a stupid idea to do this today, given that most of them hadn't slept and everything they'd been through. But she'd talked it over with Stella, and they both wanted an end as soon as possible. Stella's face was like stone, mouth in a hard line. She'd lost her mother, father and brother.

Dorothy stood next to her, still in shock. She was obviously worried about Thomas, no doubt chewing over Webster. Jenny wished she couldn't relate, but she'd been through similar with the man on the gurney, using his power to get what he wanted. Jenny had asked Dorothy if she wanted to talk, but it was too raw. Jenny understood.

It was useful that Thomas was still in hospital. The police didn't know about Jenny finding Stella and Craig. Dorothy had stuck to her word and not said anything to Thomas. Stella was a victim like everyone else, it'd taken Jenny a long time to understand that. Stella might face repercussions, but Jenny would do all she could to help. For a start, the police would never know about Craig's body.

Also in the chapel were Archie, Brodie and Indy, the Skelfs' support network.

Jenny pulled the *netsuke* fox from her pocket and stroked it. Archie smiled at her and she smiled back.

She looked at Brodie. He was embarrassed about being hailed a hero for last night, and Jenny liked that he didn't want to be in the limelight. He was still crashing in the studio upstairs.

She turned to Craig's body wrapped in a white, biodegradable sheet. She and Stella had seen his rot and decay, Hannah didn't need that image of her dad.

Jenny cleared her throat. 'Does anyone want to say anything?'

She'd looked forward to this moment for so long, it felt like a dream.

Stella swallowed and stared at the ground.

Hannah shook her head and took Indy's hand.

'OK,' Jenny said. 'Goodbye, Craig, rest in peace.'

She opened the resomator door. Archie, Brodie and Indy helped her lift Craig's body into the machine. It felt like loading your washing at a launderette. Once he was inside, Jenny closed the door and Indy made sure everything was in order.

'Do you want to do it?' Jenny said to Stella, pointing at the green button that started the water cremation.

Stella shook her head.

'Hannah?'

Another head shake.

'OK.' Jenny pressed the button.

The whoosh of water jets filled the room, steam billowing into the capsule, rivulets of water running down the window. Jenny could see Craig's winding sheet soaked through. She half-expected him to sit up and lunge for the door, escape again, trailing the sheet, leaving wet footprints for her to follow.

But he just lay there, finally at rest.

❦

Schrödinger stalked along the large hedge, following a scent. Birds warned each other about his presence. Just another day of danger for them.

Jenny sat on the bench and watched Hannah inside the wind phone. She'd been talking to her dad for ten minutes, sometimes animated, other times with her head bowed. Indy was keeping an eye on the resomator, Brodie and Archie were back at work, Dorothy had taken the van to Cramond.

Stella sat in the open door of her van, drinking tea and looking at the sky. She'd already spent a few minutes in the wind phone before Hannah.

Eventually Hannah came out of the box, wiping her eyes. Jenny rose and wrapped her arms around her. She wanted Hannah to be a baby again, or five, ten, fifteen years old, with a problem Jenny could fix. She missed those days, though they were stressful. But at least she felt like a mum, like she had purpose, some answers. Having an adult daughter meant not having answers and she felt the emptiness of that.

They hugged for a long time, Jenny smelling her daughter's sweat, feeling the greasiness of her hair. They all needed a bath and a week's sleep. But life goes on, until it doesn't.

Hannah pulled away and nodded at the wind phone. 'Do you want to have a go?'

Jenny looked at the white box and shook her head. 'I've said everything I want to him.'

And she hugged Hannah all over again.

69

DOROTHY

She was thirty yards from the caravans when Fara spotted her and ran, barrelling into her with a hug. Dorothy let herself be held. Eventually she tried to pull away, but Fara clung on.

'A little longer.'

Dorothy held the other woman, felt her energy.

'OK,' Fara said eventually, stepping back. 'Thank you.'

'I'm not sure I did anything.'

Fara shook her head. 'No, you did everything, I spoke to Griffiths earlier. They'll be prosecuted.'

Dorothy pictured the gun blazing, Webster's bloody stomach, the surprised look on his face.

'There's a long way to go,' Dorothy said.

'You have to start somewhere.'

Dorothy looked at the caravans and campers. 'Where's Ruby?'

'Sleeping, I gave her something after last night. We spent hours in police vans, they never took us to the station. That's when I knew it was bullshit. If they wanted to arrest or question us, they would've done it at the station.'

'Ruby has identified the other officers?'

Fara nodded. 'Griffiths has the ear of someone higher up, your man had something to do with it. I hope this will be taken seriously.'

Dorothy thought about Thomas in hospital, trying to do the right thing.

'And what about Parker?' she said. 'He assaulted Low, right?'

Low had come out of his coma and said as much last night.

'We haven't seen him. He's gone to ground.'

Dorothy sighed. 'That's a mistake. He needs to admit what he did.'

'If he did it.'

Dorothy gave her a look and she nodded.

'I know. He was angry about Billie, but that's no excuse.'

Out on the water, two sailing boats were heading to Port Edgar. Dorothy stared at the island and remembered walking over there in the dark, alone. Stupid, but she was still here.

'I can't imagine,' Fara said, following her gaze.

Dorothy thought about Webster's family and friends. She didn't want to know if he was married or had kids. Imagine a wife finding out what he'd done. Or maybe she wouldn't believe it, maybe she would stand by him.

'Want a cup of tea?' Fara said.

'No, I have a lot to do.' Dorothy glanced at the camp. 'What about you guys?'

Fara raised her eyebrows. 'We like it here, despite everything.'

Dorothy nodded.

'There's one other thing,' Fara said, glancing at the island. 'When you're ready. We need someone to do Billie's funeral.'

Dorothy followed her gaze. 'Out there?'

Fara placed her palm on her heart. 'I promise we'll pay attention to the tides next time.'

✤

It was hard to look at Thomas, beaten down and in pain. If she hadn't done Arlo's funeral, if she hadn't taken the arson case, maybe Webster wouldn't have murdered Billie. If Jenny hadn't seen what they did to Ruby, if she hadn't told Thomas, he wouldn't be in hospital. But she couldn't think like that, these men had to be held to account. Ruby said Billie tried to report her own rape to the police, the reason for the arson in the first place, a warning. The fact there was no record of her initial complaint was something else that needed investigating.

Thomas saw her in the doorway. 'Hey.'

She came and stood by his bed, squeezed his hand. Leaned down and kissed him. He closed his eyes longer than a blink, squeezed her hand back.

'I'm sorry,' he said. 'For everything.'

'You have nothing to apologise for.'

He cleared his throat. 'That's not true, they were under my command.'

'You're not responsible for everything that happens.'

'Of course I am, the buck stops with me.'

Dorothy held his gaze. 'Listen to me, that's bullshit. The buck stops with the men who do bad things.'

'But they felt they could,' Thomas said, voice croaky.

Dorothy shook her head and held his hand tighter that she should. 'You're a good man, Thomas Olsson.'

He didn't reply, just avoided her gaze. Her heart tightened.

He struggled to swallow, looked at a glass of water on the bedside table. 'Can you?'

She passed it to him. He took it with shaky hands, brought it to his lips, handed it back.

'I'm the one who should be sorry,' Dorothy said.

'Maybe we stop playing the blame game.'

'Good idea.'

He seemed to gather some strength. 'I've handed in my notice.'

She stayed silent for a while. 'Are you sure?'

'It's been a long time coming. I don't have a place there, not after this.'

She wanted to say so much, but also didn't see the point. Maybe he was right, he usually was. 'It's your decision. Just ... keep talking to me, OK? We need to keep talking.'

He nodded and squeezed her hand.

She saw the time on the wall clock.

'Sorry, honey,' she said. 'I have a funeral to go to.'

꠸

The chapel was full and so was her heart. They were here to pay their last respects to Johnny Sullivan. Brodie had done an amazing job. There were seventy mourners, none of whom had ever met Johnny, or even heard of him a week ago. This was the community Brodie had rustled up at short notice for the first of their communal funerals. There was a smattering of older people around Johnny's age, but also lots of younger faces in the diverse crowd.

The Multiverse had set up in the opposite corner from the resomator. They'd finished with Craig earlier, his ashes in the preparation room. Stella was here at the back, smiling at a young mother with two toddlers. Dorothy loved that someone had brought their kids. We should all learn that death was part of life, the part that made it worth living.

Brodie, Archie, Indy, Hannah and Jenny sat in the front row along with Natalya from the council.

Dorothy looked at Johnny's body, wrapped in a white sheet, ready to go into the machine. She cleared her throat.

'Thank you all for coming, it's hugely appreciated. None of us knew Johnny Sullivan but I hope he would've liked that so many people came to his funeral. We know very little of Johnny's life except he was born and raised in Leith and joined the merchant navy, which he sailed with for many years. He had no family, and we can only assume he lost contact with friends along the way. But he was a valued member of our community all the same.

'I hope he wasn't lonely in life. I looked up the opposite of "lonely" and there isn't a satisfactory word in English. "Popular" isn't right, neither is "accompanied". "Neighbourly" is a little better, or "connected". At least they give a sense of community, a sense that we are part of something. I hope Johnny felt that in his life. Being connected, being a part of something other than yourself, is the most important thing. But it's a hard thing to accomplish. We tend to close down as we get older, shut off the opportunities to engage with the world. That's understandable, but it's to our immense detriment. I hope Johnny lived a good life, an enjoyable life, a life he didn't feel was wasted. *We* know it wasn't wasted. He was a part of this great human experiment, as vital as any other. As all of us.'

She looked round the room, then at Johnny.

'Goodbye, Johnny Sullivan. Be at peace as you return to the energy of the universe.'

Will in the band started playing the riff as Dorothy walked over and got behind the drumkit. The choir were clapping along to the guitar and bass as Dorothy joined in on the kit, a roll around the toms and into the simple dance shuffle. They were playing 'Since I Left You' by The Avalanches, a laidback, patchwork summer groove that was irresistibly joyous. The choir sang the hook as Maria laid down piano parts and Gillian gave little hits on the trumpet. The original was all samples, so this sounded nothing like it, but glorious all the same. They broke it down and built it back up, feeding off each other's energy. The choir vamped around the hook, ad-libbed harmonies and overlapping lines, running through and over each other.

The music pushed through Dorothy's skin to her heart, echoed in her lungs and ribs, moved through the air around them, connecting everyone to each other, to Johnny Sullivan, to all the other people, dead and alive, who'd ever passed through here.

Dorothy looked around the chapel. Smiles on faces, feet tapping, hands clapping, hips moving. The young mum danced with her toddlers in the aisle and others joined in, an older couple dancing ballroom style, the music swelling and ebbing and flowing, waves all around them.

The band hadn't rehearsed an ending, they just watched Dorothy for a nod into the final bars. But she didn't give it, just kept drumming, kept the music going, the energy, for as long as possible. She would keep going forever, if she could.

ACKNOWLEDGEMENTS

Thanks to Karen Sullivan for her undying support for both me and the Skelfs, and everyone else at Orenda Books for their immense dedication. Thanks to Phil Patterson and all at Marjacq for their sterling work. Thanks to everyone who has supported my writing over the years, words can't express my gratitude. And all my love to Tricia, Aidan and Amber.